STAR TREK®
DARK VICTORY

Books by William Shatner

TekWar
TekLords
TekLab
Tek Vengeance
Tek Secret
Tek Power
Tek Money
Tek Kill
Man o' War
The Law of War
Believe (with Michael Tobias)
Star Trek Memories
Star Trek Movie Memories
Get a Life!
Star Trek: Odyssey
(with Judith and Garfield Reeves-Stevens)
   Book 1: The Ashes of Eden
   Book 2: The Return
   Book 3: Avenger
Star Trek: The Mirror Universe Saga
(with Judith and Garfield Reeves-Stevens)
   Book 1: Spectre
   Book 2: Dark Victory
   Book 3: Preserver (Coming April, 2000)

WILLIAM SHATNER

STAR TREK®
DARK VICTORY

with
Judith Reeves-Stevens &
Garfield Reeves-Stevens

POCKET BOOKS
New York London Toronto Sydney Tokyo Singapore

POCKET BOOKS, a division of Simon & Schuster Inc. 1230 Avenue of the Americas, New York, NY 10020

 STAR TREK is a Registered Trademark of Paramount Pictures.

A VIACOM COMPANY

This book is published by Pocket Books, a division of Simon & Schuster Inc., under exclusive license from Paramount Pictures.

ISBN: 0-671-00882-X

Printed in the U.S.A.

I have a dear friend who has been
steadfast and loving and kind and perceptive.
She is a woman of the soil and of the spirit.
Her looks are glamorous and her work makes her sweat;
her name is Donna Moore and I love her dearly.
I dedicate this book to this grand woman.

ACKNOWLEDGMENTS

To Judy and Gar Reeves-Stevens, without whom this book would not have been written.

To John Ordover, without whom this book would not have been written.

STAR TREK®
DARK VICTORY

PROLOGUE

───────── ☆ ─────────

The Enterprise *hung dead in space, surrounded by the floating ruin of the crossover device, like an ancient sunken vessel shrouded in kelp and debris.*

The mighty ship's running lights were out. Her nacelles were dark. But she was intact, and her batteries were keeping life-support at minimal levels.

Kirk and Picard stood together before the Voyager's *main screen. Spock and Teilani were with them.*

"Jean-Luc, I'm sorry," Kirk said. And he meant it. Among a handful of beings, he truly knew the force that bound a captain to his ship. He knew what must be in his friend's heart as Picard gazed upon the battered hulk before them.

"Don't be," Picard said. He flashed a smile at Kirk. A small one, but one that said he could see light shining through this dark hour. "I still have her. We saved her."

Kirk went to give Picard his hand, but both men stared awkwardly at the bandages that protected Kirk's damaged flesh. Picard put his own hands on Kirk's shoulders instead. "You saved *her," he said. "And I thank you."*

1

Then La Forge spoke up from an aft sensor station. "Captain?"

Both Kirk and Picard turned as one and said, "Yes?"

La Forge smiled. "Captain Picard. *Scotty and I have completed our structural analysis. She's not showing any sign of transporter misalignment."*

"That's a relief," Picard said. Kirk understood why. The subspace shock wave generated by the Sovereign's *warp-core explosion had shut down the transporter effect intended to beam the* Enterprise *to the mirror universe. If the shock wave had hit too late, while transport was already in progress, the huge ship might not have been properly reassembled when she had rematerialized. But all was well. Another victory to add to all the others.*

But Spock, apparently, did not think so. "Curious," he said. "I was certain I detected a full transporter-field effect before the warp-core detonation."

Kirk smiled at his old friend. "We've never seen a transporter this big before, Spock. There're bound to be engineering differences we know nothing about."

"Perhaps," Spock said, but he didn't sound convinced.

Picard looked down at his Klingon armor, as if suddenly realizing he still had it on. "I suppose I should clean up. The relief vessels will be here in two hours and . . . I imagine there's a great deal of work to be done over there."

Picard walked back to the turbolift, that small smile still on his face.

Kirk watched him go, pleased his friend still had his starship but glad that he himself had other missions to attend to now.

Then Teilani hugged him. "And I want to get you down to Dr. McCoy to get those dressings changed."

Kirk looked at his bandages. Still the least of his concerns. "I'll be fine," he said.

"You'd better be," Teilani told him. "I'm not going to change all the diapers by myself."

Kirk grinned at the thought of that one new mission in particular. He couldn't wait for it to begin. Then he saw Spock look back at T'Val, and knew his friend was also distracted by thoughts of children and parents. Of paths not taken. It pained him to think that Spock might be in distress. Kirk changed the subject.

"Spock, just when the Voyager came in on the attack, you said you and your counterpart had worked out what made the two universes diverge."

Spock returned his attention to the here and now. "Not the event," he clarified. "The time period. Approximately three hundred years ago. About the time of First Contact between humans and Vulcans. Kate Janeway gave us a clue when she referred to Lake Sloane on Alpha Centauri IV being called Lake Riker in her universe."

"One name made the difference?" Kirk asked.

"No, but it is one of the earliest signs of divergence my counterpart and I could identify. The fact that the lake was named by Zefram Cochrane, following his move from Earth to the colony he founded on that world, made us focus on the time of First Contact."

"There was First Contact in both universes, though?" Kirk asked.

"Yes. And to the best of our abilities to recall history, that event in both universes was the same. Cochrane's first warp flight attracted the attention of a Vulcan ship, and the next day, contact was made." Spock's long face took on a thoughtful expression.

"But . . . ?" Kirk prompted.

"It is the events after *First Contact that somehow seem to be at odds in the two universes. There is nothing conclusive. No key document or incident we can point to. But in one universe, our universe, humans and Vulcans shared an optimistic dream of combining their resources to seek out new life. In the mirror universe, the same cooperation followed, the same early expeditions took place, but there was a decidedly military aspect to their nature. Almost as if, somehow, those responsible for First Contact believed some grave threat was waiting for them among the stars. As if they had secret knowledge of the future and the conflicts to come."*

"What kind of conflicts?" Kirk asked.

Spock folded his hands behind his back. "Again, the differences could just be an artifact of how history is recorded. None of this might be true. But . . . in the mirror universe . . . when the Borg were first detected, far earlier than they were in our history . . . it was almost as if the Terran Empire had been expecting them. The Borg did not remain a threat there."

"How could that be?" Teilani asked.

"I do not know," Spock said. "And even if it is true, the explanation of that truth might always elude us."

Kirk looked back at the screen and the Enterprise. *There were enough mysteries in the universe for him to struggle with. He would leave the mirror universe to others. Janeway and T'Val would return to their war with all the technical information that Kirk could provide them. The mirror Spock would be treated for Bendii here and given sanctuary until T'Val judged it was safe for him to return. And then, Kirk would return to his own life.*

"What are you thinking, James?"

4

Kirk smiled at the woman with whom he had created life. "Will you marry me?" he asked.

Teilani looked at him with eyes that saw into his soul. He could have no secrets from her and he was glad of it.

"What are you going to do about that stump on Chal?"

"Phaser it out of existence," Kirk promised. "I'll borrow one from Memlon's mother."

Teilani laughed. The sweetest sound Kirk had heard in weeks.

"And then what?" she asked. "After you've planted the clearing and built us a house?" She looked to the screen, past the ship and the storms, to where the stars waited. "What about . . . out there?"

Kirk looked out as well, not through space, but through time.

He could have no secrets from her. He could tell her no lies.

"I don't know," he said. "Maybe I'll farm. Maybe we can breed that horse Jean-Luc sent me. And maybe I'll buy a starship and we can find out how many other Chals are out there. You, me, and our son."

"Or our daughter."

"All our children," Kirk said with a smile, and he pulled her closer to him, so she could rest her head on his shoulder. "I don't know what I'll do, Teilani, or where I'll go. But what I do know, without question, without doubt, is that whatever waits for me, I'm going to face it with you."

Teilani smiled at him, and in the love she shared with him, Kirk knew he had found what she had sent him out to discover.

His place in the universe.

It was not a world. Not a time. Not any physical place at all.

Instead, it was every place and every time. As long as he was at her side.

"I love you," she whispered, next to his cheek.

"I love you," he whispered back.

A perfect moment.

And then an alarm blared on the bridge.

Instantly Kirk and Teilani broke apart.

"What is it?" Kirk demanded.

"Weapons lock!" T'Val said.

Janeway was on her feet, reading the tactical boards. "It's the Enterprise! *All systems . . . they're coming back online."*

"What?" Kirk said. "How can that be possible?"

"We're being hailed," T'Val called out.

"Onscreen," Janeway said.

All eyes went to the main screen as the image of the drifting Enterprise *winked out, to be replaced by a transmission from that ship's bridge.*

It was fully staffed. All consoles lit and active.

But none of that mattered.

Because of the man who sat in her center chair.

If there were gasps on the bridge of the Voyager, *Kirk didn't hear them.*

If Teilani grabbed his arm in fear, he did not feel her grip.

His heart thundered in his ears.

His breath caught in his throat.

Every thought in his mind was banished, replaced by a primal dread that lived deep in the darkness of his mind.

Because when he looked at the man in the center chair—

—the face he saw was his own.

And that face laughed at him.

"James T. Kirk," *the man in the center chair said.* "I've heard so much about you. I owe you . . . so much more."

"They are powering phasers," *T'Val said.*

Kirk struggled through his shock to find his voice. "Who . . . are you?" *Though he already knew the answer.*

The man in the center chair leaned forward, and the smile that split his face was the grin of the devil.

"You can call me . . . Tiberius."

Kirk leaned against the helm console for support. "Why are you here?"

His mirror counterpart answered as if it were the most obvious question ever asked. "You stole a universe from me, James. And now I'm here to do the same to you."

"Never," *Kirk said.*

"The choice is yours. Lower your shields and surrender. You have ten seconds to comply. Or you will die."

Emperor Tiberius sat back in the center chair of the Enterprise.

The waiting began.

ONE

The waiting was over . . .

"Ten," the emperor said.

It was the number of seconds James T. Kirk had to live.

Behind him on the mirror *Voyager*'s bridge, Kathryn Janeway lunged for the conn. Kirk knew her well enough to understand her intention.

Once, it would have been his as well.

"Nine."

Kirk turned from the viewscreen, from the man in the mirror, and shouted at the *Voyager*'s captain. "No!"

Spock, following his captain's lead, now pushed ahead, one hand extended, fingers ready to remove Janeway from the equation of this moment.

But he was blocked by T'Val, the young, drawn Vulcan woman who haunted him, the ghost of a possibility unexplored, child of his mirror counterpart and the mirror Saavik. The follower of Janeway.

"Eight."

T'Val's mechanized hand swung up to divert Spock's attack. Janeway reached the controls. Kirk felt the ship's

9

warp-core generator sing its song in the vibration of the deck.

The stunning blow of T'Val's mechanized hand swept Spock to the side. Then T'Val joined her leader.

"Seven." Tiberius laughed mockingly, seeing everything, the chaos that he had brought.

Kirk leaned over the central flight-control console, to reach the controls on the captain's side, then gasped with pain as the ruins of his hands strained but did nothing.

Hours ago, transtator feedback had destroyed the controls of the runabout he had piloted. He had kept the craft on course, completed his mission, but had paid the price in charred flesh, shattered bones, now wrapped in McCoy's glittering bandages.

Kirk called for help from the one person left to give it. "Teilani!"

"Six."

No more than a moment ago, his beloved had agreed to become his wife. No more than a month ago, in the peace of a glade on Chal, their love had quickened their child within her.

Now, for him, their child, and their future, she became the fighter Kirk needed at his side.

Teilani, child of *Qo'noS* and of Romulus, Klingon warrior and Romulan tactician, vaulted over the console.

T'Val had no chance.

Teilani's boot made contact with the Vulcan female's jaw. Teilani's arm cut across Janeway's neck.

All three women flew back from the console. T'Val crumpled to the floor, unconscious. Janeway fought unsuccessfully against Teilani's grip.

"Five."

Without functioning hands, Kirk did what he could. He ran. Charging around the console to reach the empty conn, even as the bridge tilted in the lag of the inertial dampeners and the *Voyager* began her suicidal run, just as Janeway had intended.

But in the mirror universe, this Janeway had lived as a Terran slave to the Klingon–Cardassian Alliance, cursed with the burden of a scientist's intellect and dreams.

This Janeway knew what had been taken from her. This Janeway burned with hate.

Directed at one man—Tiberius—just as her starship was now directed in a deadly collision course with the *Enterprise.*

But on the viewscreen, Tiberius did the unexpected. He abruptly broke off his countdown and commanded his gunner to target the *Voyager.*

Hunched over the keyboards of the flight-control console, Kirk tore with his teeth at the bandage on his right hand, like an animal gnawing at its own limb to escape a trap. As the sparkling bandages fluttered to the floor, they took with them shreds of torn flesh. Kirk's mouth bore fresh bloodstains.

The *Voyager* shuddered and he swayed as the first salvo from the *Enterprise*'s aft phasers blazed around her shields, but he remained on his feet.

On the screen, Tiberius grinned fiercely. His long white hair was tied back in an immaculate warrior's queue, his deeply tanned skin unblemished and un-marked, his face the face of triumph.

On the *Voyager*'s bridge, it seemed as if Kirk was now the beast. Broken, bleeding, desperate.

But not desperate to kill.

On his right hand, his thumb was still intact. He jammed it down on the helm controls, gasping as a blade of fire shot through his raw palm, up his arm.

"Scotty! La Forge!" he cried out to the two engineers. "Everything to the starboard shields, *now!*"

A second salvo blasted the *Voyager*. But her weakened forward shields had not been the target.

Kirk had succeeded in forcing the ship into a turn. Her undamaged starboard shields had absorbed the full charge.

The bridge lights flickered. The deck and bulkheads echoed with the groaning of metal as the structural integrity field fluctuated.

"We've lost half the shield nodes," Scott called out. "We cannae go to warp."

La Forge's urgent voice rose above the ship's din. "We'll barely be able to manage half impulse!"

Suddenly, Janeway broke free of Teilani and rushed Kirk at the console, trying to drag him from the helm.

"We *can't* run! We *can't* protect ourselves! Let it end *now!*"

But Kirk shouldered her away even as Teilani recaptured her. Even as the ship rocked and bucked violently. The readouts confirming that *Voyager* was spinning on her central axis, her inertial control damaged by the last phaser hit.

"It's not your decision," Kirk shouted at her. "You're not alone on this ship!"

Hate had blinded Janeway. But not Kirk. Spock and Scott and La Forge were on the bridge of this ship. On the other decks were McCoy, Picard, Spock's counterpart, Data, Dr. Crusher, Will Riker, Deanna Troi, and dozens more from Starfleet who had been rescued from the asteroid labor camp below. *No one* had the right to force death upon others without giving them a say.

Teilani held Janeway secure at Kirk's side, ready to deliver a deathblow if that was what was required.

The grinning image of Tiberius vanished from the viewscreen, leaving in its place a blur of streaming images: the roiling clouds of the Goldin Discontinuity in which the two starships were embedded; the two asteroids in their decaying orbit rushing dangerously closer to each other; the *Enterprise* encased in her metallic, webbed cage.

"You're weak," Janeway screamed at Kirk. "Letting that monster live because of *her!*" She struggled in vain to escape Teilani's hold.

Kirk clenched his teeth as he forced his right thumb over the controls, bringing the ship back into trim. "There's been too much death already."

"It's him or us!"

But Kirk could not be distracted. He was focused on his ship and survival. "There is *always* another way!"

Recovered from T'Val's attack, Spock was on his feet again, already at tactical. "Phasers, captain?"

"On my mark!" Kirk answered.

Janeway exploded in fury and frustration. *"We can't outfight that ship!"*

Kirk grunted to mask the agonizing pain he felt as his thumb and bloody knuckles stabilized the *Voyager.* He brought her around to face the *Enterprise*'s stern again, and then moved her forward. But not on a collision course. "We don't have to outfight the *ship,"* he gasped. "Just the *man!"*

More vibrations coursed through the bridge, but they

were weaker this time. The *Enterprise* had scored only a glancing blow.

And then the *Voyager* was to the port of the larger ship, moving slowly, a perfect target. Yet untouched.

Confusion dampened Janeway's rage. "He's not firing."

Kirk's attention was on the positions of the *Enterprise* and the intricate construction that wrapped her like a mechanistic cocoon. "Of course he's not firing," he said. "Not after what he went through to build that thing. He's not about to risk shooting it." He turned to Spock. "Spock, has the *Enterprise* enlarged her shields to protect the device?"

"She has."

Kirk nodded, unsurprised. It was what he would have done in the same situation.

Then the turbolift doors opened and Jean-Luc Picard rushed onto the bridge, still in the Klingon armor he had taken from his mirror counterpart. The captain of the *Enterprise* looked at the viewscreen in shock. "Kirk, what is this?"

But Kirk could not respond. There was no time. Already the vastly more powerful starship was beginning to slip out of its metallic cage. Once the *Enterprise* was free, the *Voyager*'s remaining lifetime would be measured in seconds.

"Watch the shield intensity on the forward section," Kirk told Spock. "When the tip of it shows through the shields . . ."

"Understood," Spock said.

Kirk brought the Voyager about to face the closed end of the device, even as the *Enterprise* had backed halfway out. Sweat poured from Kirk's brow. "Spock—"

"Shield strength over the device is at eleven percent . . . six . . . three . . . zero."

"Fire!" Kirk commanded.

Teilani released Janeway.

On the screen, a thin blue stream of phased energy shot from the *Voyager* to find its target—a few square meters of metal and wire no longer protected by the *Enterprise*'s shields.

At once, those copper-colored plates and strands lost all molecular cohesion. And as they blew apart into quantum mist, a chain reaction spread as if a fuse had been lit. Now the full power of the *Voyager*'s weapons raced along the web of metal, *through* the *Enterprise*'s shields, to explosively detonate the entire crossover device.

In the same instant, the shields of the great starship began to act against her. Instead of keeping energy away from her, they did not allow energy out.

"No . . ." Picard whispered. An eruption of phased energy now enveloped his ship within the perfect curved perimeter of her shields.

Then the ovoid shape vanished as the *Enterprise*'s shield generators failed, and the contained explosion rebounded into space.

A subspace compression wave swept out to engulf *Voyager.*

Impact with the massive wave struck the ship. The deck pitched. The bridge lights flickered again.

"I've no idea what ye just exploded in there," Scott announced, "but it's done in our shields. We've got nothing protecting us now."

Then, on the screen, the *Enterprise* reappeared from the fire, free of the crossover device, still intact.

Janeway's bitter accusation was directed at Kirk. "You've killed us all anyway. And for what?"

But Kirk was not listening to her. He hugged his hands against his body, fighting the sensation that *Voyager* was still spinning, still vibrating, out of control. "Spock, does the *Enterprise* have shields?"

"Her shields are down," Spock's calm voice confirmed. "Storage batteries are exhausted. Life support failing."

The gamble had worked. He had won again. Kirk allowed himself to fall back heavily in the helmsman's chair. "Lock transporters on all life signs on the bridge. Beam everyone directly to the brig." He felt Teilani's touch as she placed both hands on his shoulders. He could stop fighting the pain. Safe in her arms, he could yield to the darkness that called him. He needed to sleep, to rest . . .

"No life signs detected," Spock said. "There is no one left aboard her."

Kirk's eyes widened. "Scotty! Transporter trace!"

"Aye, that's it, sir. Nine people beamed directly to . . . the asteroid labor camp?"

Kirk struggled to his feet. He had to stop Tiberius. He could have anything hidden down there.

But now Picard's hand was on him, gently but firmly forcing him back into the chair. "You've done enough, Captain. My people and I have spent the last three weeks down there. We'll find Tiberius."

At any other time, Kirk might have resisted Picard's offer to help. That was Kirk's own counterpart down there. This was Kirk's battle. But there were limits to what one man could do. Limits to the pain he could

16

withstand. Perhaps Teilani was right. It was time to pass the burden to others.

Then La Forge shouted out: "Captain Picard! The *Enterprise!*"

And on the screen, to Kirk it was as if the starship had begun to disassemble herself, breaking up into a flurry of subcomponents like a puzzle being shattered.

"The escape pods . . . ?" Picard said. "Mr. La Forge, what is the status of *Enterprise*'s security systems?"

Of course, Kirk thought. He knew what La Forge's answer would be before the engineer began to speak. *Exactly what I would have done to buy time.*

"Captain, she's on a ten-minute countdown to self-destruct."

Kirk had no strength left within him, no reserves on which to draw. But he knew the look of loss on Picard's face. Understood it all too well.

He rose to his feet, forced his hands to hang at his sides as if they were undamaged, willed his voice to remain strong.

"You have to save your ship, Captain," he told Picard. "I'll find Tiberius."

Kirk shook his head once at Teilani to stop her protest before it could begin. "Spock, tell Dr. McCoy to meet us in the transporter room. Scotty, we'll need environment suits for the landing party and I'll need you up here to run the sensor sweep."

As he headed for the turbolift, Kirk heard Picard already giving orders to his command crew on the *Voyager,* having them assemble in the transporter room, as well.

In the turbolift car, with Spock on one side of him,

Teilani on the other, Kirk looked toward the flight-control console. "Captain Janeway," he said. "You have the bridge."

If there were limits to what one man could do, to how much pain he could withstand, Kirk hadn't found them yet.

The burden still was his.

Then the turbolift doors closed and James T. Kirk began his descent.

TWO

———————————— ☆ ————————————

It had been known for centuries that the vacuum of interstellar space was more than simple nothingness. Instead, it seethed with quantum fluctuations, infinite amounts of energy and matter—created and annihilated so rapidly that the net effect was zero.

Most of the time.

But in rare places, for unknown reasons, the odds of nature broke down and the balance shifted from one side to another. All things were possible then. Wormholes. Rifts. Time loops. Spatial interphase. And plasma storms.

Some of those regions were torn by immense discharges of energy that extended for light-years, as if a cluster of stars had been stretched into long tendrils of plasma fire instead of contracting into compact spheres.

One such region was near the Cardassian border. It was called the Badlands.

Another was within a few hundred light-years of the Vulcan Colonial Protectorates. It was called the Goldin Discontinuity.

Less than four weeks ago, the *Enterprise,* under Jean-Luc Picard, entered that discontinuity, searching for signs that Dominion and Cardassian forces might be trying to exploit the region's unstable spacetime to create a wormhole.

Instead, Picard's ship was captured by Alliance forces from the mirror universe and her crew enslaved in a labor camp built on a nickel–iron asteroid, no more than 15 kilometers in diameter.

Before the camp had been attacked by Kirk and his team on the duplicate *Voyager,* a force-field generator had maintained an atmosphere over the camp. Now, an hour later, the camp was exposed to vacuum. And in one precise location near the center of that camp, that vacuum began to glow, then shimmer, as it was forced apart by the sudden intrusion of phased matter.

Then, on the gleaming metal surface of the asteroid, nine figures materialized, resolving from the light to become dark silhouettes against the burning sky. Though all were humanoid, the armor of their pressurized battle suits gave them an exaggerated, harsh, and alien appearance.

In the sky beyond the boundaries of the camp, the ion distortions of the Goldin Discontinuity writhed in a constant war of color. Red clouds swept over blue. Golden streamers flashed with silent, pinpoint explosions of blinding white energy like sparks from primitive chemical reactions. But the canvas of the discontinuity was light-years deep and distant, and its power was no threat to those in properly shielded suits—provided they did not remain in one place too long.

Directly above the nine battle-suited figures loomed the oppressive mass of the second asteroid, also nickel–iron, also 15 kilometers in diameter, that was spinning slowly on its axis, moving on a newly disturbed orbit that in minutes would bring it within 200 meters of the first asteroid.

But as spectacular and awe inspiring as the discontinuity's display of plasma energy was, as threatening as the descending second asteroid appeared to be, nothing in this environment distracted the nine from their mission.

The moment transport was complete, they began to run in military formation. Their destination was the cluster of low, circular barracks of rough-finished, rust-colored metal, surrounding a central overseer's command station. That building of Cardassian design was double the height of the others, bristling with sensor dishes and antenna masts and linked with all the other structures by a network of raised plasteel walkways and platforms.

Running easily, despite the extra mass of his armor, Tiberius led his six samurai and two commandants to the overseer's station. The battle suit he wore was of Klingon design, smoothly sculpted to depict the heroic musculature of Kahless himself. Its dull metallic finish was so deeply red it verged on black. Built for ease of motion and the speed and grace and intimacy of hand-to-hand combat, Tiberius's battle suit was also more lightly armored than his soldiers' ebony Cardassian suits of sharply angled insectlike wedges.

Rounded jewels and bloodstones were embedded on the arms and across the chest of Tiberius's suit. To any other warrior of *Qo'noS,* they told the story of the wearer's victories in battle. To any denizen of the mirror universe, it identified that wearer as the monster who had caused the deaths of untold worlds and civilizations. The madman who had lost an empire and consigned the once great people of Vulcan and of Earth to abject slavery at the hands of the Klingon–Cardassian Alliance.

But to Tiberius, all the decades of his life that had elapsed since the fall of the Terran Empire, since Vulcan was conquered and Earth laid waste, had merely been a setback. A minor deviation on his way to claiming absolute and inevitable control of known space.

Born on a farm in Iowa, this James T. Kirk had risen above his station as captain of the *I.S.S. Enterprise* to become Emperor Tiberius I. He had survived both the treachery of his prime minister, Spock, son of Sarek, and the betrayal of the Klingons and Cardassians whose alliance he himself forged.

But then, surviving even death itself, Tiberius had found himself in a new era, 78 years beyond his own.

How could any man blessed with such immortality not believe he had been touched by the gods to put his mark not just upon a world, but upon the very universe?

Tiberius had no doubts about the destiny he would make for himself. The universe would be his. It was just a matter of time until every other living being— including the false reflections of the ghost universe— realized that truth, as well, and gave up their struggles against him.

The nine reached the command station. Though its main entrance was up above, on the raised plasteel platform, Tiberius led his soldiers to the side of the building. There were cooling grids inset in the wall there, radiator panels for shedding excess heat. But Tiberius knew that one grid did not function.

He swung open the cover of a radiator-adjustment terminal, then pushed back the dummy-control surface inside to reveal the cavity of a hololock. He inserted his gloved hand into the dark opening and spread his fingers until the hololock's sensors identified the unique structure of the bones in his hand. Responding as if it were a miniature holodeck, the hololock then created five solid buttons in the empty space before his hands.

Before the buttons could fade, Tiberius tapped out his imperial code. As the machinery within the wall accepted the code, the false radiator panel slid open, exposing a circular Cardassian airlock. The disc door rolled to the side. As it did so, a sudden wind of ice crystals from a pocket of trapped air rushed past the nine.

When his soldiers were in the airlock at his side, Tiberius entered the code that would put it through its cycle. As the disc door rolled closed again, he took one last look upward.

The *Enterprise* hung lifeless in space a kilometer overhead. Beside her, the duplicate *Voyager* began to pull away. The enemy had realized that he and his soldiers had beamed from the ghost Picard's ship. *They're coming closer for transport and high-resolution sensor sweeps,* Tiberius thought. That's what *he* would do next.

Tiberius also knew the enemy would trace his beam-in coordinates. Which is why he had had his team set down in a place well away from his true destination.

A few more minutes, Tiberius thought. Some of the ghosts would be boarding the *Enterprise,* he knew, in a desperate attempt to save her from self-destruction. But the real enemy—the ghost Kirk—would be coming to this asteroid, for him. And there would be nothing for him to find.

The door clanked shut. Tiberius heard the whistle of wind outside his helmet as the airlock was repressurized.

He snapped the seals on the neck of his suit, pulled off his helmet while the atmospheric pressure was dangerously low, felt the air in his suit rush up around his face.

He inhaled deeply, the pitifully thin air that made it into his lungs like that on a kilometers-high mountain, barely enough to sustain life.

But Tiberius inhaled deeply anyway, as if through his actions and his force of will he could bring life-giving air into the chamber for his soldiers.

Those eight began to take off their helmets now. The whistle of the wind grew softer as equalization was achieved. The inner door of the airlock began to roll once more.

Before the door had stopped moving, Tiberius stepped through the opening and into the hot, oppressive air of the command center. The foul stench suited his mood.

Regent Picard awaited him, out of uniform, in a simple brown Klingon tunic and trousers. Even his long warrior's queue was missing, leaving him with only a wavy fringe of ragged white hair.

The regent touched his fist to his heart and flung his arm out level in a salute of loyalty. "Emperor, I—"

Tiberius ended the greeting by swinging the back of his hand against Picard's face.

"You allowed your ghost to *live*," Tiberius snarled. "I saw him on the bridge of the *Voyager*, wearing *your* armor, with the Spock of this false universe *and* the ghost Kirk."

A thin thread of blood trickled from Picard's torn lip. "Nechayev failed to protect the camp! I cannot be held responsible for the failures of others."

"Yes, Jean-Luc, you can. And you will be. Count on it." He held his gaze on Picard, neither man wavering, neither man showing fear.

"You need me," Regent Picard said, not even bothering to hide the intonation of a threat.

Tiberius touched the handle of the jewelled *d'k tahg* at his belt. "Shall we see how much?" he asked.

Then the moment was broken by his commandant of weapons, Geordi La Forge. "Emperor! We have beamins!"

Tiberius turned from Picard to face his weapons master. The brilliant human, whose skin was as dark as the armor he wore, had been born without functioning eyes. So to tap his genius, Tiberius had gifted him with ocular grafts—Borg-like holographic lenses surrounded by dull gray metal, implanted deeply in each empty socket. Like insect legs, extra tendrils of nerve transducers pierced La Forge's forehead and cheeks to hold the implants in place. Now the enhanced weapons master could see in energy realms even tricorders were unable to detect.

La Forge held up his Cardassian combat sensor. "Four intruders, Federation transport signatures." The indicator lights on the sensor display shifted. "Four more."

Tiberius pointed to three of his samurai. The glittering jeweled slashes of red on their dark suits' chests were symbolic of their blood, which they had sworn to sacrifice in the name of their emperor. "Take cover by those converters. Let the ghosts cycle through the lock, then kill them all. *Except* for Kirk."

The three samurai saluted their emperor and quickly took up their positions by the large power converters that rose from the polished metal floor of the command station. Around each converter coiled narrow-channel plasma conduits through which pulsed golden light, its glow rhythmically undulating across the floor like light reflections off water.

Tiberius turned to his commandant of security. "The regent is in your charge. The first sign of treachery, gut him."

William Riker's grin crinkled the long white scar that slashed his face, a reminder of the long-ago kiss of an Iopene cutter. The lightning-bolt pattern of damaged skin ran across his forehead, beneath his leather eye patch, and reemerged to crease his cheek and leave a narrow path of shiny skin through his full, dark beard. "With pleasure," he said.

Tiberius checked the tactical display on the forearm of his battle suit. "Seventeen minutes to crossover. Stay close."

He led his remaining soldiers through a maze of additional power converters and storage containers to the hidden subspace station at the command center's core. His pace was swift and sure, without hesitation. He had studied the plans for this hidden facility only once, two years ago. But that had been enough to etch the layout in his memory. He never forgot what was important. But he gave no more thought to the three samurai he had left behind. He had no doubt they would die when the enemy attacked. But that was their duty. It was everyone's duty to die for their emperor.

Tiberius, his five remaining soldiers, and Regent Picard came to a large, black storage container against a silver metal wall. In Cardassian script, the container's contents were described as dehydrated vole bellies. No Klingon would bother to open such a container. The Cardassians that had run this camp had known better than to try.

Tiberius traced his fingers across an unmarked pattern on the shipping label. At once, a section of the container's side swung open to reveal a narrow passageway with a spiral staircase. Tiberius stood back as his weapons master, unasked, scanned ahead.

"Clear," La Forge reported.

Tiberius descended the stairs.

The control room was circular, five meters across, and contained everything Tiberius needed. The vast subspace transmitter nodes and inactive power couplings were hidden elsewhere on the asteroid. They had to be. When the signal pulse went out, any living thing within a kilometer of the nodes would die. Tiberius had wished the camp to survive his use of the system. Though because Regent Picard had failed and the ghost Kirk had interfered, the camp was already a total loss.

However, Tiberius had not survived this long without an appreciation for contingencies. Whatever the situation, he always thought of the worst possible result and devised a strategy to contend with it. And that strategy, more often than not, was simply to change the rules.

That is what he planned to do now.

Tiberius powered up the consoles, brought the subspace nodes online, and started the warm-up of the long-dormant power couplings.

By now, Regent Picard and Commandant Riker had joined him.

"How can you proceed like this?" Picard demanded.

Tiberius was almost amused to see that the regent seemed appalled. "This has always been part of the plan, Jean-Luc. Once the device holding the *Enterprise* has fulfilled its function, all the other pieces must be brought to the board."

"But the device failed! I saw it destroyed! The *Enterprise* is still up there!"

Tiberius allowed a small smile to touch his lips. He took no small pleasure in tormenting the Klingon quisling. But he didn't take his eyes from the controls he adjusted. "Where else would it be?"

"The ship didn't pass through the portal."

"What portal, Jean-Luc?"

Tiberius stiffened as Regent Picard now dared to lay his hand on Tiberius's shoulder and force him around. "I have risked *everything* to bring you this far!"

From the corner of his eye, Tiberius saw Riker instantly snap his wrist to unfurl a Mobius blade from the forearm of his battle suit. He knew the commandant of security had simply to press the tip of the needlelike weapon into Picard's flesh and the blade itself would complete the attack, propelling itself forward with millions of nanomolecular arms. Once inside a victim's body, fluctuating currents would compel it to twist like a snake, to literally—and painfully—carve its way through its victim's soft flesh and organs.

But Tiberius raised a hand and Riker stopped as swiftly as a machine might respond.

"And your reward," Tiberius icily reminded the foolhardy regent, "is *everything* you can imagine. Your own system, your own fleet, and escape from your own side." Tiberius roughly pulled Picard's hand from his shoulder. "The device worked, Jean-Luc. It was never intended to be a portal to our universe. No transporter can be built on such a scale."

Picard's mouth opened in shock. Tiberius smiled cruelly. The regent had spent more than a year here, running the labor camp, overseeing the construction of the duplicate *Voyager* and the device. And Tiberius had never once revealed to him what he was actually doing.

"Then . . . then what was that thing?"

"All you need to know is that it functioned as designed." Tiberius nodded at Riker and the commandant flicked his wrist again, making the Mobius blade recurl itself into its forearm pocket. "And the next time you touch me," he said sharply, "you will die. Slowly enough that your regret will be worse than your agony."

Tiberius turned back to the controls. The power couplings were almost at full readiness. Another minute and everything would be in place. The plan would go forward, unstoppable, just as he was.

Then he heard the distant whine of phaser fire and an answering volley of disrupter bolts. Slightly sooner than he had expected. But expected, nonetheless.

"They're here!" La Forge shouted down the entry shaft.

Tiberius ordered his commandant of weapons to come down into the control room, then had him seal the door. The other three samurai were lost to him now. But in truth, their function had been to fly the *Enterprise* out of the Goldin Discontinuity so she could be destroyed where her debris would be easily found. And what had been done to her, never discovered.

Since their original mission would no longer be possible, the three soldiers could now die more humanely by slowing his enemy's approach, instead of merely being eliminated later, through an airlock, as surplus personnel. Tiberius cared for his followers. Whenever he could, he thought of their welfare first.

The control room's Cardassian display screens shifted colors, indicating the power couplings were on full standby.

Tiberius sealed the controls. Nothing could stop the signal now.

He saw the slight glimmer of fear in Riker's eyes. The commandant obviously knew what the close-range subspace distortions could do to living flesh. "Emperor, what if we don't cross over in time?"

Tiberius opened one hand. "We will die like *targs.*" Then he closed that hand in a fist. "Are you a *targ,* Commandant?"

As he had intended, the humiliating insult helped drive the fear from Riker's eyes.

Then Tiberius turned away from his soldiers and the regent, to locate the hidden panel in the curved wall. He held out his hand and his disrupter, plated in gold-pressed latinum, sprang from its holster on his thigh and into his grip. In that same instant, he fired and the wall panel melted into a spray of white light.

Beyond was a small alcove, and in its floor a single transporter disc.

Regent Picard's protest was immediate. "That's a Federation transporter! That can't get us across without a multidimensional transporter device!"

Tiberius paused, rapidly losing his patience. "It's preset to take us back to the surface. If we cross over by transporter from this camp, you know where we'll appear. And you know we can be followed. I'm not willing to give up yet." He tightened his grip on his disruptor. "Are you?"

"Never," Picard said.

Tiberius released his disruptor and the weapon leaped back to its holster, reclaimed by his battle suit's force manipulators. "La Forge," he said.

Instantly his commandant of weapons stepped into the small transporter chamber, pulled on his helmet, sealed it, drew both of his disruptors, and nodded once.

Tiberius touched the wall control. La Forge passed into the light.

An explosion shook the control room's door at the top of the spiral stairway. Picard and Riker looked up in anticipation, but Tiberius kept his eye on the transporter control. When its power levels were restored, a five-second process, he ordered the intendant to go next.

Picard pulled on his helmet, but before he had sealed it, Tiberius deliberately started the transport. "Next time, move more quickly."

Commandant Riker laughed at the regent's panicky fumbling at the neck of his suit even as his body dissolved.

Then the control room door began to hum. Tiberius recognized the sound as phaser harmonics. A beam was burning into the door from the other side. But the door had heavy shielding and a low-power force field running within it. It would last long enough, he knew.

"They're coming through," Riker said. "You go. I'll hold them here."

Tiberius refused. "It might be James. Get on the pad."

Riker sealed his helmet smartly and Tiberius energized just as an incandescent fountain of molten metal and phaser sparks punched through the door above. Flashes of blue light and curls of white smoke swept down into the control room.

Tiberius calmly watched the transporter power display as it recycled, then smoothly pulled on his Klingon helmet, sealed it with a quick twist of the neck ring, and held out his hand for his disruptor.

The transporter power was restored. Tiberius stepped up on the pad, then turned to face the control room. The transporter activation switch was just within reach on the wall outside the alcove. All he had to do was touch it, and he would be on the surface with the others.

He checked the countdown display on the transmitter console. Eight minutes. *Not quite* enough time for everything he had yet to do. But enough to make the challenge interesting.

So he decided to wait. To see who would come down the stairs.

If the situation were reversed, he knew what *he* would do.

Kirk breathed hard in his environment suit, fogging the thin faceplate. Ahead of him, the edges of the hidden door still glowed from the phaser fire it had taken to burn through it.

Spock held a tricorder to that opening. Like Kirk, T'Val, and Teilani, the Vulcan was also in his full environment suit, despite the fact that the labor camp command center was pressurized. Opening one remotely controlled airlock was all it would take to explosively decompress the entire building.

"One life sign," Spock said.

Kirk knew who it would be.

Nine had beamed down from the *Enterprise*. Six were now dead. They had tried to ambush Kirk's party at the airlock and near this deceptive storage crate in the bottom level of the command center.

But both ambushes had failed for the same reason Spock had been able to track the landing party so quickly. The Vulcan had reset a basic tricorder to register quantum signatures. Everyone and everything from the mirror universe had a quantum signature unique to the mirror reality, easily distinguished from the quantum signature of this existence.

To Spock, the molecular debris scuffed from the boots of Tiberius's soldiers had stood out against the metal surface of the asteroid as if they had been footprints tracked through red paint.

The hidden airlock had been easy to find for the same reason. Bypassing its lock had been as simple as asking the *Voyager* to beam Kirk's team from one side of the airlock to the other. Then Spock had registered the exhalations of the concealed soldiers and Teilani had phasered away the power converters they hid behind, exposing them.

Not unexpectedly, instead of surrendering, Tiberius's men had fought, though not for long. Without cover, they had fallen victim to the unerring speed and aim of T'Val's artificial hand.

The attack by the storage crate had been the same. If prevented from launching a surprise attack of their own, it seemed Tiberius's soldiers knew only how to die, not how to fight.

Kirk had not taken part in either attack. He'd been forced to stand by, doing nothing.

At least his hands no longer hurt. McCoy had injected him with something to numb them. He had also administered a tri-ox compound to counter fatigue, saying he was tempted once again to slip in a neural paralyzer as he had more than a century ago on Vulcan.

Then McCoy and Teilani had replicated insulated construction mitts and attached them to the arms of Kirk's environment suit. The bulky mitts were designed to be worn over gloves on ice worlds, so Kirk's bandaged hands fit into them easily.

Between the cumbersome mitts and McCoy's numbing injection, Kirk could do nothing with his hands. But this would be the end of his inaction.

He knew Tiberius was the single life sign in the hidden control room beneath the false crate.

"I'm going first," Kirk said. He stepped through the phaser-blasted opening.

"No, James," Teilani protested. Her voice sounded distant in the helmet's speakers. "I'll go, or T'Val— someone who can carry a weapon."

Kirk held his position. "He doesn't want to kill me."

Spock raised an eyebrow behind his faceplate. "Jim, he tried to destroy the *Voyager.*"

"He fought the ship, not the man," Kirk argued. "Killing me won't be enough. Remember what he said when he was on the viewscreen. 'You stole a universe from me. Now I'm here to do the same to you.' He needs me alive so I can see his victory. But any of you three, he'd kill right away."

Kirk saw that Teilani wasn't convinced, but the silence from the Vulcans told him his logic was sound.

"I'll keep talking," Kirk said. Then he started down the rust-red plasteel stairs, sliding one insensate, useless hand along the metallic railing to help him keep his balance.

The control room was at the bottom of the stairs. His first glance at the consoles told him a countdown was underway, though he didn't recognize the Cardassian engineering glyphs. *It could be a self-destruct setting,* Kirk thought. But that didn't feel right. If the situation had been reversed, it wasn't what he would have done. Defeat was not yet that certain for Tiberius.

Then he saw the figure in the alcove: massive, monstrous, and threatening in a combat environment suit, Klingon in design, though more extreme than anything Kirk had ever seen.

He knew at once the figure was Tiberius. And that the alcove held a transporter.

He knew why Tiberius had waited.

"There's a countdown on a Cardassian control system," Kirk said into his helmet communicator. He did the time-unit conversion in his head. "I think there're six minutes left."

"Do you see the source of life sign?" Spock's voice echoed in his ear.

Kirk looked across the control room, directly at Tiberius in the shadowed alcove. The emperor hadn't moved.

"It's him."

T'Val's cool tones came over Kirk's helmet speaker. "Is he conscious?" It was obvious the Vulcan couldn't understand why nothing had happened.

But Kirk did.

He stepped forward, arms open. "Are you on this frequency?" he asked his counterpart.

Tiberius shifted forward on the pad. Kirk saw a gleaming gold disruptor appear in a shaft of white light. But he wasn't afraid.

Tiberius's hand reached around the edge of the alcove wall. Kirk saw a control padd there.

Of course, he thought. *He wants me to follow.*

Tiberius pressed a control on the padd. An instant later, a transporter claimed him.

"He just beamed out," Kirk said into his helmet communicator. "Probably into the mirror universe. I'm following."

He ran to the alcove, pressed his unwieldy mitt against the control padd until he saw an activation light glow, then stepped up onto the transporter disk.

He knew without turning that Spock and T'Val and Teilani would be right behind him. He could hear them shouting at him to stop.

But this was time to act, not listen.

Kirk turned back to see the alcove, the control room, and his three companions fade into a sparkling curtain of light, and then the radiance cleared and—

A heavy fist drove into his stomach.

Kirk's breath exploded from him as he fell back upon the slick, metal surface of the asteroid.

Tiberius was standing over him like an avenging Klingon demon.

He could see Tiberius's mouth moving behind his faceplate. But he heard nothing through his helmet speakers.

He tried to put a hand to the side of his helmet, to let

Tiberius know he couldn't hear. But the moment he raised his hand, Tiberius kicked him in the side.

Kirk's breath was driven from his lungs again. Wheezing, he looked up at Tiberius through watering eyes.

His counterpart impatiently gestured at him as if a question had been asked. As if he were waiting for an answer.

Gasping for air, Kirk forced himself to concentrate on Tiberius's lips, to read what he was saying.

". . . a ghost! A shadow . . . nightmare . . ." Five meaningless words, they were all that Kirk could make out.

Then a shadow fell over Tiberius and he looked up. A moment later, he looked down at Kirk. He said nothing. But Kirk could see the contempt in his eyes.

Tiberius wheeled and ran off.

Kirk looked overhead to see where the shadow had come from. His eyes widened.

The second asteroid now filled the sky completely. Darkness replaced the wild, shifting colors of the Goldin Discontinuity.

Kirk heaved himself to his feet. "Spock, can you hear me?" He looked all around. He was *still* in the labor camp. But why would Tiberius build a duplicate camp in *his own* universe? *Unless,* Kirk thought, *I'm still in* my own.

He saw Tiberius fifty meters away, swiftly running beyond the cluster of barracks.

"Spock! Teilani! I'm on the surface of the asteroid." He located the building he had entered only minutes ago. "I'm about half a klick from the command station."

Still no answer. Kirk peered down at the status lights shining up from the inner collar of his suit.

His communicator wasn't functioning. The fall must have damaged circuitry in his helmet.

Kirk began running after his counterpart, hoping Spock's tricorder or the *Voyager*'s sensors would find him.

He glanced up at the asteroid above him, now so close he felt he could almost jump up and touch its speeding bulk.

As he ran, he thought of the *Enterprise,* somewhere beyond, on a ten-minute countdown to self-destruct. Jean-Luc Picard's time to save her was almost up.

But why would Tiberius want the *Enterprise* destroyed?

Or to put it another way, Kirk thought, *why would I want to destroy that ship?* Could there be something on the *Enterprise* that Tiberius did not want them to see? Some evidence he wanted to be obliterated? But evidence of what, he didn't know.

Pursued by mysteries only one man could answer, Kirk did the only thing he could.

He ran faster.

THREE

———— ☆ ————

The transporter's beam delivered Picard to the bridge of his ship. At once, his eyes sought out all the displays that were still functioning.

Only a handful were. Like the ceiling illuminators, most of the screens and consoles were dark. The only light on the bridge came from the safety glowstrips at the base of the walls and along the steps.

The darkness confirmed to Picard what the few working displays told him.

The *Enterprise* was dying.

But she wasn't dead yet.

Picard was already on his way to the security station as Riker and Data resolved from their beams. His first thought was that the station was offline, but then he almost stepped into a circular opening in the wall and deck where the station used to be, almost invisible in the darkness.

"Will—the security station's *gone!*" Picard turned to summon his first officer, but Riker and Data were astounded by a discovery of their own.

The command chair was also missing. In its place,

another circular hole in the deck, as if a Borg tractor beam had been at work.

Data rapidly examined the rest of the bridge. "That is not all, sir," the android said. "Fifteen key control units have been removed from the bridge in the same manner."

Just then the ship's computer announced, in the same calm, unflappable tones that had served more than a century of starships, "Self-destruct in five minutes."

"Find me a working station," Picard told his officers. "Anything I can use to input my access code."

La Forge's voice suddenly came over the communicator Picard had attached to his Klingon armor. "Captain, I'm in Engineering, and—"

"Key components are missing," Picard said. "Excised in perfect circles."

"Yes, sir, that's it exactly."

Riker interrupted. "Geordi, are the power systems stable? Have we lost warp controls?"

"All the power systems and generators are shut down, Commander. The warp core's cold. So as long as we don't self-destruct, we'll be okay. But I have no idea what happened down here."

"Stand by," Riker said.

Data was now at the auxiliary engineering station. It was intact. "Captain, this console will permit you to contact the secondary computers."

Picard swiftly crossed the bridge, avoiding the hole in the deck where his chair used to be. "What about the primaries?"

"They no longer appear to be on board, sir."

Picard entered his access code.

The screen above the control surface changed to show the autodestruct countdown in progress.

"At least I haven't been locked out," Picard said. He entered the deactivation sequence.

"Self-destruct in four minutes, thirty seconds," the computer said.

"What? How can it accept my code and not the deactivation command?" Picard moved away from the console. "Data, input the override sequence you used when the Borg had possession of the ship."

But Data made no move. "Unfortunately, Captain, the override codes I used were based on a programming flaw that had gone undetected by Starfleet computer operations. The flaw has since been corrected."

Picard tugged at the leather collar of his armor, far too hot. "Computer. This is Picard, four seven alpha tango."

"Identity accepted," the computer replied.

"Cancel destruct sequence alpha one. Enable."

"You do not have authorization to disable autodestruct," the computer said.

Picard felt himself flush. "I am the captain of this ship. Cancel destruct sequence alpha one!"

"Self-destruct in four minutes."

Riker tapped his communicator. "Riker to *Voyager*. We need you standing by for emergency beam-out."

Captain Scott replied. "Aye, I've locked on to you, lad. But I have to warn you, these transporters are getting touchy from all the site-to-site beaming they've been doing. I don't know if I can get you all out in one go."

Riker frowned. "Understood."

"Data," Picard said, "what's wrong with it?"

"Perhaps it will not accept your authorization because you are not one of the officers who initiated autodestruct." Data glanced up at the dark ceiling. "Computer, this is Commander Data. Authorization delta india zero one. Replay command sequence authorizing autodestruct."

From all the bridge speakers, the audio recording began. The first voice Picard heard was unmistakable.

"Begin autodestruct sequence. Authorization Kirk. Eight eight alpha kilo."

"Tiberius," Picard said bitterly. "He made the computer think he was Kirk, and Nechayev reinstated Kirk as a Starfleet officer with command authority."

"Sir," Data said, "I suggest we beam the real Captain Kirk to the *Enterprise* so he can order the sequence to be cancelled."

Picard turned to Riker to tell him to do exactly that, when a second voice came from the speakers.

"Computer, Commander William Riker. Confirm autodestruct sequence. Authorization Riker. Two five sierra tango."

Picard saw the shock on his first officer's face. So Riker had a counterpart as well.

And then the third officer necessary to initiate autodestruct was heard.

"Computer, Commander La Forge. Confirm autodestruct sequence. Authorization La Forge. One nine x-ray lima."

"Self-destruct in three minutes, thirty seconds."

"Commander Riker," Data said in the profound silence that had settled on the bridge of the *Enterprise,* "I believe the computer will listen to you."

Riker, still visibly shaken, spoke to the console where

the countdown continued. "Computer, this is . . . *Com-mander . . . William . . . Riker.* Cancel destruct sequence alpha one." He glanced over at Picard before adding the final word: "Enable."

On the small display, Picard watched as the countdown numbers froze, replaced a heartbeat later by the alert screen: AUTODESTRUCT DEACTIVATED.

He and Riker exhaled deeply in relief, then looked at Data, who had also done the same, despite the fact the android did not have to breathe.

Data shrugged. "I was simply getting into the spirit of the moment."

Picard nodded. He looked around at the ruins of his bridge. "We've done what we can here." He tapped his communicator. "Picard to *Voyager.* Self-destruct has been canceled. We're ready to beam back and go down to the asteroid to help Kirk."

"Energizing," Captain Scott replied.

Picard braced himself for the cool wash of the transporter beam.

Nothing happened.

He tapped his communicator again. "Captain Scott . . . ?"

After a moment, Scott's strained voice came back. "We've had a . . . wee bit of a problem. The main transporter circuits have fused. I'm afraid ye'll have t' stay put for a while. And at the rate your life-support is failing, I'd find some environment suits as quickly as ye can."

Picard felt a moment of relief that the circuits had fused before transport, and not during the process. But that relief was quickly replaced by concern.

"What about Kirk and the search party?"

"I'm afraid they're on their own," Scott said. "This poor ship's been through too much. We've no way of helping them until the rescue ships arrive."

Picard, Riker, and Data had one reply to that situation, and all three said it at the same time.

"Hangar deck."

The *Enterprise* had shuttlecraft. To help Kirk, it was time to use them.

As he ran across the metal surface of the asteroid, Tiberius had no need to check his tactical display. His sense of time was absolute. He knew he had two minutes left. Long enough to win a universe—or lose one. The challenge invigorated him.

But still, despite the perfect plan of conquest he was about to set in motion, his confrontation with the other Kirk, that pale imitation of the original, had been disappointing. Tiberius had planned to kill his ghost universe double. The other Kirk's existence was an affront to Tiberius's own. And the shock of learning that this other Kirk had somehow survived his age to reach this new era, just as Tiberius had engineered his own escape across time, had been unnerving. It baffled him still that they could be so much alike, yet so different.

In both universes, Tiberius had learned, the great warlords of history were the same. Alexander, the caesars, Washington, Khan . . . both versions of each had attained their greatness equally, proving that indeed it was their *destiny* to be what they became, independent of any other conditions.

So how then to account for the fact that in this universe, Kirk was little more than a vassal to an ineffectual Starfleet, serving the spineless Federation?

How could Tiberius claim that *he* was destined for incomparable greatness, if in an identical setting, his ghost universe double had failed to achieve *any* accomplishments of note?

His Spock, once his friend, now his betrayer, years ago had said that the differences between the universes might come down to nothing more than random chance.

But Tiberius could not, would not, accept such a definition of his destiny.

Chance controlled fate, and fate was what claimed the weak and the helpless. But men of vision and iron will could *control* their own destiny, independent of chance and circumstance.

The other Kirk was a mistake. Erasing this ghost of himself from existence was the only way he would be able to erase all doubt about what he was born to achieve.

But still, it wasn't enough to merely kill the other Kirk. He needed the other Kirk to understand *why* he was being destroyed—an error being corrected.

Though he would never say these words to anyone but himself, Tiberius knew that before he could conquer the universe, first he must conquer himself.

A moment ago, he had stayed his hand against Kirk because his ghost had been unable to hear him. Kirk had not experienced or witnessed Tiberius's full power.

Tiberius was confident he and his ghost would meet again. A public execution would have more finality, more satisfaction. They had certainly worked well in the past.

The emperor tapped the forearm control that activated his helmet's tactical display. A holographic projection of flashing green dots within a small circle on his faceplate showed him he was being followed by four pursuers. One far ahead of the others.

The ghost Kirk.

Strangely tenacious for a weakling. But he couldn't possibly cover the required distance in time.

Tiberius was only 100 meters from the edge of the asteroid. He was aware that artificial-gravity generators had been installed to make this flattened section of the nickel–iron mountain an arbitrary surface. But he also knew that the gravity field ended at the sharp ridge ahead.

Tiberius stared up, through the topmost curve of his faceplate. The other asteroid was 200 meters overhead, spinning as if it were about to scrape everyone and everything from the surfaces of both. But 200 meters was the limit of its approach on this orbit.

He looked ahead. His two commandants were waiting for him with Regent Picard. In his holographic helmet display, Kirk's green dot was still chasing him. Gaining.

Commandants Riker and La Forge had each drawn their disruptors. Tiberius signaled to them to put their weapons away.

If the ghost Kirk was that eager to meet his death, then Tiberius would take full responsibility for seeing he wasn't disappointed.

For Kirk, each breath was agony. But he refused to stop his mad run across the asteroid. A countdown was underway. For what, he didn't know. But he'd be damned before he'd let Tiberius escape.

Kirk needed answers.

He had to know if he himself was the cause of what befell the humans and the Vulcans in the mirror universe. Not Tiberius, but James T. Kirk, the starship captain who crossed from one universe to another 108 years ago, who had a single conversation with the mirror counterpart of Mr. Spock. Was he personally *responsible* for the total chaos that had consumed that other universe? Was that all it had taken? If he had not crossed over, if he had not planted the idea of revolution in that other Spock's mind, would humans and Vulcans have never become slaves to the Alliance? Or was what happened inevitable? A confluence of events and history that would have occurred in some form, whether or not he had ever played a role?

Fate or destiny?

Kirk had to know.

And Tiberius was the key.

That same Tiberius who now waited for him at the edge of the asteroid, only 20 meters away.

Tiberius was not alone. Kirk saw three other figures with him, in Cardassian battle suits, weapons drawn. It seemed to Kirk that two of the faces might be human, though true detail was hard to perceive at this distance, especially through faceplates that reflected the blue and red plasma fires of the Goldin Discontinuity.

He ran closer, one part of his mind already working on the tactics of the situation. He wondered if he launched himself at Tiberius, could he manage to propel both their bodies out of the artificial gravity field and across the 200-meter gap to the second asteroid. If he could keep Tiberius occupied, that might give Scott the chance he needed to lock on and beam them both back to the *Voyager*.

Ten meters from the group, Kirk slowed his pace as if he were planning to stop, though he was, in fact, still trying to calculate the speed and distance he'd need to hit Tiberius cleanly.

The second asteroid was just now passing the edge of this flat surface, giving Kirk the illusion that the second asteroid was standing still and he was rushing straight up past it. Like falling from El Capitan in reverse.

Kirk saw that the other three figures had put away their weapons.

He realized they had done so because Tiberius had ordered them to do so.

It seemed the emperor intended to meet his double on an equal basis.

If so, Kirk decided, then Tiberius was going to be disappointed.

Tiberius detected indecision in the ghost Kirk's eyes.

Until the moment he put on a burst of speed and his target became obvious.

Tiberius shouted for his soldiers to move out of the way. The regent and the commandants were now unarmed.

But Kirk had timed his approach perfectly, heading straight for Tiberius as if he, too, intended to face his double, one-on-one, until at the last possible moment Kirk pivoted to barrel-roll into the three bystanders.

La Forge leapt clear, but Riker and Picard both jerked away in the same direction at the same time and collided with each other.

An instant later, Kirk's body had slammed into both.

Commandant Riker fell back to the very edge of the asteroid, his helmet hanging over the side. Tiberius watched with surprise, and grudging admiration, as Kirk threw himself at Riker's life-support module and pounded both of his hands on one side of it. Suddenly, its backmounted air replenisher purged itself, expelling a burst of vapor strong enough to push Riker off the edge and out of the gravity field. The commandant's flailing form accelerated toward the other asteroid in an expanding cloud of vapor.

Kirk didn't stop to observe the results of his actions. He kept moving, driving his shoulder into Regent Picard's back before the regent could regain his feet, knocking him down again. Tiberius saw the regent twist as he fell to keep his helmet from hitting the asteroid's metal surface. Kirk took advantage of the regent's panic to relieve him of the only weapon Tiberius had allowed him to carry, his Klingon *mek'leth.*

But Kirk's move, as assured as it was, came too late. Tiberius was now to one side of Kirk, far enough away to draw and fire his disruptor should Kirk attempt to charge him. And Commandant La Forge was on the other side, his disruptor already in hand.

Exhausted, outnumbered, Kirk was caught in a hopeless situation. Tiberius was curious to see what his ghost would do next. Though inept, he was resourceful. But then Tiberius saw that Kirk was holding the regent's short-bladed weapon like a child, squeezing both hands against its rear hilt.

Construction mitts? Tiberius thought. *What's wrong with him?* Kirk hadn't even bent his fingers around the hilt. Then Tiberius remembered what he had seen on the viewscreen. Kirk's hands had been bandaged. *He can't use his hands.*

La Forge's voice came over the helmet speakers. "Emperor, it's time. Give me the word."

One minute, Tiberius thought. There were sixty seconds left in the countdown. He could see Kirk glance at La Forge, then back at him. Regent Picard was crawling toward the edge of the asteroid. Neither Kirk nor Tiberius was interested in stopping him.

"Put your weapon away," Tiberius told La Forge. "Prepare to cross over."

La Forge put his disruptor back on his belt at once. Kirk, as if he had anticipated Tiberius's order, now turned toward the emperor with the *mek'leth* held in attack position.

Maybe that explains it, Tiberius thought. The reason why the other Kirk had not amounted to anything in the ghost universe. He was insane.

Tiberius strode toward his ghost, not even hurrying.

Kirk thrust the *mek'leth* forward.

Pathetic, Tiberius thought. *The weakling's trying for my leg. He has no desire to kill me.*

With a basic defensive move, Tiberius swung his arm down to deflect the attack, then grabbed both of Kirk's wrists as the *mek'leth* tumbled away.

He drew Kirk up to face him, their helmets only centimeters apart.

Kirk's face dripped with sweat. Tiberius experimented by changing his grip so he could squeeze one of Kirk's hands.

Kirk's eyes narrowed. His face paled.

Tiberius squeezed again, fascinated to see the mirror image of his own face contort in agony.

Even through his environment suit, he could feel Kirk's body tremble.

He leaned forward until their helmets touched, allowing sound vibrations to pass from one to another. "You know my works," he said. "You know they could have

50

been yours as well, in your existence. Having betrayed your destiny by not achieving my greatness, how can you even bear to live?"

"Your works." Kirk's voice was faint, muffled, but its scorn burned as it passed between their helmets. "I've seen Earth laid waste and dying because of you."

"Spoils of war, James." There would be no reasoning with his ghost, Tiberius decided. But he could still be humane to this pale reflection of his glory. "You, on the other hand, have achieved nothing but a nightmare of your own making. Let me free you."

Tiberius moved to reach behind and release the seal on Kirk's helmet.

From the way Kirk's eyes tried to follow the movement, Tiberius was certain his ghost knew what was going to happen. Tiberius paused a moment, curious to see if Kirk would manifest relief. People whose lives Tiberius ended often did that in the moment when they realized they no longer had to struggle, that all their pain would soon be over.

Yes, there it is, Tiberius thought. Kirk rocked back his head as if relaxing, in the final surrender.

He reached for Kirk's helmet release.

And then Kirk's head suddenly snapped forward in his helmet, driving that helmet forward so that it smashed directly into Tiberius's helmet, the two faceplates impacting dead center with unexpected force. The low-power structural integrity fields of both helmets were cancelled out by the impact, and cracks spread through both faceplates as through breaking ice.

Tiberius released Kirk in shock, pressing his gloves to his faceplate as his suit's pressure alarm sounded and he heard the high-pitched hiss of escaping atmosphere.

Tiberius bolted for the edge of the asteroid, leaving Kirk behind.

But Tiberius felt his boot catch on something.

It was Kirk!

Tiberius began to fall. He shot out both arms to keep his helmet from hitting the solid metal surface. The ghost had stuck out one of his useless hands to trip Tiberius, even though the act must have caused him unspeakable pain.

The ghost Kirk was wounded, without weapons, or soldiers. Yet he had dared try to kill the emperor at the cost of his own worthless life. His action made no sense.

Unless he truly *was* insane. It was the only answer for his unpredictability.

Tiberius rolled onto his back and kicked out at Kirk.

"Kill him!" Tiberius shouted to La Forge and Picard, even as he felt air rush past his face from his suit's interior. He had experienced the same sensation less than an hour ago. But, then, he had known the command-station airlock was repressurizing. Now, Tiberius didn't know if all the facilities were in place on the other side. "Kill him!"

Kirk was crawling toward him, his own faceplate crazed with dark lines. And not one lance of disruptor fire was reaching out for him.

Tiberius dared turn his head for a second to see why La Forge and Picard had refused to obey his order.

He was just in time to see the regent throw himself from the edge of the asteroid, his body beginning its downward arc with the rushing bulk of the second asteroid.

Commandant La Forge, though, was on one knee,

firing his disruptor at—the others. The ghost Kirk was not alone.

Tiberius saw Kirk's followers charging forward. The two in the lead were firing phasers.

"No!" Tiberius screamed. He had not come this far to be beaten by ghosts!

This was not his destiny.

Kirk felt as if he were trailing his hands through molten lava, but still he crawled forward. Tiberius would not escape. Kirk would not let him escape.

Flashes of phaser and disruptor fire! T'Val and Teilani and Spock! Kirk knew his team could deal with Tiberius's soldiers. Tiberius was his responsibility. Either he and Tiberius would beam up to the *Voyager* together, or they would die here, together. In this situation, for once there was no third way out.

"Life-support failure in thirty seconds," the computer voice said in his helmet.

Kirk knew he was almost in position to pin Tiberius. If he could just hold on a few more seconds till Scotty got a lock on them.

At that moment, Tiberius lifted his head and angled his helmet so that once again Kirk looked into the face of his double. Both of them were equally aware that they were seconds from suffocation, that each of them was driven by the same relentless, unthinking drive to go further than any before them. An irrepressible compulsion that exploded from the same recesses deep within their hearts. Except that one had learned to use that compulsion, and one had let that compulsion use him.

Face-to-face, gasping their last breaths, both Kirks

stared at each other, unmindful of death, focused only on their struggle.

They spoke the same words at the same time.

"Give up!"

Both answered with the same word, spoken with the same conviction.

"Never!"

And then as Kirk struggled to attach a magnetic lock to Tiberius's belt, Tiberius savagely jammed his elbow into Kirk's fractured faceplate.

Kirk saw the elbow coming, knew his suit's structural integrity field was no longer functioning, drew in a last breath, and then felt it explode past his lips in sudden, utter silence as the last of the atmosphere blasted from his suit.

His vision blurred as Tiberius rolled out from under him. He felt the pure cold of vacuum suck the moisture from his skin.

He reached out to grab Tiberius just as the monster reached the edge of the asteroid, then pushed himself off.

Kirk pulled himself to that edge, determined to follow, even as darkness swirled at the edge of his vision.

He saw three figures floating away from him, toward the asteroid.

No, that's wrong, Kirk thought with perfect clarity.

Now there were two figures. One figure. *Tiberius.*

Kirk's vision shrank to just that one image of that red-black suit, that figure clutching at his helmet as—

—a flash of phaser fire—

And Tiberius was consumed.

Gone.

Like the other figures.

Like life itself.

At least he died first, Kirk thought, even as a fading image of Teilani and the child he would never know flickered from his awareness.

Then the darkness was absolute.

FOUR

☆

Dr. Andrea M'Benga wanted answers and she wanted them *now.*

But the runabout pilot had nothing to say to her, beyond a few muttered and insincere apologies.

"I'm a doctor, not a navigator," M'Benga said, angrily pointing through the forward viewport. "But I know what Vulcan looks like. My great-grandfather lived on Vulcan. And that planet down there is *not* Vulcan."

Without looking back at the Starfleet physician who was literally breathing down his neck, the young pilot moved his fingers over the control surfaces. "Uh, no, ma'am—Doctor—it's not Vulcan. I'm sorry."

M'Benga studied the reflection of herself and the pilot in the slanted viewport, contemplating her next move. The pilot's confusing answer was definitely not helpful. He was young, maybe 22, with his Academy sideburns as sharp as trillium facets—which meant daily cutting, not weekly depilation—and a gray-shouldered uniform that looked fresh from the replicator—which meant evenings spent at the recyclermats, and not with friends.

In contrast, M'Benga knew, her uniform had a more

relaxed appearance. After 10 years in Starfleet, she preferred the softness of replicated fabric when it had been through the sonic washers a few times. Also, 24-hour shifts in a battle zone had taught her that a comfortable uniform was a necessity, not an indulgence. For the same reason, she liked to keep her black hair sleek and close to her skull. And further accentuating the difference between her and her young, by-the-book pilot, there was the item of nonstandard apparel she'd lately been wearing with her uniform—a narrow headband of green, yellow, and red kente cloth. Up till a few months ago, she had worn the colorful headband only with her off-duty clothes. But after a few days at her current posting on Deep Space 9, with the number of elaborate Bajoran earrings she'd seen on the station's Starfleet staff, she'd thought, *Why not?* She could always take it off if Command objected.

But when Captain Sisko had noticed it, not only had he recognized the kente design but they had ended up having weekly lunches together during which she attempted to teach him Swahili. Starfleet protocol was a bit more relaxed on the frontier. She had always appreciated that kind of extra latitude, and it only made her miss her old ship, the *Tobias,* and Captain Christine MacDonald all the more.

But thinking about the past wasn't helping her deal with this obstructionist pilot. Truth be told, what she really wanted to do was to whup him upside the head. A good expression, that. She could remember her great-grandfather saying it to her when she got too rambunctious with the *sehlats* he kept on the little *plomeek* farm he'd retired to near Vulcan's Voroth Sea. *You watch out, girl, or else they'll whup you upside the head,* she could hear him say. Who knew how far back the saying went in her family's history?

But since Starfleet frowned on senior officers striking junior officers, no matter how deserving said junior officer might be, the good doctor decided on another tactic.

She slipped into the empty copilot's chair. "Ensign Adamski, let's start at the beginning. You came to Deep Space 9 to take me from my duties there to attend a classified Starfleet Medical seminar on new biological weapons being used by the Dominion. Is that correct?"

The pilot finally deigned to glance at her. "Doctor, I really am sorry, but there is no medical seminar. And my name isn't Adamski."

M'Benga sat back in her chair. The runabout pilot still looked like he was no more than two minutes older than a wet-behind-the ears cadet, fresh from the Academy. But there *was* something much older and more assured about the way he was refusing to give her any more information. Her initial annoyance, which had been threatening to become anger, shifted closer to sudden apprehension. There was a war on. And the Founders were shape-shifters. "Answer me this. Is this or is this not a Starfleet runabout?"

The pilot nodded. "That I can answer. Yes. This is a Starfleet runabout. This is a Starfleet mission."

"Then why in blazes have you shanghaied me?"

The pilot chewed his lower lip. "Uh, I'm unfamiliar with the word *shanghaied*. Is it . . . Vulcan?"

"Oh, for . . . okay, from the top. Whatever your name is, you're wearing ensign's pips. I'm a commander. I order you to take me back to DS9."

Instead of replying, the pilot made some adjustments

and the runabout entered into a standard orbit of the world below. M'Benga still had no idea which world it was. If not for the shape of its continents and seas, it might have been Earth. All the colors were right. And from the size and number of the cities and the transportation network she could see on the night side, lit up like sparkling jewels, it probably wasn't a colony world.

"Did you hear me?" she asked testily. "I gave you an order."

"Um, I'm already under orders, Commander. From Admiral Jorge Santos."

"Never heard of him," M'Benga said. Through the slanted viewport, she saw flashing lights ahead. They were coming up on an orbital facility of some kind.

"I think that's the idea," the pilot told her.

M'Benga's apprehension reverted to profound irritation. She folded her arms and narrowed her eyes at the young man. "You sound like someone who knows a lot more than he's saying."

"I'm really just a transport pilot for the admiral. Commodore Twining will be able to answer your questions."

"Commodore Twining. And when might I be meeting him?"

The pilot pointed ahead. They had almost reached the orbital facility. "Just a few more minutes. We're about to dock."

From her seat in the copilot's station, M'Benga observed their destination as it grew larger. It appeared to her to be a standard Starfleet design: a series of large, disc-shaped habitats stacked together, one atop the other on a central spine, with a few smaller discs held at a distance by radial arms.

As the pilot skilfully eased the runabout to one side of the facility, M'Benga caught sight of a Starfleet emblem on the topmost habitat disc. The familiar insignia made her feel a little more at ease, though she was still going to demand some answers of whoever Commodore Twining might be. Squinting, she could just make out that there were letters beneath the emblem, though she wasn't yet close enough to read them.

The pilot touched a communications control. "This is the *Runabout Ohio* requesting docking information."

As M'Benga listened intently, the unmistakable Starfleet computer voice answered. *"Runabout Ohio,* you are cleared for docking in Bay Five. Drop shields for sensor sweep."

"That was a computer," M'Benga said.

"Yes, ma'am." The pilot shut down the shields. The doctor was immediately uncomfortable with the sudden knowledge that only a few centimeters of duranium were between her and the void of space, completely unprotected by force fields. What if a tiny piece of ice or a leftover bolt or two from the construction of that orbital facility were to strike the viewport at 30,000 kilometers an hour? The hair on the back of her neck prickled. She'd much rather be beamed.

"Is this an automated station of some kind?"

"No, ma'am."

"Sensor sweep completed," the computer announced. "Dr. M'Benga, please confirm your identity through voice authorization."

"What? Listen here, you lump of isolinear circuit droppings, I have no intention of—"

"M'Benga, Andrea Nyota, identity confirmed. Stand by for tractor beam."

M'Benga pressed her lips tightly together, really angry now.

"Last chance, Ensign. Either put me in contact with someone in authority, or you get me the hell out of here—*now!*"

A lavender beam shot out from the facility and glimmered over the viewport. The facility began to fill the viewport as the runabout was drawn toward the opening pressure doors of Docking Bay 5.

Then two details moved her apprehension closer to fear.

The letters beneath the Starfleet emblem spelled out AGRICULTURAL RESEARCH STATION 51. ALPHA CENTAURI IV.

And in the area directly above the docking-bay doors, she saw phaser emitters, poorly disguised as an old-fashioned subspace relay, and big enough for a starship.

M'Benga abandoned her half-worked-out plan to give her pilot a nerve pinch, then hijack the runabout.

Now she wanted to know why Starfleet had used subterfuge to bring her to humanity's oldest colony world. Why an agricultural research station in one of the safest sectors of space needed starship-class firepower.

And most of all, she wanted to know why she suddenly had the feeling she had been here before.

The airlock door puffed open and M'Benga hesitated before stepping through. It had been a long time since she had seen an airlock in a docking bay, as if the pressure door and forcefield weren't protection enough.

She had only been on Agricultural Research Station 51 for five minutes, and already it was looking more like a fortress than a science facility.

"Dr. M'Benga, a pleasure."

The man striding toward her was a Starfleet commodore, shorter than she was, but with the same impossibly crisp, by-the-book appearance her nameless pilot had displayed.

"Commodore Twining?" M'Benga asked.

"Call me Nate. We don't stand on ceremony here."

M'Benga shook hands with the man, from force of habit rather than any desire to be polite. Even he was looking familiar. "Have we met?"

Twining smiled. "Oh, I'm sure we've seen each other at medical conferences over the years. You know what they're like."

"I do. I also have a very good memory for faces. But . . . I can't place yours."

Commodore Twining gestured for the doctor to proceed along the corridor. "After our meeting, we'll compare our schedules. I'm certain we'll find we've attended many conferences in common."

M'Benga walked at the commodore's side. She noticed that the corridor was deserted, despite the fact that a station this size should have a crew numbering close to 500. "What meeting might that be?" she asked.

"It will be easier to show you."

They'd reached a turbolift. Surprisingly, the commodore had to put his hand on an identity-scanning plate. Then he stepped aside, indicating that she had to do the same.

"All this for a turbolift?" she asked.

"There's a war on, Commander," the commodore replied easily.

But something else wasn't right to M'Benga. "From the looks of things, this station has been around a lot longer than we've even known about the Dominion."

The turbolift doors opened. The commodore waved her inside, then stepped in after her. "You're very observant, doctor. That's why we enjoy working with you."

M'Benga felt her stomach tighten. "So . . . I *have* been here before?"

Twining smiled pleasantly. "Do you think you have?"

"I have to tell you, Commodore, you're making me feel distinctly uneasy."

"I know. But it will pass."

The turbolift stopped, the doors opened, and M'Benga paused in surprise. She had fully expected to see another corridor. But what waited before her seemed to be a spacedock installation, as if the center of Facility 51 were hollow, with enough room to contain a starship.

"If you please, doctor," Twining said. He waited for M'Benga to exit the turbolift first.

She did. And through the towering viewports that lay before her, she found herself gazing into a spherical chamber large enough to encompass a Sovereign-class vessel. Though she could see no way a starship could enter the chamber—there were no docking doors visible from her perspective.

However, the docking sphere did contain a ship, though the vessel was only about one-third the length of a Sovereign-class warp nacelle.

M'Benga walked forward to the viewports. She looked from the small craft floating in complete isolation beyond the viewports to the chamber's white ceilings twenty meters above her, laced with power conduits and pipes worthy of a terraforming station. All around her on the deck were control consoles, transporter pads, science stations; the chamber that looked into the improbable spacedock was the largest and most complete lab M'Benga had ever seen. Some of the equipment was completely unknown to her.

"All this," she said, pointing to the small ship, "for that?"

The commodore stood beside her at the viewport, hands behind his back. "Do you recognize it?"

M'Benga frowned. Another of her questions answered with a question. The inductive discovery method was so very tedious. "Have I seen that before, too?"

"Doubtful. But perhaps something like it."

M'Benga sighed but thought back to the dreary ship identification classes she'd been forced to take at the Academy. It *was* somehow familiar. And yet bizarre. Almost as if an old-style submarine hull had been—she had it.

"It's a DY-100! One of the old sleeper ships from . . . I don't know, centuries ago, at least."

Commodore Twining nodded. "That's certainly what it appears to be."

The commodore had her full attention now. " 'What it appears to be'?" Then M'Benga remembered something else. "I heard some engineers talking in a bar a few months ago. About rumors that another group of the so-called genetic supermen from the twentieth century had been found." M'Benga fixed her eyes firmly on her host. "And they were being examined on Alpha Centauri IV."

The commodore nodded. "I've heard that rumor. Actually, I created it."

M'Benga snorted. "Commodore, you'd better start giving me some answers if you want me to continue this discussion."

Twining motioned toward a science station farther

along the lab's spacious floor. "That ship is only about eighty years old, though it was deliberately designed to look like one much older."

"Why?"

"That's one of the questions we hope you'll be able to help us with."

"If it's not a sleeper ship, then what is it?" M'Benga asked briskly, more interested in answers than questions at the moment.

"Oh, it *is* a sleeper ship. It has twenty-two hibernation compartments, and seventeen are occupied."

Twining led M'Benga to the science station, where he input a security code. A display screen flickered to show an image of a cramped cargo hold, with horizontal doors on either side, stacked two at a time. M'Benga realized the doors were reflective, as if they were transparent, but from the angle of the visual sensor, she couldn't see through any of them.

"Occupied by whom?" she asked. "Or should I say, what?"

"You be the judge." The commodore touched a communications control. "Doctor, are you there?"

"Where else would I be?" A figure moved in front of the sensor in the cargo hold. Startled, M'Benga recognized him at once.

"Dr. Zimmerman?"

The bald doctor on the screen frowned at her. "Would Dr. Zimmerman be in a class-eleven biological quarantine zone without protective clothing?"

"Oh," M'Benga said. "You're an EMH."

The holographic doctor rolled his eyes. "Sorry to disappoint you, Doctor . . . ?"

"Doctor Andrea M'Benga."

At that, the holographic doctor brightened. "Ah, author of *Medical Melds: A Millennium of Vulcan Healers*. And the exquisite piece in the *Journal of Federation Medicine* about cloning drift and quantum uncertainty. Delighted to meet you."

"Thank you," M'Benga said. She knew she was interacting with only a holographic interpretation of Dr. Lewis Zimmerman, but she had learned that the best way to deal with artificial life forms was to simply take them at face value. Perhaps somewhere in the mathematical algorithms that made this simulation possible, some numeric equivalent of delight had been calculated. Who was any organic being to say that the equations of joy were less valid than their emotional analogs?

"Doctor," Twining said, "I hate to interrupt." The EMH grimaced as if he had heard that phrase a thousand times before. "But could you move the visual sensor so Dr. M'Benga can see one of the . . . patients."

"I live to serve," the EMH retorted, but he reached up, and for a moment, his out-of-focus holographic hand blocked the view on the screen.

"Are there really class-eleven organisms in there?" M'Benga asked the commodore.

"None we've detected, but . . . until we know exactly what we're dealing with . . . we thought it best to take no chances."

M'Benga watched the image on the screen jiggle as the EMH carried it to a better vantage point. "I'm not aware of any type of disease organism from eight decades in the past that would be more than an inconvenience today," she said. "Alien microbes, yes. New mutations, perhaps. But germs from the recent past . . . ?"

"Technically, Commander, this sleeper ship is not from the past."

Before M'Benga could ask the commodore what he meant by *technically,* the image on the screen stabilized. Now the sensor was aimed directly into a hibernation chamber.

M'Benga's interest sharpened. "Is that . . . ?"

"Yes," the commodore said. "Doctor, if you could show us the rest of the chambers?"

The EMH's petulant disembodied voice came back from the console speaker. "It's not as if I have anything important to do."

Then one by one, all the hibernation chambers passed before the sensor.

"They're just children . . ." M'Benga said wonderingly. "Human children. All of them?"

"All of them."

"How long have they been in hibernation?"

"About eighty years."

"But, you said they weren't from the past."

"Technically, they're not." The commodore held her eyes with his. "Technically, they're from another universe. And technically, they're like no human we've ever seen."

M'Benga folded her arms, anticipating the challenge before her, all feelings of annoyance or anger or unease banished from her being.

There was a mystery before her of epic proportions.

And somehow she knew there was nothing she liked better than to solve mysteries for the commodore.

But when had she met him before? And what other mysteries had she solved?

FIVE

Kirk realized he must be dead.

Then he realized that if he was aware of being dead, he must still be alive. But he couldn't feel his body, had no sense of position, not even the sensation of floating weightlessly.

He tried to remember how this had come about. He recalled running across an asteroid, heading for the edge of an artificial-gravity field.

That's it, he thought. *I fell off the edge of the world.*

For reasons he didn't understand, he pictured himself hanging between two nearly colliding asteroids as they spun past each other in the void.

But in that picture, his environment suit was all wrong. It wasn't Starfleet high-visibility white for easy identification and rescue in space. It was so darkly red it could almost be black.

No, that's not me. That's—

Then he remembered who he had been chasing. That final fight. How, faceplate shattered, he had crawled to the edge of the asteroid, only to see himself—*no,*

Tiberius!—tumbling in free fall until the phaser hit and he himself vanished like the others.

But I *didn't vanish,* Kirk thought. I . . .

He opened his eyes.

Then gasped in surprise at the face that was only centimeters from his: young, narrow, and topped with a shock of unruly blond hair.

"Now what's the matter?" the holographic doctor asked.

"Nothing . . ." Kirk croaked. His throat was raw. His voice was barely audible. "I was just . . . surprised."

"Well, who wouldn't be? I mean, imagine waking up in sickbay and finding a *doctor.* What are the odds of that?"

Kirk realized he was stretched out on a diagnostic bed. He tried to sit up but a surgical palette covered his chest and it was all he could do to lift his head.

He tried to remember where he had met this particular Emergency Medical Hologram before, the Mark II version whose personality programming seemed to be a few q-bits short of a kiloquad. "Am I . . . on the *Sovereign?"* This version of the EMH had been installed on Nechayev's ship and had behaved quite courageously, Kirk recalled.

But the EMH gazed down at Kirk with pity. "The *Sovereign* is last year's model. Does this *look* like the *Sovereign?"* He gestured expansively around the sickbay. "Do we see any buckets of leeches? Phlebotomy troughs? I don't think so."

Kirk had to admit the sickbay was unlike any he had been in before. Almost every surface was a smooth, oddly matte-finished white, with bulkheads rising from the deck in elegant curves that blended seamlessly into the sculpted ceiling. He lay back again. Incredibly, just that amount of movement had drained him. "No offense. What ship is this?"

With evident smugness, the EMH said, "You are onboard the pride of Starfleet, the *Leviathan*-class science vessel, *U.S.S. Heisenberg.*"

Kirk couldn't resist. "You're certain?"

The EMH frowned. "That's the first time I've heard that. *Today.*"

Kirk licked at his dry lips, tried shifting on the diagnostic bed, experienced a strange ripple of discomfort deep inside his chest. He decided much of his grogginess and inability to move was the result of some kind of anesthetic. At least, he hoped so.

"Have I had surgery?"

The EMH shrugged. "Minor. A trifle. Hardly worth mentioning. A little matter of *all the alveoli in your lungs* being ruptured by exposure to vacuum. But the replacement lungs seem to be working well. So far."

Kirk sighed. Maybe he was dead after all. And his hell was being trapped for eternity with a computer with a bad attitude. He tried again. "Where is everybody?"

"Let's see now," the EMH said thoughtfully. "Current Federation figures suggest a total human galactic population of one hundred billion. Would you like me to run through the list of their whereabouts *alphabetically?*"

"Spock? Or Dr. McCoy? Anyone else?"

"As long as they aren't an artificial life form, is that it?"

Kirk stared fixedly at the hologram, remembering three of the best words he had learned in the twenty-fourth century. "Computer . . ."

"Don't you *dare,*" the EMH warned.

70

". . . end program."

The Mark Two blurred in a flurry of holographic static, then was gone.

Kirk felt better already. He cleared his throat, dismissing its painful protests. "Kirk to Spock."

He waited less than two seconds for the response.

"Spock here. I am pleased to hear that you are awake."

Kirk smiled. Now he would get answers to his questions. "I'd be pleased if someone could tell me exactly *where* I am, *how long* I've been out, and *what* I've missed."

"The holographic doctor was supposed to brief you after he alerted us you were awake."

"He . . . had better things to do."

"Indeed. I am on my way. Please do not leave sickbay."

Kirk glanced at the surgical palette holding him in place. "That sounds . . . logical."

"Tri-ox," McCoy said as he positioned a pillow behind Kirk's neck a few minutes later. "That's what kept you going after you blacked out."

"Aye," Scott said, "that and Captain Picard in his shuttle."

Kirk pushed his bandaged hands against the arms of the chair he'd moved to and took a deliberately slow, deep breath, trying to detect any sensation that would let him know he was breathing with anything other than the lungs he'd been born with. As he exhaled, he looked around again at the unusual sickbay—it seemed so modern and advanced he almost felt as if he had jumped another 78 years into the future. He risked another deep breath, and other than a slight stiffness beneath his sternum, felt no difference.

"Amazing," he said.

"What is?" McCoy growled. "The fact that you've made a fool of yourself again? I told you not to go down there. I told you—"

Kirk narrowed his eyes at McCoy. "End program," he said. But it didn't work. His old friend remained firm and solid—and determined not to let him forget his frailties.

"You can't get rid of me that easily," McCoy said.

Kirk nodded, looking up at his three companions through time: Spock, McCoy, and Scotty. "I wouldn't want to." He paused for a moment, remembering those who were missing, who had so often helped him before. And then his thoughts turned, as always, to the future.

"Where's Teilani?"

"She is on the *Pauli,*" Spock said. "There is a Romulan physician on the ship's medical staff. Considering Teilani's pregnancy, we felt examination by a specialist would be prudent."

"Of course," Kirk agreed. But now there was something else he didn't understand. "Is the *Pauli* a Romulan ship?"

"It is a Starfleet science vessel," Spock said. "And, as yet, I have no information on its unusual staffing arrangements—there are a great many exchange officers onboard. The ships do, however, appear to be prototypes of some kind."

"If they are prototypes," Scott added, "then they're the strangest ones I've ever seen. All three of them."

Kirk knew Spock could see that he was bursting with questions but was still too weak to ask all of them.

Spock folded his hands behind his back. "To put it briefly, Jim, less than sixty seconds after Tiberius vanished—"

"Vanished? I saw him get shot . . . didn't I?"

"I am surprised you could see anything, given the fact you were exposed to vacuum at the time. However, T'Val does claim to have scored a direct hit on Tiberius, just before he dematerialized."

"Dematerialized how?"

"We don't know," McCoy said. "Tiberius. His men. They all . . . *phht.* That's what these ships are here for. They're all science vessels: the *Heisenberg,* the *Schrödinger,* and the *Pauli.*"

"Twentieth-century physicists," Scott added. "Quantum physics. At least, what they called quantum physics back then, even though they had no idea that—"

Spock interrupted. "Another time, Mr. Scott. Suffice it to say that Tiberius's fate is still being investigated. You, however, were beamed to Captain Picard's shuttle. Commanders Riker and Data were able to stabilize you, and Dr. Crusher managed to restore enough of the *Enterprise*'s sickbay facilities to maintain you on a pulmonary support unit. She thought you would have to be taken back to a starbase under medical stasis, but the *Heisenberg* proved to have exceptional medical facilities. So your lung replacement surgery was carried out here."

"How long since Tiberius . . . dematerialized?"

"Six hours," McCoy said. "How's it feel to breathe through those things?"

"Same as always."

"Good. It'll be a few weeks before the blood supply is fully restored at the capillary level, so you're apt to feel breathless if you exert yourself. But we'll keep you on tri-ox compound and set up a daily routine of tissue regeneration." McCoy tapped his own chest. "I had mine done years . . . decades ago. Haven't had a problem with them since."

"So I've noticed," Kirk said with a wry smile. He looked up at Spock. "So the *Enterprise* survived?" For Picard's sake, he was relieved, and happy.

But then he noticed the way his three friends exchanged almost furtive glances. *"Is* there something wrong with the ship?"

Again his friends hesitated, until through some unspoken agreement, Scott took over. He spoke haltingly, as if not all was known to him either. "It's difficult to say, one way or the other. They were able to stop the autodestruct without much fuss. But . . . the ship seems t' have suffered some peculiar interior damage."

"Because of the failed transport?" Kirk asked, puzzled.

Scott's next words spilled out in a rush of frustration. "Jim, the fact of the matter is, I don't know because she won't let me talk to Geordi."

"Who won't let you?"

"Hu-Lin Radisson," Spock said. "Captain of the *Heisenberg.*"

"And commander of the science convoy," McCoy added.

"She's not letting us talk to anyone from the *Enterprise,*" Scott continued. "Or from the rescue convoy. Or—"

Kirk held up a newly wrapped hand to stop Scott. The replacement bandages were thinner, less bulky, than before, but now he couldn't feel a thing past the middle of each forearm. *McCoy must have me on some type of neural block,* he guessed.

"Scotty, just a minute. There're *two* different convoys here?"

"Aye. Captain Radisson and the science vessels were here within an hour after Tiberius escaped—vanished—dematerialized—whatever the blaggard did. The relief convoy arrived about an hour after that."

Spock added, "And Captain Radisson is apparently making them hold position half a light-year from the labor-camp asteroid while the *Schrödinger* ferries survivors to them."

"Apparently?" Kirk asked. His brain was struggling to make sense of all the new details of the latest mystery surrounding his mirror universe counterpart.

"In addition to the restrictions established by Captain Radisson," Spock continued, "it appears communications have been badly affected by a local disturbance in the subspace medium. About the time Tiberius vanished, our suit communicators were overloaded by a powerful subspace pulse. Logically, that is the most likely cause of the disruption. But what caused that disruption, I cannot say."

Kirk looked from one friend to the other. "I take it I'm not the only one who thinks there's something wrong here."

Spock answered for them all. "Despite having been caught up in the middle of these events since the beginning, I am left with the strong suspicion that Captain Radisson knows even more about them than do we."

"I'd like to meet Captain Radisson," Kirk said.

"That is fortunate for all of us."

Kirk waited for Spock to explain himself.

"Because the captain has stated in no uncertain terms that until you and she come to some agreement, the four of us, and Teilani, are to consider ourselves under ship arrest."

"What have we done *this* time?" Kirk asked.

"It's not what we've done," McCoy said.

"Apparently," Spock added, "it is because of what we know."

But as far as Kirk was concerned, no one seemed to know anything.

At least not what he needed to know.

Where had Tiberius gone?

And who was helping him now?

SIX

———————— ☆ ————————

Dr. M'Benga watched the genetic profiles of the children move across the screen of her science station. And it was *her* science station. These control surfaces were configured to her preferences. She recognized the layout of the screen displays. It was her own idiosyncratic system of organization.

This was no longer a case of some ill-defined feeling of déjà vu. There was no doubt in M'Benga's mind that she *had* been to Station 51 before, probably more than once. Nor that, somehow, all memories she had of previous visits here had been wiped from her mind.

She was well aware that there were many methods of doing so, from bi–neural neutralizers to engrammatic agonists. And even as she searched for clues in the data that streamed by, M'Benga worked out a plan for avoiding such memory theft today.

Then an incongruous pattern caught her attention. "Computer, stop. Reverse two screens."

As the data streamed backward, M'Benga became aware of Commodore Twining suddenly at her side. "You found something?"

"Maybe." M'Benga looked up at the commodore. His short hair, more white than black in it, was as perfectly groomed as the rest of him, a match for his precisely arranged uniform with its phaser-straight jacket seam bisecting him with geometric exactitude. She doubted a full sensor sweep would turn up one loose thread.

The computer displayed the screen she had requested. It was a fractal graph of amino-acid distribution in the genetic structure of child 7. She'd chosen this type of fractal representation, a method of her own devising, because it was a technique that enabled the human eye and mind to quickly grasp the totality of an individual's genetic code. Seeing the visual relationship of the code's different amino acids was infinitely more efficient than spending hours viewing the complete, base pair–by–base pair listing of a human genotype. M'Benga knew that in such inspections the constant stream of letter combinations quickly became nonsensical.

Pictures and patterns, on the other hand, were what the human mind had evolved to understand. And M'Benga understood the pattern she was seeing now.

She pointed to the screen where a spiked curl of yellow unfurled like the tip of a fern from a central spiral of red. "There," M'Benga said. "That's not human."

She saw the commodore step back from her, as if startled, to glance beyond her science station, through the enormous viewport, and to the sleeper ship floating in its web of tractor beams at the center of the docking chamber.

"Can you tell what it is?" he asked.

M'Benga placed her hands to either side of the computer's control surface. She needed more information and she needed it now. "Commodore, if they're from another universe, how can it be that their DNA is so similar to ours?"

"Maybe *universe* isn't the word for it. Another quantum reality."

Now M'Benga was startled. She twisted around to confront the commodore. "The *mirror* universe?"

M'Benga whistled as she saw Twining's nod of assent. As chief medical officer of the *Tobias,* she had read the classified standing orders detailing protocols to be followed upon contact with beings from that parallel existence, beings known to Starfleet for more than a century. Her level of clearance hadn't allowed her to access all the details of conditions in that other reality, but the few warnings that were available to her made it sound extremely disturbing. An alternate universe in which humans and Vulcans had been subjugated by an alliance of Klingons and Cardassians wasn't an existence she wished to experience.

And even more unusual than the protocols had been the procedures that were to be followed in the event a Starfleet vessel made contact with *duplicates* of its command staff and/or crew . . . M'Benga had found even the possibility of such contact bordering on the surreal.

"That means that genetically, they're *exactly* like us," she said, seeking absolute confirmation.

"Exactly."

"Then I should be able to get the computer to identify any standard deviations. You do keep the *Federation Genetic Atlas* online?"

The commodore flashed a quick, nervous smile. "You ask that every time."

"So we're not playing games anymore? You admit I've been here before?"

"No games. I'm sorry, Doctor. You have been here many times."

"How did—how do you erase my memories?"

The commodore put his hand on her shoulder as if he were an old friend. M'Benga's first thought was to push his hand away, but then she had the distinctly unsettling feeling that Twining *was* an old friend of hers.

"Andrea," he said, "I know this is difficult, but you have to trust me on two very important points."

Struggling to suspend her natural pragmatism and rationality, M'Benga forced herself to listen. Already, though, it almost seemed to her as if she could remember each word he was about to say, but only in the instant before he said it.

"First, years ago, when we told you about our work here, you volunteered to help us, and we hid nothing from you. You knew and accepted that your memories of your time with the project would be suppressed after each visit."

M'Benga was taken by his choice of words.

As if he had read her mind, Twining said, "That's right. Suppressed. Not erased. This is still a Starfleet operation. Rather than practicing mind control, we prefer to think of what we do to your memories as merely enforcing a long period of communications blackout." Another fleeting smile transformed his lined face, and M'Benga had a sudden memory of what he had looked like when his hair had been completely black. She had known him that long. "The same type of blackout that any Starfleet facility might enforce in a time of war to prevent the chance that unauthorized information might be inadvertently spread."

M'Benga spoke haltingly. "You say a time of war, and you say I've been helping you for many years. So . . . we're not talking about the war with the Dominion, are we?"

Twining shook his head, and M'Benga had no trouble detecting the sadness within him.

"If my memories are going to be suppressed again, why can't you tell me more?"

"Because they *are* only suppressed. If we wiped them out completely, I could tell you everything. But the next time you came here, I'd have to tell it to you all over again. And again. And again. And after too many treatments, we'd run the risk of carving out parts of your memory that have nothing to do with your work here." He gave her shoulder a final, paternal squeeze, then took his hand away. "You must have noticed by now that you haven't seen any of the other people who work here. And when you need to know something about this facility, it comes to mind."

"Sometimes," M'Benga said slowly, *knowing* he was right but not yet *feeling* that he was.

The commodore looked back at the sleeper ship. "Because we'd rather keep certain information from you than risk permanently erasing it. Accept our intentions for your well-being as evidence that you are here of your own free will, even if you don't remember giving it."

"Do I have a choice?"

"Not now. Not when we're so close." Twining turned back to her, and M'Benga suddenly knew she had seen that intense face a thousand times before, anxious, caring, upset, jubilant. "Please, Andrea . . . identify the nonhuman genetic information in that child."

M'Benga sighed, still disconcerted. Perhaps her subconscious would work out the problem while her conscious attention was directed elsewhere. "Let me set up the search."

As Twining left her side, M'Benga turned back to the console to link the fractal display to the *Federation Genetic Atlas*. She knew it could take days to run a full comparison of all recorded genetic structures encountered in the known galaxy, so she set limits to narrow the search to the most obvious possibilities. The yellow spiral of nonhuman DNA in the child might indicate he had an alien ancestor, perhaps Vulcan or Betazoid, four or five generations ago. She selected HUMANOIDS, POST-CONTACT from the menu and put the computer to work comparing the DNA fragment from child 7 to the complete genetic sequences of some 320 warp-capable humanoid species to which the Prime Directive would not apply. One of those would be the most likely source of a human–alien hybrid.

Knowing the comparison would take a few minutes, she got up to stretch her legs.

The commodore was back again, offering her a tumbler filled with a carbonated dark brown liquid. M'Benga smiled as she recognized its sweet scent. Twining *was* her friend. "Cola! You know, there's a bar on Deep Space 9 that claims to have every drink in the universe, and the owner can't even get his replicators to come anywhere near this." She took a tentative sip. "Magnificent."

"They make it down on Alpha IV. A very old factory. One of the first ever built here. But with the carbonation, it doesn't travel well. We always have some here for you."

"No wonder I took the job."

Twining stood beside her at the viewport, watching the ship as she did.

"How did it get here?" she asked.

"To this universe? We don't know. A Starfleet tanker found it in a parking orbit near Rigel VII. The commander recognized the type of ship it is from his history lessons at the Academy."

M'Benga nodded. She had had the same lessons. "Captain Kirk and Khan Noonien Singh."

M'Benga smiled to herself as she remembered her assignment on Chal during the virogen crisis. "I met him, you know. Captain Kirk."

The commodore nodded. "I know."

M'Benga glanced sideways at Twining, wondering if she'd told him her entire life story, perhaps all her secrets. If so, she still couldn't remember. "How many years did you say we've been working together?"

"I didn't. But it's ten. We recruited you right after you graduated."

Now that *made no sense whatsoever,* M'Benga thought. "Who have we been fighting for ten years? The Borg?"

"Those children aren't Borg, Andrea. You saw their profiles. They're all human. The EMH has scanned every cubic centimeter. No nanoprobes. No symbionts."

"Then why are you—we—so . . . afraid of them? I mean, to keep them in such extreme bio-isolation."

"Afraid is not a strong enough word."

At that, M'Benga made a concentrated mental effort to see if she could dredge up anything more about her work here, to help explain the commodore's fears. But absolutely nothing relevant surfaced in her mind. She turned her attention back to the present. "Have you tried waking one of the children?"

The commodore frowned. "A few of them did come out of hibernation once."

"When?"

"Sometime after the tanker commander reported finding the ship."

M'Benga didn't like the sound of that. Somehow, she knew that Commodore Twining was a man for whom everything must be precise. Yet he had used the word *sometime*. "What happened?"

"The tanker crew conducted a preliminary inventory of the ship. A five-person away team. Some type of automated system revived one of the children. What happened next, we don't know. Except that all five members of the away team were killed."

"How?"

The commodore sighed. "You name it. There were bruises, cuts, gouges, several broken arms. But the cause of death for each member of the team was different. Neurotoxins, mostly. Synapse inhibitors. Adrenaline accelerators. For one of the bodies, we still can't even identify the toxin that was used."

M'Benga looked at him sharply. "Have I studied these children before?"

"No," the commodore said firmly. "This is the first time we've brought you in about this ship."

Her workstation chimed to indicate its search was over, and M'Benga left the viewport to view the result. Commodore Twining followed after her.

A series of graphs scrolled by on one of M'Benga's

display screens, marking the percentage of correlation between the alien DNA in child 7 and the genetic structure of all the warp-capable humanoids known to the Federation. She turned to Twining. "This ship. You've found others?"

But the commodore ignored her question. He was staring intently at the screen. "No match."

Surprised, M'Benga addressed the computer. "Display full correlation results."

There was a 22 percent correlation to Vulcans, but that was the strongest, not enough to confirm that it was a Vulcan gene sequence. All the other species comparisons hovered around the 10 to 15 percent range. M'Benga knew that one school of thought claimed this was the figure to be expected of blind chance, whereas another believed it was evidence that all species in the galaxy had been seeded by an earlier race of starfarers.

"Could it be an artificial gene?" the commodore asked.

"Doubtful," M'Benga answered. She toggled the display back to the fractal graph of child 7's genotype. "See how chaotic the pattern is? If there were artificial-gene sequences in there, something inserted through genetic engineering, the fractal pattern would be noticeably disturbed. We'd see some straight lines, discrete blocks of color, clear signs of order in what should be an almost random structure."

The commodore bit his lip, apparently troubled. "But surely the very fact that it's a *structure* implies that there is some order to it."

"Now we're leaving biology and heading into philosophy." M'Benga hesitated for a moment, unsure how much the commodore already knew but was not telling her. But Twining merely waited, as if wanting her to continue.

"Our universe," M'Benga began, "however it came into being, is a result of the fundamental forces of nature—that is, electromagnetism, quantum gravity, and the strong, weak, and subspatial nuclear forces—all of them operating in accordance with the fundamental principles of nature. And those principles include entropy, quintessential inflation, the broken symmetry of time, and self-organization.

"The self-organizing principle is the one that most directly affects the development of life. It is simply the tendency of matter and energy in our universe to form associations that are stable over time. At its most basic level, life is a form of self-organized matter and energy that is not only stable but capable of reproduction. And in nature, the most successful forms of life are usually those that end up reshaping their environment—most often blindly, occasionally with intelligence—to make that environment more conducive to the continued existence of life."

M'Benga paused, but again the commodore said nothing. So she continued. "Centuries ago, there used to be a rancorous debate about whether life existed only on Earth or if it was common throughout the universe. Now we know the answer. It's everywhere. And one of the reasons it was so difficult to determine the origins of life is because it has so many. Life arises from clay substrates, geothermal vents, solar-heated tidal pools, lightning discharges in atmosphere . . . Virtually any planet, moon, or asteroid with an environment in the right temperature range will almost inevitably give rise to life of some kind. But because there are so many ways for life to get started, and so many paths it can take once it's established, the end result at a genetic level is invariably random."

M'Benga was about to go on with her discourse when the commodore finally reacted to what she was saying. "But so many species are humanoid in appearance. That's not random."

"No, that's convergent evolution, a natural process that's an inevitable result of the self-organizing principle." M'Benga saw the frown on Twining's face. "Similar habitats tending to force the appearance of similar adaptations. On Earth, penguins are birds and killer whales are mammals, yet because both have evolved to exploit the same habitat, both species exhibit the same type of protective coloration. Another example—the eye. It's such a useful organ for perceiving the environment that it independently evolved more than forty separate times on Earth. Again, it's the result of the many random processes of life being shaped by a common feature of the environment—in this case, visible light."

M'Benga adapted her argument to the case at hand. "The bipedal humanoid form is an efficient design for coping with the common ecological features found on Class-M planets. We know evolution produces random mutations but that the mutations that persist are usually those which increase the likelihood of an individual's or a group's survival within a given environment. Thus," she looked directly at Twining, "whether a life form evolved from the iron seas of Earth or the copper seas of Vulcan, what is important is the fact that both planets have similar habitats. This is what led to the development of life forms with dissimilar blood chemistry nevertheless taking on the same overall physical arrangement."

Twining hadn't taken his eyes off the fractal pattern on the screen. "So it's all random to you. Leaving these children aside for the moment, in your study of galactic biology, and given the similarities among many of the species from different planets, you don't see any indications of deliberate genetic manipulation, seeding, anything like that?"

"You mean like the Preservers?" M'Benga asked. "Some ancient alien race that roamed the stars like Johnny Appleseed?" *Surely I've had* this *conversation with Twining before,* she thought. It was a standard ongoing debate on any starship. She couldn't count the number of long nights on the *Tobias* that she and Captain MacDonald and Chief Engineer Barc had argued it back and forth and back again.

"The Preservers," Twining said. "Or Dr. Galen's ancestral race."

M'Benga had also heard those arguments before, so many times that her response now was nearly automatic. Even as she spoke, she was beginning another search on her workstation. Instead of looking for another species that might account for the nonhuman DNA in child 7, this time she instructed the computer to compare the child's genetic sequence with all known genotypes of lifeforms of any kind on Vulcan. Maybe one of the child's ancestors had merely caught a Vulcan flu or cold, and some of the disease organism's genes ended up being incorporated in its host's genotype.

"I've read Captain Picard's papers about Galen's ancestral race," M'Benga said as she input the new search parameters, "and I don't dispute they existed." The race in question, still unnamed, had apparently been the first species in the galaxy to develop a starfaring society, more than 4 billion years ago, when the Earth was still cooling after coalescing from a planetary nebula. As this first race had explored the galaxy and found no other intelligent species, in their loneliness they had seeded the oceans of many promising worlds with the precursors of life. Their story had been revealed in a remarkable piece of genetic detective work begun by Dr. Richard Galen and completed by Captain Jean-Luc Picard. The two men, teacher and student, had made the astounding discovery that a sophisticated holographic message from that ancestral race was actually encoded in the genetic structure of four humanoid species—humans, Klingons, Cardassians, and Vulcans, including the Vulcans' offshoot race, the Romulans.

M'Benga herself had seen recordings of that message, a message assembled from long stretches of genes that appeared to have no discernible role in the normal function of healthy cells.

"But what about the Bajorans and Andorians, Tellarites and Trills, Betazoids, Orions, Ferengi . . . ?" she asked the commodore. "They're all humanoid, all capable of bearing children together—with appropriate medical support, of course. And that type of genetic relationship among the older species goes back well more than four billion years."

M'Benga sat back as the computer went to work on its new series of genetic comparisons. "Galen's ancestral race quite possibly did have a hand in establishing life on some of the planets in local space, but I think the argument can be made that Galen's race is another *result* of the same processes that brought forth life in the galaxy, not its ultimate cause."

Now the commodore directed his full attention to M'Benga, not her display screen, as if this was the most fascinating conversation he had had in years. "So you are a supporter of the Preserver theory?"

She snorted. "From the studies I've read, I'd say the whole concept of a race called the Preservers arises from our human need to see a pattern in the archeological record, even when there is no pattern there. When you think about it, every spacegoing culture behaves in some way like the Preservers. All colony worlds act to preserve specialized cultures and ways of life. The Federation is no exception. It has an active program for distributing animals and plants from one world to another, to preserve life in the event of planetary disaster."

M'Benga glanced at her screen. Nothing yet. "I think that when we look back at the archeological records of a thousand extinct cultures and we see evidence of Preserver-like activity, it's much more likely that we're seeing a thousand different preservation initiatives that had arisen independently, like the more than forty different forms of eyes on Earth.

"It takes a huge leap of faith to interpret *all* preservation efforts over the eons as the result of *one* virtually omnipotent race operating consistently over . . . well, billions upon billions of years. I just don't accept that's likely, or even possible."

"What about the Preserver artifacts?" the commodore asked. "It was your Captain Kirk who found one of the first."

M'Benga grimaced. "First of all, he's not *my* Captain

Kirk. And second, what *about* the Preserver artifacts? There're what? Six of them?"

"One hundred and eighteen, actually."

That number took M'Benga by surprise. "Oh?" She frowned, wondering how that discovery had bypassed her. And just when. "I see I haven't been keeping up."

She automatically checked her display screen again, but the computer was still engaged in its new search. "Still," she said, "if we postulate a race that had a cultural, industrial, and economic structure that was stable over eons, enabling it to visit every planet in the galaxy and move whole populations of species and even cultures around like chess pieces, one hundred eighteen artifacts isn't much of a legacy to leave behind.

"I mean, where are the ruins of their colonies? Where are their derelict ships? Every dead culture leaves *something* behind, even if it's just a garbage dump."

The commodore rubbed at his chin. "Maybe they're not dead."

If he hadn't said that with such a serious expression, M'Benga would have scoffed at him openly. "Well, you've just abandoned philosophy," she said. "Now you're on the very fringes of lunatic science. I mean, really, Commodore—if there is such a thing as Preservers, or whatever you want to call them, omnipotent aliens who travel among us without us ever spotting them on our sensors or recording images of them, how do you account for it?"

Commodore Twining shrugged. "Highly advanced alien technology."

M'Benga's eyes narrowed. "Arthur Clarke, one of the great scientific minds of the twentieth century, said something that was as true then as it is today: 'Any sufficiently advanced technology is indistinguishable from magic.' Magic is fantasy. And that's what the Preservers are."

"Lots of people believe in them."

"Commodore," M'Benga said, studying Twining. "People always want to believe in something bigger than themselves. Since the beginning of space travel, one of the most enduring myths of humanity has been that somewhere out among the stars will be an omnipotent race of aliens who will answer all of our questions, solve all our problems, and take away all our fears."

M'Benga pursed her lips, puzzled. The commodore had seemed a reasonable man. So why did he seem to be promoting unreasonable beliefs? The contradiction was worth exploring. She decided another example might make her argument clearer. "I mean, remember how the euphoria of our First Contact with the Vulcans was replaced by an incredible social letdown? Earth had been through a nuclear war. We needed a future to look forward to, and suddenly we had the answer to our prayers—contact with an advanced alien race. The world was supposed to change overnight. But it didn't, did it? Because, in the end, the Vulcans were just like us. Their starship technology was more established, but even so, Cochrane was able to make improvements on the Vulcans' designs. And although their medical knowledge was vast, even then, it was more than a century before any of it could be adapted for humans.

"This time we live in, Commodore, as miraculous as it might seem to someone from Cochrane's era, wasn't given to us by aliens. It's one we made ourselves, day by day. And we still have to work at it. This . . . fantasy of the Preservers, it's a fairy tale. Lots of people might believe in it, but I'm a scientist. I need proof. And as another great scientific mind of the twentieth century once said, 'Extraordinary claims require extraordinary evidence.'"

"That was Carl Sagan, an astronomer," the commodore said with a smile. "And if I recall correctly, that statement of his had to do with that same rancorous debate you just mentioned, about whether life was just on Earth or throughout the galaxy. Sagan was responding to people who claimed to have seen alien starships on Earth and to have met with aliens, prior to First Contact."

That was news to M'Benga. *Why would anyone have thought that?* she wondered. But then, the twentieth century had been one of the most peculiar times in human history. She shrugged and made the point that mattered now. "Then I submit," she said, "that the landing of the Vulcan ship at Cochrane's base was the extraordinary proof that Dr. Sagan would have accepted. The same way the day the Preservers land in front of me is the day I'll accept them."

Intriguingly, Twining looked as if he had something more to say but for some reason was choosing not to. Then M'Benga's computer chimed again.

And even given everything that had happened to her today, for the first time M'Benga could say she was truly disturbed by the results she saw on her screen.

"One hundred percent correlation?" Commodore Twining exclaimed. "With what?"

M'Benga's fingers flew over the control surfaces. She was just as anxious as he to know the answer to his question. According to the graph now on her display screen, that anomalous piece of genetic information in child 7 was an exact match for a genetic sequence from a life form on Vulcan. But which one?

The sudden blare of a warning horn and the flashing of red lights caused M'Benga to lose her place in the command instructions she input.

"The ship!" the commodore said. His communicator chirped and he tapped it. "Twining here."

The voice that came from the small device spoke in Federation standard, requiring no automatic translation. Nonetheless, M'Benga heard a distinct Klingon accent. *"Commodore, the EMH is reporting that the children are coming out of hibernation. All of them."*

Immediately, M'Benga's eyes looked past her workstation to the sleeper ship beyond the viewport. She saw nothing different.

"What did the EMH do?" Twining asked sharply.

Now the EMH himself responded from a display screen on the console. "Nothing!" He seemed, to M'Benga, extremely indignant for a hologram. "I was running a dust-particle analysis of the cabin air, looking for errant traces of DNA, when . . . well, see for yourself."

On the screen, the EMH stepped to the side of the visual sensor mounted on the wall of the sleeper ship's cargo hold. Now M'Benga saw a flashing green light over each hibernation chamber door in view.

"Something must have happened to cause this," Twining said.

Then another display screen came to life with an image of a young Klingon male. M'Benga didn't know what to make of his uniform. It looked as if it was a Starfleet uniform conceived by a Klingon. The design of the jacket was Starfleet's latest, but instead of gray shoulders on a black jacket, the color combination was Klingon blood-lavender on an almost metallic silvergray. And the communicator pin the Klingon wore was not a Starfleet delta, but a yellow, red, and green Klingon trefoil.

"Commodore," the Klingon said, "moments before the revival process began on board the ship, communications reported an anomalous subspace pulse. There's a complex pattern encoded in it, but it was so powerful, we might not have been able to record its entire contents."

"You think it might be a signal?" Twining asked.

"I am doubtful the connection to the sleepers' revival is coincidental."

"Do what you can to decode it," Twining said. "And get me a point of origin. I want to know who sent it."

The Klingon huffed as if preparing to do battle, then cut the connection.

"What kind of uniform was that?" M'Benga asked.

But instead of answering her, the commodore said, "Here they come."

On the screen, a clear door rose up and slid out of the way on one of the chambers. A moment later, a small pair of legs swung over the side and a child dropped free of the chamber.

It was a young girl. Perhaps ten. Short, unkempt blond hair was standing up on the back of her head, and she looked confused.

M'Benga's first thought was, *What a pretty child.*

She watched, fascinated, as the young girl began performing a ritual Vulcan *kata,* a series of slow and deliberate movements intended to focus the mind on its connection to the body. M'Benga's great-grandfather had shown her some of them and had said that they could take more than a hundred years to master.

But this apparently human child was moving with a breathtaking precision M'Benga had only seen in masters of the *Kolinahr*.

"That's . . . unbelievable," M'Benga said.

"You mean the way she's moving through that *kata?*"

M'Benga nodded. It seemed the commodore was also a knowledgeable man—which made it even more surprising that he could believe in the Preserver fantasy.

"Doctor," Twining said abruptly, "see if you can establish contact."

On the screen, the EMH approached the child. When it seemed she was looking at him, he said. "Hello, little girl. Can you tell me your name?"

The little girl held up her hand. The EMH reached down for it.

At once, the child yanked the EMH's head down to her level, secured a hold on his neck, and *bit* into his neck.

The EMH leaped back, arms outspread, the girl's arms wrapped around his shoulders. For an instant, his holographic body lost focus and the young girl fell through him. The EMH had obviously adjusted his cohesiveness.

"Good grief," the EMH said. "That was completely uncalled for, young—"

The EMH was cut off as another small form lunged at him from offscreen, and then another and another until it seemed he'd disappeared into a swarm of young children.

Just as M'Benga was wondering if she was actually hearing the sounds of *snarling* over the workstation speakers, a familiar hum vibrated the air next to her, and the holographic doctor took shape beside her. He was busily brushing off his trousers and jacket. "They're little savages," he said.

"Small, yes," Twining said, "savage, perhaps not. They seem to know what they're doing."

On the screen, M'Benga saw a small, pudgy hand reach in front of the visual sensor and then the picture was gone.

Twining tapped his communicator. "Twining to Observation. Do we have any visual sensors left onboard the ship?"

A standard computer voice answered. "All visual sensors have been taken offline."

"Go to sensors. Send the reconstruction to Dr. M'Benga's station."

At once, on the science station, a graphic, wire-frame version of the sleeper ship appeared. M'Benga saw 17 yellow dots in constant motion within, many of them moving toward the bow. She turned to the commodore.

"They're all awake," he said.

M'Benga had a worrisome thought. "Any chance they can try to move that thing?"

Twining nervously tapped his fingers on the top of M'Benga's station. "No, we removed its propulsion system. Left it just enough power for life-support."

"At least it's not going anywhere."

"Good," the holographic doctor said. "They were entirely too aggressive for my liking. Did you see that one of the little monsters tried to *bite* me?"

And then all conversation stopped as the main dorsal airlock on the sleeper ship opened with a puff of frozen atmosphere.

The Klingon was immediately back onscreen. "Sir! They have decompressed the entire ship!"

"Committed suicide?" the commodore asked in disbelief.

"No! Look!" M'Benga said.

Figures were appearing on the topmost surface of the sleeper ship. The children were leaving.

Commodore Twining stared at the screen. "But there were no environment suits on that ship."

M'Benga felt an icy chill flow through her. The children were not wearing suits.

Ten children, 12, finally 17 of them, 8 to 15 years old, were now clustered together on the exterior of the sleeper ship, kept in place by the edges of the gravity generators that served the ship's interior.

But that was impossible, M'Benga knew. The children were in a vacuum. Exposed. They couldn't last more than a minute or two without air.

"What are they doing?" Twining addressed himself to the Klingon.

"Gesturing to each other," the Klingon said. "I don't know if—"

Then M'Benga watched unbelievingly as two of the children jumped from the top of the sleeper ship and floated toward a maintenance airlock in the wall of the docking chamber.

Twining jabbed his fingers against his communicator so powerfully that M'Benga thought he might break it. *"Wildfire! Wildfire!"* he shouted.

On the screen, the Klingon had jumped to his feet. "Full implementation?"

"Now!" Twining ordered.

M'Benga was on her feet, too, as more alarms

sounded. In the chamber, more children were leaping from the ship, floating over to equipment bays and airlocks. Not only were these "children" surviving in vacuum, they were fully functional, and they were trying to escape.

Then she saw panels in the curved wall of the chamber begin to slide open as equipment rolled out.

She recognized the equipment.

Phaser cannons. Just like the ones she had seen on the exterior of Station 51, defending the docking bay.

She grabbed Twining's arm. "Get those children out of there!"

"We're following procedure," Twining said as he pulled his arm away.

"All phasers standing by to fire," the Klingon announced.

M'Benga forced Twining to turn to face her. "You can't kill them! *You're Starfleet!*"

Twining pointed at something behind her, as if giving a signal.

Suddenly, M'Benga felt a powerful hand grip her shoulder and pull her back from the commodore. She tried to struggle, to escape, but the hand was unyielding.

"Implement full Wildfire procedure," Twining commanded.

The emitter coils on the cannon began to glow as the children flew through the empty space before them.

"No," M'benga said in horror as she turned to see who had captured her.

It was the EMH. He had a hypospray in his free hand.

"Stop him!" she demanded of the EMH. "You're a doctor! Do no harm!"

"That is what we are attempting," the EMH said.

M'Benga couldn't fight the strength of the force fields that gave the doctor form. She heard the hiss of the hypospray as it kissed her neck. She felt its cold pinprick, felt the rush of medication, and saw the darkness that instantly shrank her vision and engulfed her.

As she fell, she just had time to see the docking chamber fill with silent phaser fire.

The ship and the children vanished into oblivion.

Then so did she.

SEVEN

☆

Kirk thought of the captain of the *Enterprise.*

Christopher Pike.

He had been one of Starfleet's finest. A dynamic officer who had commanded the first *Enterprise* on two five-year missions. It was Pike whom Kirk had followed as captain of that ship, inheriting a crew and a science officer who had inspired him to become a leader worthy of them.

Pike had set an example for Kirk, perhaps *the* example. Kirk remembered how often he would tell himself to approach a situation like Chris, resolve a problem like Chris, to *be* like Chris.

Then he had had his final voyage with Chris Pike, to Talos IV. By then, Chris was little more than the pilot of a life-support chair. So severely blasted by delta radiation, he'd been incapable of doing anything for himself, except, perhaps, to dream.

All the rest of his career, Kirk had worried that he himself would meet a fate that might incapacitate him. And if he did, how *he*'d cope with it.

He knew he lived for action, thrived on physical

challenge. He'd fought McCoy tooth and nail every time the doctor dared suggest it might be time to ease up. That he should think before horseback riding. That he should avoid throwing himself out the airlock of low-orbiting skimmers to paraglide in on tricky reentry parabolas. *Et cetera, et cetera, et cetera.* But Kirk had always known that going down that road would lead to his eventually giving up everything he loved to do.

For some time he had been living in dreadful anticipation, not of the day that the death he had cheated so often would finally, inevitably claim him, but of the little deaths he might face along the way. The day he could no longer ride. No longer run or even walk. Or make love. He might deny the need to stop, but stop he would, no matter how much he fought it. As much as he railed against it, he was mortal.

And now, as he rolled toward the captain's ready room on the *Heisenberg,* in the medical antigrav chair that Spock had programmed for him, Kirk feared he might be on the threshold of personal decay. With his new lungs, he was still unable to draw enough oxygen to stand on his own feet. With his ruined hands, he was unable to dress or take care of himself. The irony was he might finally have achieved what he had long ago set out as his primary goal.

He had become just like Chris Pike.

Kirk paused, in his chair, in the narrow service corridor before the doors to the ready room. But the chair must have announced itself through the ship's computer system, Kirk supposed, because after a moment, the doors opened and the antigrav chair floated forward again.

The *Heisenberg*'s ready room was a surprise. In fact,

this ship was entirely different from any other Starfleet vessel Kirk had ever encountered. The turbolift he'd ridden in had betrayed no sense of motion, with absolutely no detectable change between its up, down, and sideways movement. And the ship's smoothly flowing corridors had seemed more like works of sculpture than utilitarian passageways.

But in the midst of all this sleek, futuristic splendor, the ready room was outfitted like a library reading room from the 1800s. Wood paneling, book shelves with real books, even a large wooden desk for the captain, with intricately carved panels. Kirk was certain he could smell the leather of the books' bindings, the clean scent of wood polish, even the subtle mustiness of centuries-old paper.

"Captain Kirk, how good to meet you at last."

Kirk turned his head in surprise and the floating chair automatically adjusted its position to point him in the direction he had looked.

Captain Hu-Lin Radisson was watering a vividly green plant. The exuberantly healthy plant, with lush, dark green leaves embroidered in pale green spirals, was the same height as the captain, no more than a meter and half.

Radisson set down her copper watering can on a wooden side table, which also held a small wood and metal trowel and garden rake, then wiped her hand on a red gingham cloth at the table's side.

"Captain," Kirk said. "Forgive me for not getting up."

Radisson chuckled. She was an older woman, looked 60, which Kirk knew meant she could be over a hundred, given twenty-fourth-century medicine and nutrition. And though she was small and slight, as she walked over to Kirk, he could see that under her uniform was a wiry frame that could likely take on a Klingon or two in hand-to-hand combat.

"Forgive me," she said, "for not offering to shake."

Kirk looked down at his bandaged hands. "Another time."

Radisson nodded, smiling. "They'll grow back soon."

"I beg your pardon?"

"Your hands. We already have our biolab culturing the clone buds. Before you leave today, we'll implant them and you'll have a new pair of hands in . . . let's say, four to five months." It seemed to Kirk that Radisson spoke as if she were talking about refinishing one of the pieces of wooden furniture in her ready room.

Kirk held out what until just now he had thought were his hands, obscured as they were by bandages. He stared at Captain Radisson. He knew his face must be betraying his shock.

"I'm so sorry," she said. "Didn't anyone tell you?" Her face was a study in sincere concern. "They amputated your hands. But I can personally assure you, reconstruction was not an option."

Kirk felt dizzy. He desperately needed air, but his new lungs were not up to the extra demand. Glittering stars sparkled at the edge of his vision.

Radisson immediately approached him, placing a solicitous hand on the back of his chair, leaning down close to him. "Are you all right, Captain Kirk?"

Kirk pressed one of his bandaged . . . he could barely think the word, let alone say it . . . stumps to his chest. "Can't . . . breathe . . ."

Radisson spoke quietly, but it was the voice of command. "Doctor, you're needed in the ready room."

A moment later, though it seemed a lifetime, Kirk heard a familiar voice. "Please state the nature of the . . . oh, it's you again."

Kirk, by now suffocating, glimpsed through the increasing darkness the Mark Two EMH at his side.

"He's had a bit of a shock, I'm afraid," the captain said.

Kirk's eyes followed the EMH as he moved to the wood-paneled wall, touched a hidden control, and what appeared to be a food-replicator slot appeared. But instead of food, there was a hypospray inside.

"Typical," the hologram complained as he returned with the hypo. "Give someone a new set of lungs, and do they read the instruction files? No." He touched the hypo to Kirk's neck. Kirk felt the momentary coolness of a transdermal injection, then his vision cleared. He sighed in relief.

The EMH shook his head disapprovingly. "I expect you'll have to go through a lot of this in the next few weeks. It's tri-ox compound, emphasis on the *ox.*" He wedged the hypospray down between the side of the chair and its cushion. "I'll just leave it right here."

Kirk found his voice. "How can you project yourself beyond sickbay?" he asked the EMH.

"Maybe I can't," the hologram said, raising an eyebrow. "Maybe I'm just a hallucination of your oxygen-starved brain."

"That's enough, thank you," Radisson told him. "You may go."

The EMH rolled his eyes. "That's right. Use me.

Abuse me. Then beam me up." He dissolved into holographic static, which quickly faded.

"To answer your question," Radisson said to Kirk, "the whole ship is outfitted with holoemitters. That way the Emergency Medical Hologram can come to us when there's an emergency. It's something new Starfleet's experimenting with. Many benefits." She smiled at Kirk as if she hadn't just told him his body had been mutilated forever. "I'll show you. Computer, the ninth configuration, please."

Once again Kirk lost orientation as the ready room seemed to spin around him. And then he was on a large, open-air patio, under a bright sun in a sky so blue it had to be Earth's. To one side of him was a long, low, white house framed by palm trees. To the other, the edge of a 100-meter cliff that overlooked a spectacular view of a blue-gray ocean, about a kilometer away.

Recovering from his sudden vertigo, Kirk inhaled deeply, smelling the salt spray of the sea, erasing all sensory impressions of the *Heisenberg*'s musty library. He heard the piercing cry of seagulls and looked up to see several wheel by overhead. The rays of the sun were so intense, beads of moisture formed on his brow.

"Myself, I find it makes a starship a more interesting place." Radisson put her hands on her hips and gazed up at the sky, breathing deeply. "And each crew member's cabin is infinitely adjustable."

Wonderingly, Kirk saw that where the captain's desk had been was now a stone-and-ceramic countertop, still covered with Starfleet padds and a captain's terminal. The green plant was still with them as well.

"Malibu, California, April 26, 2005." Radisson said with satisfaction. "Exactly as it was the day before the offshore quake generated the tsunami that wiped it clean. I call it Camelot."

The need to return to a dark, quiet room swept over Kirk. "You wanted to see me?" he said wearily, squinting in the bright sunlight.

"Ah, but you're not comfortable," Radisson said solicitously.

"A bit hot and bright," Kirk admitted.

"Computer, advance time reference by twelve hours."

Suddenly, the sun became a streak that blurred down to the horizon and the blue sky abruptly changed to black, now studded with the twinkling starfield of Earth. A crisp full moon rose in the sky, its pale light bright enough to cast shadows. Burning torches ringed the patio now, their red-gold flames fluttering in the soft onshore breeze. From the windows of the house behind them came the warm glow of golden lights, old-style electricity, Kirk guessed.

"Better?" Radisson asked.

The night air was cool. Kirk caught the scent of something sweet, a night-blooming flower of some kind. "Yes," Kirk said. "Thank you."

Radisson remained silent, studying him, waiting.

Kirk began by forcing all thoughts about his hands from his mind. It was done. He would deal with it on his own terms, later, in his own way. Radisson had surprised him with the revelation, but, on second thought, he half suspected she had done so deliberately, ordering Spock, McCoy, and Scotty not to say a word. He could think of no other reason why his friends would not have told him.

In that case, Kirk thought, *I'll concede she won the first round. But only because I was unaware there was a game underway.*

He opened with an attack, jumping to an extreme, though likely, conclusion. "How long have you known about Tiberius?"

Radisson shrugged and walked over to a small, round table set with a blue-and-white-striped linen cloth and ivory candles in glass chimneys. "You submitted your first report on the mirror universe one hundred and eight years ago. Mr. Spock's account, detailing his inter-actions with your counterpart, was part of that report. Have you forgotten?"

Kirk's antigrav chair followed her. "That's not what I mean. How long have you known about what Tiberius is doing here, in the Goldin Discontinuity?"

Radisson sat down in a white-painted wrought-iron chair, took a bright blue linen napkin from the table, and folded it in her lap. Then she steepled her hands, tapping her index fingers together.

"Take your time," Kirk said. "I have all night."

Radisson began to serve herself salad from the oiled teak bowl on a tripod stand beside the table. "Actually, you don't. The quake hits in about fifteen minutes. The tsunami strikes three minutes fifty-five seconds after that. Twenty-seven hundred people killed just on this stretch of coastline. Then when the San Andreas went two days later . . ."

"Captain Radisson, you have placed my associates and me under ship arrest. As I understand it, we will remain under arrest until you and I have had a chance to talk. I'm here, but you're not talking."

Radisson clapped her hands once, then lifted an open bottle of white wine from the silver bucket on the other side of the table. Each bead of moisture on the green glass stood out in sharp relief, perfectly reflecting the light of the candles and the surrounding torches. Kirk had never seen a holographic simulation so exquisitely detailed. "I'm not here to talk, Captain Kirk. You are. How long have *you* known about what Tiberius was doing here?"

"I didn't even know Tiberius existed until eight hours ago. What I know about his historic actions in the mirror universe, I learned in the past four weeks from Intendant Spock and the mirror counterpart of Kathryn Janeway. Are they under arrest as well?"

Radisson poured herself a glass of wine, then looked inquiringly at Kirk, in a mute offer to do the same for him. He shook his head. "They're in protective custody," the captain of the *Heisenberg* said. "Admiral Nechayev is one of perhaps a hundred Starfleet officers who have been replaced by exact mirror duplicates. Intendant Spock, his daughter, T'Val, and Janeway's counterpart are in very real danger of assassination if they remain free."

Kirk leaned forward in his antigrav chair. "But they aren't *exact* duplicates. People from the mirror universe, their quantum signatures are different. All it takes is a tricorder to tell the difference."

"At first, Captain. Only at first." Radisson took a delicate forkful of her salad, pausing to savor it, before continuing. "Let's say I was from the mirror universe. I come over by transporter, and everything about me, every molecule in my body, carries the quantum signature of the universe I was born in. But then . . ."—she took a sip of her wine—". . . I live in this universe. I breathe the air of this universe, eat the food, drink the wine. As my body goes about its normal processes, I grow new tissue, using molecules of *this* universe as the building blocks. In a year, a tricorder doesn't do it. My skin is completely replaced with local molecules. If I cut my hair short, it's all local growth. I'll have a few pockets of cells and bone inside that still have mirror-universe molecules and a mirror-universe signature, but not enough for a tricorder to pick up." She took another sip of wine. "You see, Captain Kirk, in time, they *become* exact duplicates."

"Then . . . how can you tell which officers are real and which are counterparts?"

"Right now, we can't. It's as simple as that." Radisson touched her lips with her bright blue linen napkin, then put it down with a sigh. "That's what makes this one faction of the mirror-universe Alliance even more of a threat to the Federation than the Borg ever could be. We're working on identification techniques. We think we have a good shot at using transporter ID traces to make the kind of detailed comparisons we need."

"But . . ."—Radisson picked up her wineglass by its fragile stem and swirled the pale gold liquid under her nose—". . . if a counterpart manages to replace original transporter IDs with new ones without our knowing, then we'll be right back where we started from."

Kirk read between the lines. "Who is this 'we' you mention? It's not Starfleet, is it?"

Radisson's eyebrows lifted as if she were impressed. "Let's just say we're part of Starfleet."

"That's not good enough."

"Really?" Radisson pushed back her chair and stood up, still holding her wineglass.

Kirk persisted. "I'm here because you want information from me. All right, I'll give it to you. But I want information in return."

Radisson took another sip of her wine as she stared out at ghostly white-capped waves sweeping into shore. A shimmer of moonlight played across the scalloped surface of the ocean. But other than that, there was little difference between the black of the sky and the black of the sea. Stars danced in each.

"You're only half right, Captain. I do want something from you. But it's not information. And as for getting something from me in return . . ."—she turned to him, the torches making her dark eyes gleam—". . . Very well."

Kirk waited, wondering if the game was going to continue or if this actually was the end. He heard the distant crash of breakers on the rocks far below.

"This convoy of science vessels is part of what Starfleet calls Project Sign."

"Never heard of it," Kirk said.

"I'm not surprised. It's one of the most highly classified operations within the fleet. But the irony is, you started it." Radisson gave a little laugh.

"I don't understand."

"In your first five-year mission. You made a . . . shall we say . . . discovery. And that led to an ultrasecret Starfleet research effort to determine all the ramifications that might result from what you found."

Finally, understanding welled up in Kirk. "When I crossed over into the mirror universe."

The captain of the *Heisenberg* smiled enigmatically at him. Kirk wasn't sure if her smile confirmed his conclusion or if Radisson was about to surprise him with some other revelation.

"That research effort," Radisson said, "went on to make many startling discoveries of its own. Today, a century later, Project Sign is an active detachment within Starfleet, and it is still classified. My ship is one of the remarkable vessels assigned to the project. And— I am free to tell you at least this—one of the things we do is watch for any and all signs of incursions from the mirror universe."

But Kirk wanted to know what the captain was not free to tell him. "Do you use these . . . remarkable vessels to go *into* the mirror universe yourself?"

Radisson shrugged. "They're not that remarkable, Captain. And besides, for most of the history of the project, the mirror universe fell under the protection of the Prime Directive."

"That's absurd!" Kirk knew there was something else, something Radisson was deliberately leaving out of her explanation.

"It was a special case, I admit. And the decision was made before I was born. But . . ."—Radisson put her wineglass down on the table before her. ". . . once again, you've made a difference, Captain. As long as the mirror universe stayed on its side of the quantum divide, the special implementation of the Prime Directive held. Certainly, there have been a number of incursions near Deep Space 9, but those are local matters. However, now that we have absolute proof of a concerted effort by at least one faction within the Alliance to take hostile action against the Federation, the Prime Directive no longer applies."

Kirk felt the stirrings of alarm. "Are you talking about going to war with another *universe?*"

"No, no, no. But what we will be able to do is become *involved.* You've put us in touch with Intendant Spock.

Through him, we can work directly with the Vulcan Resistance. We can make a difference over there now. Because of you.''

Kirk hadn't been expecting that. If this was all that Radisson and the mysterious Project Sign was up to, then he had no real cause for concern. He felt both flattered and relieved. "I'd . . . I'd like to keep helping.''

Radisson regarded him seriously. "Which brings me to what I—to what Project Sign—needs from you.''

"If it's not information, I don't know what it is.''

"We need a promise.''

Automatically, Kirk felt himself go on alert. "Go on.''

"It is absolutely imperative that you remain completely uninvolved in our further dealings with the mirror-universe rebels.''

Suddenly, the glasses on the table rattled. The wine bottle sloshed back and forth in its silver wine cooler. One of the torches fell over and sputtered out on the patio tiles.

Far off, in the canyons behind them, Kirk heard the barking of dogs, soon joined by the howling of coyotes.

"That was it,'' Radisson exclaimed. "A six point two on the old-fashioned Richter scale, back when it measured tectonic activity and not cultural development. The strength was relatively minor on a planetary scale, but enough to generate a forty-meter wave that's just now forming twenty kilometers offshore.'' She gave a rueful half laugh. "The end of an era.''

"I don't understand why you don't want me involved,'' Kirk said, ignoring the false excitement of a re-created disaster.

"Because you will be watched, Captain Kirk, and we

don't know by whom. If you were to work for us, no matter how cleverly we set up a communications method, no matter how carefully we arranged your travel schedule, you are such an obvious link to our efforts to defend ourselves from the mirror universe that it would just be a matter of time before Alliance spies in this universe traced your activities straight to us."

That was a weak excuse, Kirk knew. He probed it with his next question. "How do you know they don't already know about you?"

"Because we've been monitoring the labor camp at this location for a year, and we've detected no change in their schedule or activities that would indicate they knew they were under surveillance."

Kirk's rage was so overwhelming and so instantaneous that he struggled to stand up from his chair to confront Radisson. "People *died* down there! Captain Picard lost members of his crew! I almost lost Teilani! How dare you stand by and do nothing?!" But the effort was too great, his new lungs were too weak, and his truncated wrists could give no support.

Kirk toppled to one side in his antigrav chair, helpless, ineffectual, humiliatingly unable to right himself—the curse of Christopher Pike.

Radisson made no move to help him, clearly letting him know who was in charge.

"Listen carefully, Captain. *We* had the situation under control. *We* were in a position to rescue every captive in that labor camp *without* causing the collapse of the atmospheric force field. But then *you* inserted yourself into our mission and ruined all of our plans. Believe me when I say that your promise to remain uninvolved in our activities is one of *two* options I've been authorized to present to you. You *don't* want to know what the second one is."

Awkwardly slumped in his chair, unable to sit up, Kirk strained to at least push his elbows against the arms of the chair, but his body was shockingly weak. Alternately pushing with his feet merely succeeded in driving his floating chair backward, giving him no purchase.

"Tell me," Kirk said, his voice tight with angry chagrin. "How far are you willing to push this?"

"We gave you new lungs, Captain Kirk. It's not as easy as it sounds, especially with the vacuum trauma you experienced. Without the facilities of the *Heisenberg,* you'd have been further damaged during transport back to a properly equipped starbase. Best estimate? You'd have been looking at a minimum of six months on pulmonary support while a cloned set of lungs was grown for you. And another six months for recuperation in zero-g. Not to mention the *year* it would take you to acclimatize yourself to normal gravity again. That means it would have been *two years* before you could join your bride and your child on Chal."

Radisson put a hand on Kirk's antigrav chair to keep it steady. "And as for ever touching your bride or child . . ."

Kirk felt on the verge of hyperventilation at the threats she was making. *No one* could ever keep him from Teilani and their child. "I can have biosynthetic hands attached at any medical facility!"

"Biosynthetics," Radisson repeated. "I believe they're up to eighty percent physical function. Almost twenty-five percent tactile recovery. You'd be able to hold Teilani's hand but never feel the texture of her hair or the softness of your child's skin."

Radisson's insolently personal references filled Kirk with almost murderous rage. He fought for self-control. "Then I'll have someone else implant clone buds."

Radisson nodded coolly. "Clone buds work only if the remaining tissue and nerve bundles were properly prepared during a controlled amputation. And, for the best results, the same surgeon should perform both the removal and the implant."

"Bones is the best in Starfleet."

"He is. But he didn't perform the procedure."

Kirk hadn't known that. "Dr. Crusher . . . ?"

Radisson shook her head. "But you have met your surgeon."

"The hologram?"

"Admittedly a trifle rough around the edges when it comes to personality. But then, he is a combination of the greatest geniuses ever to practice medicine. There's even a bit of your Dr. McCoy in him."

Radisson held up her hand. "Do you hear that?"

A strange hissing noise rose in the distance. Kirk suddenly realized that the soft breeze had stiffened into a cold wind that was now blowing offshore.

"Look at the ocean," Radisson said, turning Kirk's chair toward the horizon.

He saw the shimmer of the moon shrink, then vanish.

As if they had not been discussing anything else of importance, Captain Radisson, with deep reverence, described for Kirk what was occurring. And he knew that she had done this many times before. "The water's receding now. It's being sucked back from the shore to feed the tsunami." She looked around with a half smile, excited, stimulated. "Can you feel that?"

Kirk felt nothing. His antigrav chair floated above the floor tiles of the patio, immune to the earth's upheaval.

"I wonder what it was like." Radisson said softly. "To be down there, really down there in one of those doomed beach houses, standing on a deck, seeing the ocean pull away from the shore, and then, in the moonlight, seeing its return—a wall of water coming for you like the hand of a god."

"Maybe that's where you should simulate your next ready room," Kirk said impatiently. "Right on the beach." He pushed up again, flopping a bit higher in his chair.

"That's just the point," Radisson said. "It is just a simulation. I can't ever know what it was *really* like. Oh—there! Look, Captain!"

A line of frothing white foam now stretched from horizon to horizon, illuminated by the full moon, rushing forward so quickly it looked artificial.

The tsunami struck the shore and the foam exploded upward as the wall of water gained in speed and height.

Then it disappeared from sight, beneath the edge of the cliffside patio. But even in his floating chair, Kirk finally felt the vibration of the tsunami's approach. Now it wasn't just in the ground, it also was in the air.

"Here it comes," Radisson said. There was almost passion in her exultant tone. An expectant elation. "Almost . . . almost . . ."

It's just a simulation, Kirk told himself as he stared out into the black void stretching beyond the edge of the cliff, listening to the growling roar that was growing in intensity. Something immense and lethal and unknown was approaching, hidden from view until at the last final second—

"End program," Radisson said.

Kirk blinked in the sudden flash of brilliant light as the Malibu clifftop transformed into a captain's ready room. This time, it was white walled.

He hadn't realized how strong the tension had been as he had waited for the simulated wave to hit until its release left him feeling drained, exhausted, still sprawled sideways in his chair. He looked angrily at Radisson, but she was already walking over to her desk—now a white, free-form shape that appeared to have grown up from the gray carpet of the deck. Other than the various colors of Radisson's padds and terminal, the only other source of color in the altered room was that same vivid green, leaf-covered plant.

"I love that program," Radisson said. "Every time I play it, I let the wave come a little closer."

Kirk pushed hard one more time and finally sat up in his chair. "Why not let it hit?" he asked. The simulated shock of cold salt water might do her some good.

"I couldn't do that," Radisson said. She gave him an odd, almost embarrassed smile. "I've deactivated all the safety protocols."

Kirk lost his breath as if her words had been a physical blow to his chest. Without safety protocols, people could and had died in holosimulations. "So if it *had* hit . . . ?"

"But it didn't, Captain." Radisson sat down behind her desk. "Getting back to what we discussed. Do I have your promise that you will not become involved in matters concerning Project Sign?"

"What if I go public?" Kirk said, amazed by her

coldness. "What if I go before the Federation Council and tell them that Project Sign cut off my hands and refuses to give me new ones unless I keep their secret? How long do you think you'd last then?"

Radisson folded her own hands piously. "The question is, Captain Kirk, since you have been so out of touch with the council, how long do you think *you'd* last?"

As intolerable as the situation was, Kirk knew she was right. He had no one to blame but himself. Until four weeks ago, he had lived as a virtual hermit on Chal, avoiding everyone except Teilani and a few close friends. Because she had been concerned about his well-being, Teilani had suggested he consider the invitation to return to Earth for a conference. But he was the one who had accepted it. It was the first time he had been back to Earth since the launch of the *Enterprise*-B. Then, in only a matter of hours after his arrival, he had been propelled once again into exactly the kind of situation he had sworn he wanted nothing more to do with.

And now this crazed starship captain, who had risked her life and his for the sake of a holosimulation, was asking him to do exactly what it was he had been doing a month ago. Mind his own business. Leave the affairs of the twenty-fourth century to those whose century it was. Rather than intolerable, the situation was almost laughable.

Kirk looked inside himself and realized that his reflex indignation, his desire to best Radisson, sprang from his own stubbornness, a stubbornness he thought he had finally mastered.

He thought he'd learned it wasn't necessary to win just for the sake of winning. That sometimes, what was

better for him was to stand back and let events transpire
without him.

Kirk searched his soul. *I have Teilani, a child on the
way, a real home half built in a clearing on Chal. What
more do I need? What more could I want?*

But there was one thing.

"What about Tiberius?" he asked.

"Is that all that concerns you?"

"Wouldn't it concern you?"

Radisson studied him, as if making a complex decision. "Do you understand that everything I have told
you, everything I will tell you, is completely classified? If
you repeat one word or even make the threat to say one
word of what you know, you'll be given the choice of
spending the rest of your life in solitary confinement on
a prison asteroid or having portions of your memory
permanently removed. And *that* is not an exact science."

Kirk made his own complex decision. "I understand."

Radisson pressed a control on her terminal. Kirk
heard his own voice come from the overhead speakers.
"I understand."

"Just to make it formal," Radisson said. She touched
another control. "Send them in."

A second set of doors slid open, not the set Kirk had
entered by. Beyond them, he saw the bridge of the
Heisenberg. Dazzling. It seemed to have a staff of
twenty. Holographic displays floated before each crew-
man's station. And then, before he could see more,
Spock, McCoy, and Scott entered the ready room,
accompanied by a stern-faced commander, at least half
a head taller than Spock, with a dull black phaser at his

waist and a silver-finished biological isolation case in his hands.

McCoy immediately hurried over to Kirk to help him straighten up in the chair. He found the hypospray. "I needed some tri-ox," Kirk said.

McCoy frowned, looked from Radisson to Kirk. "What did I tell you about exerting yourself?"

"Bones, I . . . never mind." Kirk looked over at Radisson. "So we're all in this?"

"That's right," the captain said. "If one of you talks about Project Sign, *all* of you pay the price."

Spock glanced at Kirk. "Captain, are you able to comply with Captain Radisson's request?"

"It appears so," Radisson said before Kirk could answer. "On one condition."

"Well, that's it," McCoy muttered. "Prison asteroid, here we come."

"On the contrary," the captain of the *Heisenberg* continued. "It is a condition I can accept." She pointed at the tall commander with the case, indicating that he should place it on her desk. He did.

"You may go offline now," Radisson said.

The tall commander dissolved into holographic static. "Is everyone on this ship a hologram?" Kirk asked.

"Not everyone," Radisson replied briskly. But she didn't expand on her answer. "Dr. McCoy, please open the case. Captain Kirk, you'll want to come closer."

Kirk nodded his head forward as McCoy had explained in sickbay and his antigrav chair floated toward Radisson's white desk.

The biological isolation case was open.

Kirk recognized the contents.

Fragments of an environment-suit helmet so deeply red they were almost black.

Kirk pictured the way the fragments would fit together and estimated about two thirds of the helmet was accounted for.

Radisson handed McCoy a medical force-manipulator. "You might want to use this, to prevent contamination."

McCoy switched on the slender tube and a pale purple beam shot out and attached itself to one of the larger pieces of the helmet.

McCoy used that beam to lift the fragment out of the case.

Something dripped from it.

Kirk saw it splatter on the large portion of the faceplate still contained in one of the fragments.

It was blood.

"Do you have your tricorder?" Radisson asked.

McCoy pulled it from the medical case he carried and made several passes over the fragment.

"Diagnosis?" Radisson asked.

"The DNA match is exact. It's Jim's blood." McCoy sighed. He turned the fragment so that Kirk could see that the interior curve was sprayed with blood as well as with small clumps of yellow tissue and flecks of white. "And Jim's brain matter, bone chips . . ."

"Check the quantum signature," Radisson said.

Spock did that, then handed his tricorder to Mr. Scott for verification.

"Aye," Scotty said. "That's the mirror universe signature."

Radisson's eyes fixed on Kirk's. "T'Val shot Tiberius as he was trying to escape. The phaser was set to disintegrate, but it appears the beam hit a power cell in Tiberius's battle suit and triggered a violent explosion before the full phase-disintegration effect could be established."

"So . . ." Kirk said slowly, "you're telling me he's dead."

"I'm not telling you that," Radisson said. "Why would you believe me? That's why your three friends are telling you. Feel free to use any of the facilities of the ship to confirm their findings."

Kirk was feeling wearier than he could ever remember feeling before. "That won't be necessary. I . . ." He shook his head. This wasn't the time for speeches or explanations. "It's over."

"You're certain?" Radisson asked.

"If he's gone, he's gone," Kirk said. "There's nothing more for me to do. No more battles to fight. I . . . it's time I went home."

Radisson nodded, as if she had just completed a long mission of her own. "I'll make arrangements to have you on the *Schrödinger*'s next run to the rescue convoy. There's a clipper waiting there to take you back to Chal, to Earth, to Vulcan . . . whatever destinations you choose."

"What about Teilani?" Kirk asked.

"She'll be on the *Schrödinger* with you. She's in perfect health. And so is your child."

"And what of T'Val?" Spock asked. "Intendant Spock and Kate Janeway?"

"They will be returning with us to . . . a secure starbase," Radisson said. "And we have already made arrangements with the Vulcan Healing Institute for your counterpart to receive the best treatment available for premature Bendii syndrome. In fact, we'll be looking to you to provide transplant tissue and blood."

"Of course," Spock said. "Whatever he requires."

"You'll be contacted," Radisson told him. She looked around at her guests. "I believe that's it. We're done."

Kirk closed his eyes and allowed his head to fall to the side, as if he had finally succumbed to the strains of the past day. It was the only way he knew he could take his leave of Captain Radisson without looking into her eyes.

It was crucial that he be able to do that.

Because if she was any kind of judge of people's characters, Kirk knew that one look at him now, as he struggled to contain his true emotions, would reveal to her his certain knowledge that she had just lied to him.

No matter how she had manufactured the evidence she had used to fool his friends, she had missed one crucial detail that he had not.

Despite the lies of Project Sign, Tiberius was still alive.

This wasn't over.

INTERLUDE

———————— ☆ ————————

The universe unfolded, the galaxy turned, the chaos of the life within it constantly seething and foaming like the crest of a breaking wave, forever threatening to wash the stars away.

But never quite succeeding.

Random event followed random event.

Here, *a blue-skinned bipedal humanoid, of a race unknown to the Federation, dared stand before her elders and proclaim their sun did not travel around their world, but that their world instead orbited their sun. She was put to death at once, but a revolution had begun, and within a century, all the regional systems of government on that world experienced violent upheavals, all because one female had looked at the lights in the sky and wondered why some of them moved so predictably.*

There, *a fur-covered lab assistant to a multitentacled genius, one who had just brought his planet the electric light and a method of recording sound, made a mistake. The two species, mammal and nanovore, both equally intelligent, were only one pair of five in the galaxy who had evolved a system of cooperation, not lethal competition, and created a joint civilization.*

The multitentacled genius had asked his lab assistant to install a collection of quartz crystals in the apparatus assembled on his workbench. But the lab assistant, who swung from a rope net on the lab's ceiling and in whose genetic structure lay a portion of the holographic message from Dr. Galen's ancestral race, brought rubindium crystals instead.

Because of that mistake, the genius who had been attempting to understand the phenomenon of radio-wave propagation instead stumbled onto a method of receiving subspace communications at least two centuries before the regular progression of his world's science should have made that discovery possible. At first, he was going to disassemble the apparatus and eat his assistant. But then a powerful subspace pulse arrived, transmitted months earlier from an asteroid in the Goldin Discontinuity. Upon hearing that sound, the genius decided this was a matter that deserved more careful study, and his world soon had the ability to listen into the conversations of advanced beings.

Thus it was that the world of the genius and the errant lab assistant came to unlock the secret of warp drive within 15 years, before most civilizations at their level of development had even begun to solve the rudimentary problems of heavier-than-air flight. Then, within a mere 20 years, because of its inhabitants' inability to deal with technologies they had not developed for themselves, that precocious world became a radioactive slag heap, all life extinguished. All because the Emperor Tiberius had sent a message intended for others and a junior lab assistant hundreds of thousands of light-years away made a minor mistake.

Throughout the galaxy, the cycle persisted. Intelligent beings were born. Intelligent beings died. One species of intelligent beings had hosts who died, though they themselves could live again in new hosts.

Chaos and more chaos. Events triggering events like intersecting ripples in a pond in a rainstorm.

Given enough random events, patterns began to be perceived.

In the Delta Quadrant, a tiny starship moved 25 years closer to home.

In the Alpha and Gamma Quadrants, a war made possible by what some thought was a wormhole continued to ebb and flow according to the strengths of its combatants and the seeming capriciousness of beings who lived outside linear time.

In the Briar Patch, Captain Jean-Luc Picard of the starship Enterprise *found a world of eternal youth torn by intergenerational conflict and fell in love with a woman of that world, just as his predecessor had done, years ago on Chal.*

In the Beta Quadrant, on a world where a tribe of reptilian creatures had flourished for a year because one of their number had learned to make fire on demand, a massive asteroid hit and an entire race died in the ensuing firestorm. And on one of that world's plains of blackened ash, a flash of silver could be seen, had anyone been there to see it. An obelisk with raised pictograms, standing where it had been placed a billion years earlier.

According to a pattern.

A pattern within chaos.

Seven months passed. During that time, in one small section of the galaxy, an arbitrary numbering system of stardates rolled over from 51999.9 to 52000.0. The Dominion War moved toward its inevitable end but had not ended yet. And on one small secluded oasis of a planet, two beings who meant nothing in the vast scope of the universe, and who meant everything, prepared for their marriage.

The universe unfolded, the galaxy turned, the chaos of the life within it merely an illusion—had anyone been there to see the pattern.

EIGHT

☆

"Do I look fat?" Teilani asked.

She watched Spock closely for any signs of equivocation as she smoothed the red leather of her wedding dress over her swollen belly.

"You look . . . pregnant," Spock said.

"She *is* pregnant, you diplomatic android," McCoy snapped.

"Gentlemen, this isn't th' time t' be arguin'," Montgomery Scott insisted. "This is a special day for Teilani and Jim, and . . ."—he beamed at the bride, his face almost as rosy as her traditional Klingon wedding garb—". . . ye dinnae look anything other than absolutely radiant, lass. A supernova among all the stars of th' galaxy and then some."

Scott looked around at the suddenly silent gathering. He shrugged, then took another sip of Romulan ale. "If this isn't a day for celebrating, I dinnae know which day is."

McCoy patted Scott on the back. "You're absolutely right, Mr. Scott." Then he added in a whisper. "And when we go back to town, I'm driving."

Teilani took one last look at herself in the full-length mirror Scott had erected in the minute gathering room of her half-built home, and tugged down on her leather outer dress again. Once more, she wondered if she and James should have waited the extra month for their baby to be born, so she could be married looking something like her real self. If she *were* a star, then rather than a radiant supernova, she felt more like an ancient, bloated red giant.

"Well, I'd feel much more like celebrating if James were here."

"He will be, lass."

Teilani moved toward the large picture window and carefully drew aside a corner of the cloud-soft finnellian fabric that covered it. Outside, in the clearing, the guests had already gathered beneath the stars and the floating fusion bubbles that slowly drifted overhead. She could hear the happy murmur of their conversations, wafting in and out of the sounds from the string quartet who played the unusual though harmonious music of James's native Earth. Something by Brahms, he had insisted, as if he had known the composer personally. "Everyone else is here," Teilani said.

McCoy joined her at the window. "He will be, too."

Teilani turned to face James's best friends. The three were fast becoming hers, as well. And though she hadn't seen much of Spock over the past few months, McCoy and Scott had been frequent enough visitors to Chal that she had come to know them well.

Well enough that she knew they were hiding something from her.

"James sent you to keep me distracted, didn't he?"

"Company," Spock said. "We are to keep you company."

"That's right," McCoy added much too quickly.

"He dinnae want ye t' worry."

Trust Scotty, Teilani thought. "Worry about what?"

Scott blinked as if he had just realized he had said something he should not have said. "About . . ." He looked at Spock and McCoy in desperation.

Teilani studied them herself. Spock was unsuccessfully trying to look innocent, and the doctor had already lost the battle to hide his annoyance with Scott.

The flushed engineer blustered on. ". . . about nothing, lass. There's absolutely nothing t' worry about."

Teilani reached out and put her hand to Scott's warm cheek. She wasn't beyond using her Romulan pheromones to rattle the engineer's concentration. Romulans had had such a violent early history that pregnant females produced pheromones which inspired males of any age to protect them. As the signs of pregnancy became more visible, the production of those pheromones declined. But even this far along, Teilani knew she could talk Montgomery Scott into just about anything.

"Scotty," she crooned. "Where *is* James?"

The engineer swallowed hard and was just about to blurt out the answer she wanted when Spock's cool voice interrupted.

"He wants to surprise you."

Teilani looked skeptically at Spock. The craggy Vulcan was certainly an impressive wedding guest, outfitted as he was in his formal diplomatic robes. And the doctor and the engineer were looking their best, too, in their dress Starfleet uniforms.

"Spock," Teilani said seductively, "this is my wedding day. I don't want to be surprised. I want my husband to be here. Now, where is he?"

The three friends looked at each other. This time, McCoy intervened before Spock could answer. "He's not far," McCoy offered brightly, his brow moist with the effort to resist her entreaty.

Irritatedly, Teilani tugged on her red leather headgear. "Look, if James wanted you to keep me company so I wouldn't be upset, it's not working. When you four get together, I don't know if it's because you're going to spend all night sitting out there around the firepit with a bottle of ale to reminisce about the *Enterprise* or because you're all going to disappear suddenly on another . . . secret mission. I don't care what James *asked* you to do; I'm telling you to tell me *why* I don't have to be worried." Teilani hated herself for sounding so petulant, and even worse, she felt the sting of hot tears in her eyes.

McCoy took her hand in his at once. "It's all right, m'dear. There're no secret missions. He's just down at Memlon's farm. There was something he needed to borrow for the ceremony."

Teilani couldn't speak, her relief was so powerful. She had feared that James might be somewhere off Chal. McCoy seemed to intuitively understand what she'd been feeling and opened his arms to her.

She fell against his chest, allowing herself to be comforted. "It's just . . . the last time he left . . ." She wept, unable and unwilling to fight her emotions in this company. "I came so close to losing him. . . ."

McCoy patted her back. "Now, now. We all came close. But we didn't lose him, did we?"

Then Teilani realized that Spock was to one side of

her, Scott to the other, and she knew that she was absolutely protected from harm. Whatever bond had been forged over the years between these three humans and her husband-to-be, it was as strong as any blood tie. She knew she wasn't just marrying James today; she and their child were joining his family, *this* family.

She tried to brush the tears from her cheek. Spock offered her a small cloth. She used it to wipe her eyes, then took a deep breath, willing the tempestuous emotions of her pregnancy into submission. She drew herself up to face the three humans. "Promise me that James will never go away again. Not another mission. Not another Starfleet request."

"'But 'tis not up t' us, lass." Scott looked distressed. The other two were silent.

Teilani shook her head. "If *James* decides to go off somewhere, then that will be between him and me. But I must have your promise that the three of you won't lure him away."

McCoy smiled as if her fear was groundless. "Why would we?"

Teilani wondered if, after all these months, this was the time. She decided to try. She had to know. "What happened to James on the *Heisenberg*?"

McCoy and Scott looked startled, then relieved as Spock answered with bland equanimity. "His lungs were replaced, his hands amputated, and clone buds implanted."

Teilani did not accept Spock's attempt to deflect her inquiry. "That's not what I meant. Beyond the physical. Something happened to him over there. Something he learned, something he was told . . ."

"What has he told you?" McCoy asked disingenuously.

"Nothing. But thank you, Bones. Your question tells me there *is* something to tell."

"Now hold on," McCoy objected.

"No!" Teilani said fiercely, not knowing or caring if her unsettlingly emotional state was the result of the stress of this day or her pregnancy or a combination of both. "James still hasn't recovered from what happened in the discontinuity. And I don't mean it's because he's sometimes short of breath or his hands aren't quite right. There's something missing in his . . . his spirit. As if when Tiberius died, part of James died, too. That's illogical, I know. But whatever happened there, whatever he learned onboard the *Heisenberg,* it's as if nothing's ended."

"Kin ye be more specific, lass?"

"Scotty, look over there." Teilani pointed to a corner of the gathering room, at James's desk, one of the first pieces of wooden furniture he had made for their house. It was simple but solid. And sitting in the middle of it was a piece of completely out of place Starfleet equipment. "James has a computer terminal. In this house. I mean, this is the home he was determined to build solely by hand, using only materials he could find on Chal. You know he cleared the field out there by himself. He cut the wood for this house and framed its walls himself. Only once did he accept the help of our neighbors, and that was to raise the roof. And he did everything without antigravs or construction drones or . . . Scotty, he even drew the plans himself. By hand! He used a . . . writing . . . the thing for writing that doesn't have any moving parts?"

"A pencil?" Spock suggested.

"That's it!" Teilani said. "A pencil on paper. Paper. I love that he found a new way of living that not only fit in with my world—his world—but that gave him the peace I think he'd been without for almost all of his life.

"But when he came back from the *Heisenberg,* when we came back to Chal, the first thing James did was have that *computer link* installed. And he used to be adamant that he would never have one here. So don't tell me nothing has changed. *Something* changed him. Tell me."

Teilani waited, impatient, apprehensive, as Spock, Scott, and McCoy glanced from one to the other.

Finally, Spock answered. "We are profoundly sorry. But we are unable to do as you wish."

"I don't believe you."

"Lass, it's true," Scott said sadly. "And furthermore, as t' what happened on that ship that day, the four of us hae never discussed it."

"The three of you and James *not* discuss something? I don't believe you."

Spock cleared his throat. "What Mr. Scott means to say is that Starfleet regulations forbid us to discuss it."

"Since when did any of you let regulations stand in the way of your friendship? Spock, James hijacked a starship to bring you back on Mount Seleya. I mean, don't you see that that's part of the reason for the bond between you?" Teilani could see the confusion in their eyes. How could they not know? "Spock, you died on the *Enterprise.* Scotty, you were killed by that space probe, *Nomad.* Bones, you died on the amusement-park planet. And my James died on Veridian III. But you're all still here, still together. It's almost as if some reason greater than you has kept you together and . . . and hasn't finished with you yet."

After a brief moment of silence, McCoy said, "Frankly, I don't know whether to be flattered or frightened."

"However it happened," Teilani said, "from all the stories James has told me, from everything I've read myself, you four have stood apart from everyone else because, in the end, you've always managed to figure out some way to make your friendship come first, without abandoning your duty or your principles. You've done it all your lives. I can't believe that you aren't willing to do it again."

But before any of them could respond to her, a muffled cheer rose outside.

Teilani's heart raced and the new life within her kicked her soundly, making her gasp. She turned to the window to pull aside its covering and—

James had come back to her.

He burst into the clearing in his red-leather Klingon garb, astride Iowa Dream, the Terran quarter horse, his gift from Jean-Luc Picard.

The guests parted as James rode slowly into the center of the clearing, Iowa moving proudly on an angle, lifting each hoof in the precise gait his master rider had taught him.

And on the horse with James, little Memlon, the irrepressible six-year-old from the neighboring farm, from Teilani's reading group. The small boy had become James's shadow, following him everywhere, peppering him with incessant questions about everything as James worked to clear their land and build their new home. And James's apparent exasperation had been belied by the time he never begrudged Memlon, the way he always treated each rambling question as worthy of his best answer.

James brought Iowa to a stop in the clearing, dismounted, and carefully lowered Memlon to the ground.

Then she saw her beloved look around expectantly, shaking hands with all the guests who closed around him, some to take his holo-image, but still looking past them even as he smiled and spoke to them, eyes never ceasing their search until—

He saw her in the window.

In that moment—and as surely as Teilani felt it she saw that same completion in his eyes—they were made whole again, the unbearable separation as if it had never occurred.

She blew him a kiss, then let the window covering fall teasingly between them. Now it was time to make *him* wait.

She turned to face the three friends. James's family. Her family. All looked thoughtful, somehow subdued.

"You are very wise, Teilani," Spock said gravely.

In her joy, Teilani now held out a hand each to McCoy and to Scott. Respectfully, she did not touch the Vulcan who stood between his two friends.

"You forget," she told her new family. "When the virogen struck Chal, I had no immunity. In the hospice, my doctor told me I was in the last stages, already in a coma, less than a day from my death. But that's when

James came back for me, with the *trannin* that brought me back to life, too."

Teilani let go of their hands to stroke her stomach, caressing the child within that she and James had made. "Perhaps whatever has brought the *six* of us together isn't finished with any of us yet."

NINE

Kirk caught his breath, overcome by the simple majesty and wonder of the moment.

She was before him.

His love, his bride, his universe.

Teilani.

The beauty that flowed from her came from a heart and soul that had been forever bound with his. Its radiance and its power eclipsed the silver of her hair, made inconsequential the disfiguring virogen scar that twisted across her subtle Klingon head ridges to her once flawless cheek. And though she was of an age with him, together in their love they were timeless beings, existing in a perfect moment, with no regrets for the past, no fears for the future.

Overwhelmed by his love for Teilani and the child they would soon have, Kirk . . . wondered why his beloved was gazing at him with such concern, nodding her head as if to urge him to . . . to what?

Kirk realized the crowd of guests on his left had gone silent.

The hulking Chal magistrate to his right, much more

Klingon than Romulan, was whispering something he couldn't quite—

"Oh!" Kirk said as he suddenly pulled himself from his reverie and realized what was expected of him. "Yes, yes, I *do!"*

He couldn't believe it. He had forgotten his line. And that *never* happened.

Well, not often, at least.

A murmur of laughter ran through their audience. Teilani shook her head, her face full of love. Kirk shot a glance at his three best men. Spock's face was a study in neutrality. McCoy was rolling his eyes. Scott was smiling broadly.

Then Teilani nodded at him again, just as Kirk felt a tug at the hem of his leather surplice. He looked down to see Memlon holding up a folded piece of *targ* hide on which rested two rings.

With both joy and sorrow, Kirk picked up the smaller ring. Like its partner, it was made of three strands of braided metal: gold-pressed latinum for their love, silvery diargonite—an alloy found only on Chal—for their home; and gleaming white duranium—a key component of a starship's hull—because Teilani had insisted.

The joy was because he was a heartbeat away from being joined with his true love. The sorrow was because he could not feel the ring between his fingers. Though the tendons and muscles of his newly cloned hands finally operated with some precision, tactile nerve function had yet to be established. This was his wedding day, and he could not caress his bride or feel her hand on his.

But that would not keep him from their moment.

Following an ancient tradition of his family, he

slipped the ring on her right index finger. *"jiH Saw SoH, be'nal,"* he said in Klingon.

Teilani placed the larger ring on Kirk's right index finger. *"jiH nay SoH, loDnal,"* she replied.

And in Romulan, they both recited, *"Jolu seela, true nusee,"* and they held their right hands together so the magistrate could sprinkle their eternal clasp with red ashes from the Firefalls of Gal Gath'thong on Romulus.

Finally, from the small table before them, Kirk picked up the glittering crystal wineglass they had used throughout the ceremony, and held it for Teilani to sip from. Then she took it from him and held it so he could sip. It had taken many nights of practice, but now Kirk could quaff Klingon bloodwine without gagging.

The magistrate, unfamiliar with this tradition from Kirk's heritage, took the glass, folded a square of white cloth around it, then placed it on the ground at Kirk's and Teilani's feet.

Together, they stepped on the glass until it shattered, sealing their vows of love with this remembrance of the past and their hopes for the future.

Then the magistrate cleared his throat noisily and, with Klingon bluntness, delivered the final words of the ceremony that Kirk and Teilani had chosen together. "I have been given authority by the people of Chal. I exercise that authority now, for Teilani, and for James. Together, we have honored the birthrights of the *three* worlds we celebrate today—of *Qo'noS, romuluS,* and *tera'.* Together we have witnessed their vows to each other. Everything that was to have been done, has been done. They are *loDnal je be'nal."*

Then the magistrate clamped his massive hands on each of their shoulders, forcing them together with a hearty laugh as he proclaimed a traditional Klingon wedding benediction: "You may now have your way with each other."

And then Kirk was in Teilani's arms and she in his and he swept her close and kissed her thoroughly, the celebratory music began, and those who were from Chal cheered, and James T. Kirk was married.

The guests whirled and danced as the final stages of the feast were laid out, ending days of preparation. Wonderful, savory scents filled the night air as the slow-roasted *targ* was unearthed from the pit in which it had been buried with heated stones two days before. As a gift, Teilani's fellow teachers arranged for the release of a dozen clouds of fire sprites, and the dazzling insects flew around the clearing, leaving tiny comet trails in their wake, a *chuppah* of stars, as if Chal really were heaven and Kirk and Teilani were blessed beyond measure.

Kirk swayed to the alien rhythms of Romulan folk wedding polkas. He joined hands with his guests and his friends and his distant relatives descended from his nephew Peter, to stomp his feet in unison to the blood-stirring beat of a Klingon stalking song. Then, like most of the other attendees, he stood in bemused wonder as Montgomery Scott played a most remarkable medley of mostly recognizable tunes on his bagpipes.

Later he sat on cushions by the low tables of Chal and fed Teilani as she fed him. As their guests recited toasts and poems and read greetings from those who could not be with them, Earth wine flowed, nectar from a small private vineyard in France—Jean-Luc Picard's own. One special bottle at Kirk's table—vintage 2293, the Earth year Kirk and Teilani had first met—commemorated the end of Kirk's old life and the beginning of his new one.

Then Spock rose to talk of the days of their first five-year mission, when neither was sure what the future would bring. McCoy shared a story from those days as well, which then digressed into a tale about a Trill gymnast he had met in his university days, and just when Kirk began to wonder if the story was about to turn into something little Memlon shouldn't hear, the eloquent doctor brought it back to an unexpected ending with an ancient Scottish toast.

Scott's story was one that Kirk had almost forgotten, about a brief shore leave they had taken together in the second five-year mission, when the engineer and he had beamed down to the wrong coordinates and thoroughly confused the penitents in a Deltan monastery, believing them to be—at this point, Kirk did put his hands over Memlon's pointed ears. Thankfully, however, Scott bypassed the actual details and ended the tale with a description of Kirk trying to explain to Spock exactly why the Deltans had given him an *illustrated* prayer scroll.

Other guests proved equally diverting. Frail-looking Admiral Demora Sulu arrived with two of her great-grandchildren, all descendants of Hikaru Sulu. She, and a dozen other Starfleet officers, had been brought to Chal on the *U.S.S. Sovereign,* courtesy of Fleet Admiral Alynna Nechayev—the real Admiral Nechayev this time. Nechayev had gone so far as to send her flagship to ferry the guests, Picard's crates of wine, holographic messages from Kirk's friends on the *Enterprise*-E, and a decidedly eclectic assortment of gifts.

Kirk's favorite, thus far, was a painting by Commander Data, showing Kirk—at least Kirk *assumed* it was a portrait of himself—dressed in the traditional costume of what had once been called a cowboy, firing a chemically powered "six-gun" into the sky while seated on a dramatically rearing golden palomino of old Earth. Data's note mentioned something about Spock's having provided the inspiration for the painting, and Kirk hadn't yet had a chance to question his Vulcan friend about that. He was sure the explanation would prove . . . fascinating.

The wedding festivities were everything Kirk had hoped they would be—a true celebration for all his friends and extended family to share. At times, he danced fast enough and sang songs loudly enough and posed for enough holo-images that he almost forgot that the *Sovereign* had brought something other than guests and gifts to his wedding.

Fleet Admiral Nechayev had also supplied security teams that now were stationed in the woods surrounding the clearing and his home. Spock had confirmed their presence earlier in the afternoon without mentioning why the admiral had felt security might be necessary. Kirk and Spock both knew the answer without discussing it. They both kept their oath to Starfleet.

High overhead, shuttles were flying past regularly, too. Kirk could see they were outfitted with the green and pink aviation running lights of Chal. But they flew too slowly to be supported solely by aerodynamics, and as Kirk had ridden over to Memlon's farm, he had seen the distinctive Starfleet silhouette of one of the craft against the setting of the suns.

Memlon! Kirk thought suddenly in the midst of an

incredibly complicated Klingon reel. The boy should still be curled up safely asleep on a cushion in the half-finished house, along with some of the other children who had come to the wedding whose parents were still celebrating. But it wasn't the boy that made Kirk's step falter in the dance. It was the memory of why he had suddenly ridden back to Memlon's farm before the ceremony.

He had made a promise to Teilani, on the bridge of the duplicate *Voyager,* just moments before she had accepted his proposal. To keep that promise, he had had to borrow a phaser from Memlon's mother.

Now the music faded to a close and Kirk stopped to catch his breath. The reel had given his new lungs their first real trial by fire. New melodies began as the band swung into something Spock had arranged. Rhythm and blues, he had called it, though it didn't sound like any Andorian music Kirk had ever heard. He reminded himself to ask Spock which planet it was from.

Kirk accepted an affectionate hug from his dancing partner, a great-grand-niece of his nephew Peter's third son with . . . someone or other. Kirk sighed. There were far too many to keep track of now. It was time he found his bride and sat down.

She was on the porch of their house with her own closest friends, the other teachers she worked with, and two elderly politicians with whom she had joined forces when she had successfully petitioned the Federation Council to bring Chal into full membership.

Both she and Kirk had long ago changed from their traditional red-leather garb. Teilani now wore a loose shift of white Chal cotton, swathed in a gauzy white wrap shot through with gold that had been a gift from Christine MacDonald and her crew. Kirk knew he couldn't have solved the mystery of the virogen crisis without MacDonald's help. He had been glad to hear that the court-martial convened to investigate the events surrounding the loss of her science vessel, the *Tobias,* had unanimously ruled in her favor, and that she had been acquitted of all charges of negligence and dereliction of duty. Having been through the same sort of inquiry after the loss of the first *Enterprise,* Kirk had sent MacDonald a personal note expressing his support.

He paused for a moment before walking up the last few dozen meters to the house. He had changed into traditional Earth casual wear, something that he had worn in the past but that McCoy couldn't help telling him, hadn't been seen on Earth for the past 50 years. But Chal was not Earth. Here his blue jeans were seen as exotic alien garb.

Kirk wore a traditional Earth shirt, too. The bold graphic on his T-shirt proclaimed the 75TH ANNUAL JAMES T. KIRK MEMORIAL CUP ORBITAL SKYDIVING COMPETITION. A few years back, the organizers had had to drop the word *Memorial* from the annual contest held on Earth, but McCoy had made a point of sleuthing out one of the old shirts and presenting it to Kirk at last night's rehearsal dinner.

A group of guests clustered around Teilani on the porch, reaching out to take her hand or kiss her cheek. A few patted her stomach as if she were a lucky Buddha. Small children from her reading group hugged her. It pleased Kirk to see her so settled and secure in their community. Though he had traveled uncounted billions of miles in both his lifetimes, he was beginning to understand the value of having a single home in a specific place, especially with Teilani.

Then she looked past the crowd of well-wishers and saw him standing on what he intended one day to be a stone-lined path from the clearing to the house.

She waved at him. He waved back. She motioned to him to come join her. But he shook his head and instead pointed to what was two meters away to his left.

The tree stump.

Eight months ago, almost to the very day, Kirk's battle with this field had been in its final round. In the previous year, he'd borrowed a team of *ordovers* to pull a hand-forged plow across the clearing, filling in the depressions and digging up large boulders. But the stumps he had vowed to remove himself, with his own two hands. And he had.

Except for this one.

He had ruined his back even attempting to shift it.

Memlon had found him lying on the ground, utterly unable to move. Puzzled, the boy had inquired why he wasn't using a phaser to blast out the stump and then had learned that "crazy Cap'n Kirk" didn't own the smallest piece of twenty-fourth-century technology. Taking pity on him, Memlon had offered to let Kirk use his mother's phaser.

Fortunately, Teilani had found him next and helped him to his feet, and had had Memlon hurry home. That was the day that she had talked Kirk into leaving Chal one final time. Wisely, she had known that his journey still was not over, that he had to complete it himself before he could finally rest with her. She chose to send him away then rather than lose him later.

But that same day before he left, beneath the suns of

Chal, in the field that he'd cleared, they'd joined in love again and conceived their child, the perfect symbol of their future.

When they reunited on the duplicate *Voyager,* Teilani had teased him about this stump and his stubbornness and his wretched back. And he had promised Teilani he would borrow that phaser from Memlon's mother and blast that stump from the ground.

Now Kirk stared down at the stump in the light from the floating fusion bubbles. Looking up, he caught Teilani's gaze as she made a face at him and touched her back to remind him of the trouble he'd gotten into the last time.

But Kirk reached into his pocket and removed the small phaser—Memlon's mother's own.

Teilani laughed out loud as Kirk brandished it theatrically and made a production out of taking careful aim at the stump.

And then Teilani's laughter turned into a guttural cry and her friends cried out as she clutched at her stomach and pitched forward, struck with convulsions.

Kirk tore through the others who crowded around her, gathered her into his arms, stared down in horror at her ashen face, closed eyes, the froth of green blood on her lips as her body arched upward in agony.

In a matter of seconds, chaos had emerged from order.

Yet the pattern had not changed.

Kirk threw his head back and cried out for McCoy.

But Teilani's convulsions had come to an end, and her body lay still and lifeless in his arms.

TEN

☆

"There's nothing like a good conspiracy to set the heart racing and the mind on fire," Garak said.

The Cardassian's eyes sparkled as his broad smile lit up his gray-skinned face. The double spinal cords that ran up his wide, cobra-shaped neck trembled ever so slightly with anticipation.

But Dr. M'Benga did not share the tailor's enthusiasm—or his conclusions.

"It's not a conspiracy," she said.

Garak looked to the left and to the right, as if carefully assessing everyone who passed by on the bustling Promenade of Deep Space 9. Then he leaned in over the small, round table in the Klingon café, motioning for M'Benga and Dr. Julian Bashir to do the same.

"But, surely, Doctor," Garak said softly, "that's just what they'd want you to think." He held his smile a moment too long, inviting her to join in his little game of paranoia.

Fortunately, Julian came to her rescue. "Come on, Garak—now you're going too far, even for you."

"Why, Dr. Bashir, I had no idea you were so emotionally involved with the troubles besetting your colleague." Garak dropped his voice again. "It's almost enough to make one think that you might also be involved in the dark forces rallied against her."

M'Benga couldn't help it. She burst out laughing, nearly spraying the table with a fountain of hot peppermint tea.

For all the abuse Garak took from the various inhabitants and crew and travelers on Deep Space 9, outright laughter was the one sure way to insult him. He sat back, cocked his head, looked ready to leave. "Refusing to believe they exist only gives them more power," he said sternly. "Believe *me,* I know."

"Wait a minute, wait a minute," Julian said, clearly trying to ease the sudden tension that had emerged at the table. "Garak, who is this *they* you keep talking about?"

Garak held up his hands. "I was merely following Dr. M'Benga's lead." And then, his mood appeared to mercurially change again as he leaned back to the center of the table, taking care to move his cup and saucer delicately to the side. "Item one: Dr. M'Benga falls asleep during her night shift just last evening."

Julian shook his head, as if already not convinced. "It's an occupational hazard, Garak. All the medical staff have to be on standby if war wounded come in. We've had a busy few weeks."

"Ah, but the good doctor herself said that she *never—"*

"Seldom," M'Benga corrected.

Garak continued without missing a beat. *"—seldom* sleeps while on duty. Yet on this singular occasion, what happens? Why, item two: Someone sneaks stealthily into the infirmary and . . . rearranges things. Coincidence? I hardly think so."

Julian frowned at the Cardassian, but M'Benga could still see the true friendships that existed beneath Garak's haughty indignation and the young doctor's annoyance.

" 'Sneaks stealthily into the infirmary'? There's your conspiracy," Julian said. He smiled at M'Benga. "That's something Garak would do."

Garak put a hand to his heart. "Dr. Bashir, you wound me. What reason would someone like myself have for . . ." The Cardassian tailor glanced at M'Benga. "What exactly did you say was missing?"

M'Benga sighed. She wondered if she could even remember, she felt so tired. "Well, my copy of the *Federation Genetic Atlas,* for one."

"Surely that's online in the medical library," Garak said. "Why would anyone steal that?"

"No," M'Benga explained, "it was *my* copy. On a permanent isolinear chip. It has all my annotations since med school. My whole tour on the *Tobias.* And everything I've done here."

Garak was about to ask something else, but M'Benga saw him stop as he looked to Julian. "Yes, Doctor? You have something to say?"

Julian looked puzzled. "Um, Andrea, you're a ship's surgeon. I mean, I've certainly appreciated your being assigned here, but I know it's just a temporary posting until Starfleet gives Captain MacDonald her new ship and recalls her crew."

"That's right," M'Benga said, unsure of what Julian was trying to say.

"Well . . . *I* have a copy of the *FGA,* and, to be honest,

I doubt if I've bothered to use it more than twice during the last six and half years on DS9."

M'Benga didn't understand his concern. "The *Tobias* was a science vessel, Julian. We encountered all sorts of alien life forms. New diseases. The medical and exobiology departments on the ship worked together every day. The *FGA* was one of my most important reference works."

"I don't doubt it," Julian said. "But why have you been using the atlas here? Are you conducting a private line of research?"

"No, I . . ." M'Benga stopped as if whatever portion of her brain was responsible for forming words had suddenly shut down. She was certain she knew what she wanted to say next. She could almost taste the words on her tongue, but she had no idea what words they were. "Isn't that strange?" She put a hand to her temple. "This is what I meant, Julian. One of the symptoms I've been having. Aphasia."

Garak smiled encouragingly at her. "If you can say *aphasia*, you don't have it." He reacted to Julian's sudden glare as if his wrist had been slapped. "In *my* experience," he added as qualification.

Pointedly ignoring Garak, Julian spoke directly to M'Benga. "You know the results of the full neurological scan I conducted. Your brain is absolutely normal. No indication of disease or damage."

"That's why I said 'relapse.' "

"Of Rudellian brain fever?" Julian said skeptically.

M'Benga knew her smile was strained. "That's my diagnosis."

The smile Julian gave her was not. "You were unconscious at the time."

Garak looked from Julian to her and back again. "Excuse me, doctors, but you, Dr. M'Benga, you were unconscious at what time?"

Julian waved his hand dismissively. "You remember, Garak. Six, eight months ago? Just before that horrible time when the O'Briens nearly lost their daughter in the temporal anomaly."

"I recall it," Garak said vaguely. "There were all sorts of Ferengi on the station then. Equal rights for Ferengi females. Something along those lines. Very messy."

"Exactly," Julian said. "That was when Andrea was invited to Vulcan for some dull medical conference on . . . what was it?"

"Fractional molecular degradation statistics relating to novel transporter-based packaging techniques for long-term storage of medical supplies." M'Benga almost yawned at the thought of what actually attending a conference on that subject would have been like. She had even forced herself to read the proceedings. They were dry and technical and repetitive; it was amazing to her that anyone other than Vulcans had been there.

"But she never made it," Julian said.

"Indeed?" Garak replied.

M'Benga offered an explanation for her decision to accept the invitation. "I was hoping to have a chance to spend some time with some old family friends."

Garak looked intrigued. "On Vulcan?"

"And I worked some extra shifts before I went, got flat-out exhausted, and—"

"And collapsed on her way to the conference," Julian concluded.

M'Benga nodded. "With symptoms exactly like those of—"

"Rudellian brain fever," Garak said. "How fascinating."

But it was clear that Julian didn't agree. "I tend to think it was more a case of severe exhaustion brought on by overwork."

"I know what I feel like when I'm overworked," M'Benga said.

"And I have all your records from the Starfleet clinic on Vulcan," Julian told her. "I've run the same tests. No trace of the Rudellian retrovirus in your system."

"What about the trianosyne spike in my blood work? That's indicative of Rudellian infection."

"But it never turned up again," Julian insisted, "which is an indication that there was no infection."

"Then where did the spike come from?"

Julian shrugged. "Faulty test equipment. They didn't find it on Vulcan. I found it here. When I looked for it again, nothing. Classic case of lab contamination."

"*Your* lab?" Garak said with mock surprise.

Julian looked as if he didn't appreciate the implication of that comment. "It happens, Garak. That's why we run tests over again. To be sure."

M'Benga wondered why she bothered having a repeat of this argument with Julian. They always ended up convinced of their own differing diagnoses.

"Regardless," she said to end the discussion, "I am afraid that last night's incident was a relapse of . . . whatever I had last year."

"And *therefore . . .*" Garak said imperiously, "we have the basis of a conspiracy."

"What?" M'Benga and Julian said together.

Garak was staring intently at Julian. "Doctor Bashir,

154

when was the last time you experienced any pilferage or theft or mere 'rearrangement' of medical supplies in your infirmary?"

Julian looked hard pressed to think of an answer. "I . . . I don't know. The Cardassians looted it when they had control of the station—"

"I would hardly call it looting when this was their station to begin with."

"I would have to check with Odo," Julian said.

"In other words, theft at the infirmary is a rare event."

"Yes."

Now Garak turned to stare with equal intensity at her. "And you, Doctor, you mysteriously come down with a fairly serious yet unremarkable and easily treatable disease common to Bajor when you leave for a weekend of fun and relaxation visiting old family friends on Vulcan. A disease that then lurks within your bloodstream— No. I take that back. It lurks *somewhere* in your body where Dr. Bashir's finest diagnostic attempts cannot find it, only to recur, after months and months of remission, on the exact same night that one of the infirmary's 'rare' break-ins takes place." Garak folded his hands before him. "Doctors, please, the more unlikely a coincidence, the more likely it is no coincidence. Would anyone care for more tea?"

M'Benga looked across the crowded café to check the time readout by the overhead menu. She had to get back to her quarters to catch up on her reports. "I don't see how that wild stretch of the imagination makes me the victim of a conspiracy," she told Garak.

Garak smiled warmly at her. "Which means the conspiracy is working perfectly."

As she began to stand up, M'Benga saw Garak instantly and gallantly rise to his feet. Julian was up a second later.

"Thank you for a most illuminating conversation," Garak said.

"The pleasure is all yours," Julian told him.

Garak eyed him gravely. "I know you think me overly dramatic, seeing conspiracies everywhere, but as a great man once said, just because you're not paranoid, that does not mean they—"

A large Klingon brushed past Garak's back with a tray of steaming bowls of odiferous skull stew and the Cardassian stopped speaking as if someone had just pressed a phaser to his exoskeleton. He looked left and right again, then stepped closer to Julian.

"May I make a suggestion?" Garak asked.

"You always do," Julian said drily.

"In your vast array of medicinal concoctions, would you by chance have some substance that, if ingested or injected in some form, would cause a specific and detectable trianosyne spike in your blood?"

Julian looked just as confused as M'Benga felt. "Yes," the doctor said.

"Good. Then, my suggestion is that you use that substance to cause a trianosyne spike, and then you test your own blood to find it. I will wager a full meal at this delightful establishment, for the three of us, that you will not find that spike."

"Well, that's ridiculous," Julian said.

"Then you may spend the meal ridiculing me, and I will be properly repentant."

M'Benga didn't know how much of what was going on between the Cardassian and the doctor was simply bantering and how much was serious. But she was feeling extremely troubled, though she didn't know exactly why.

"Garak," she said, "why do you think Julian won't be able to detect trianosyne?"

Garak paused as if carefully considering each word before he said it. "I . . . have heard, from those whom I have reason to believe would know about such things, that trianosyne by-products in the blood can be indicative of so much more than a bout of Rudellian brain fever."

"Such as?" Julian asked.

Garak gestured with empty hands. "This and that. Perhaps we can discuss it over the meal I shall buy for us here. Or . . . perhaps you'll be buying." He nodded his head to them both. "Until next time, dear doctors."

Without waiting for a reply, Garak left the Klingon café, walking away with a determined stride.

M'Benga watched him slip easily through the crowd on the Promenade, as if he were an expert on avoiding contact while remaining close. A useful skill for a tailor, she decided. Then she realized that Julian was watching her closely.

"How are you feeling now?" he asked.

M'Benga didn't believe in hiding symptoms from her doctor. "Apprehensive."

"Garak has that effect on people."

But that wasn't what M'Benga had meant. "Julian, what else does the presence of trianosyne indicate?"

"Easy enough to find out," he said. "Care to join me in the infirmary?"

M'Benga opened her mouth to say yes, but surprised herself by saying "Not right now. I have a lot of reports to complete." Then she turned away before Julian could protest, and made her own way through the crowds on the Promenade, not half as skillfully as Garak had done.

By the time she had returned to her quarters, her apprehension had lifted.

I must never talk about trianosyne with anyone else, she told herself, almost as if another person's voice was whispering in her ear. She immediately felt better. And thought no more about it.

As Garak had said, the conspiracy was working perfectly.

ELEVEN

─────────── ☆ ───────────

The *U.S.S. Sovereign* ripped through the fabric of space-time, trailing a starbow of superluminal photons, streaking from Chal to *Qo'noS* at 2,000 times the speed of light.

Still too slow.

In Engineering, a double crew adjusted her warp core and matter–antimatter mix second by second, driven by the engineer who had helped design her. Determined to work one more miracle in his remarkable career, he was willing to push the ship to the very edge of her design tolerances, and then beyond. Captain Montgomery Scott could do no less for James T. Kirk. He only wished he could do more.

On the bridge, which resonated as never before with the distant thrumming of the Cochrane generators 15 decks below, a calm voice spoke in the Vulcan diplomatic tongue. The speaker was bypassing the strict logic of a planetary bureaucracy to have Vulcan's own Starfleet vessels clear the navigation lanes to the Klingon Empire and dispatch a fighter wing at maximum warp to serve as the *Sovereign*'s escort. Spock of Vulcan could do no

WILLIAM SHATNER

less for James T. Kirk. His planet and Starfleet could do
no less.

But in the ship's sickbay, a tenacious country doctor
was about to tell James T. Kirk that he could do no
more.

Kirk understood the look in Leonard McCoy's tired
eyes, knew what it meant. Death had won.

"I'm sorry, Jim . . . I . . ."

Teilani of Chal lay motionless in the medical stasis
chamber before her husband. Her heart, and the heart of
their child, silent within her.

His child.

Kirk's hands pressed against the observation window
in the gray metallic bulk of the chamber, a twenty-
fourth-century sarcophagus bearing his queen to the
realm beyond the Nile. Unable to even feel the cool
smoothness of that window, Kirk felt instead the terrible emptiness within him. It was as if the numbness that
still claimed his hands had spread through his body to
his soul.

Kirk was aware that the sickbay's EMH, a Mark Two
model less wayward than the version on the *Heisenberg*
had been, was observing the drama unfolding in the
hologram's limited world. It was as if his body were
somehow floating above the *Sovereign*'s main medical
facility. He heard the EMH give a little cough, knew
McCoy would be staring at the hologram, wondering
why an EMH might need to clear its throat.

"Technically, she's not dead," the EMH said.

Kirk looked away from the body of his bride, to the
EMH.

"She's in stasis," the hologram continued. "She can

safely remain in that state for months while a treatment is developed."

Kirk reached for the EMH like a shipwrecked sailor reaching out for his rescuer. He had questions. He needed more information. But McCoy inserted himself between Kirk and the simulated doctor.

"You're mistaken," McCoy said roughly. "Teilani's from Chal. Her genetic structure is an artificially engineered blending of Romulan and Klingon. The same genetic strength that gave her extended life makes her body resist medical procedures as vigorously as it resists disease and injury. She can last six days in the stasis field, *maybe* seven. But then her body will have learned how to resist it, and . . ." McCoy's voice trailed off, the rest of his sentence unnecessary.

Undeterred, the EMH tapped a finger against his cheek. "I'm accessing the main medical library . . . accessing . . ." He brightened. "Chal! I have it. Yes, I understand . . . but, Dr. McCoy, she was saved once before, by *trannin* leaves. The basis of the antivirogen you discovered."

McCoy turned to Kirk as if the EMH did not exist. "Jim, I've spent two years having Starfleet Medical catalogue and test all the biotic material you brought back from the Borg recycling world. I know what's there. I know what the samples can and can't do. And none of them can reverse what's happened to Teilani."

Kirk was desperate for any chance to save his bride and child. "There has to be *something* in what I gave you that can save her."

"Jim, this isn't a disease or some physical affliction. Her whole nervous system's been affected. The baby's, too, I'm afraid."

Kirk tried to make fists, but his too-new hands still couldn't close tightly enough. "You keep saying that, but you won't tell me how it's *possible!* Bones, I was watching her. She was just on the porch. She . . . she was smiling. Laughing . . . and then . . ."

"Jim, there are no environmental controls on Chal. It could have been so many things. An insect bite—"

"I've lived on Chal for almost two years. No insect has this kind of bite."

"Not by itself. But combined with some food she might have had, the complications of her pregnancy with a human father . . . There just hasn't been enough research done on the physiology of—"

Kirk turned back to the gray chamber that held his life, suppressing even the possibility that his love for Teilani might have killed her. "There's *nothing* on Chal that can do this! I would have heard about it in the past two years. Someone at the wedding would have known what had happened. Recognized the symptoms."

The EMH cleared his throat again. "The symptoms, as I understand them, are classic examples of neural disruption."

Kirk spun around as if a phaser burst had passed through him. The EMH had just changed the rules. It was a completely different way to look at what had befallen Teilani. "As in a weapon? A disruptor?"

"Not a weapon, as such." Seemingly taken aback by the intensity of Kirk's reaction to his statement, the hologram looked at McCoy as if trying to draw another doctor to his defense. "But Dr. McCoy did say half her genetic structure was Klingon, and we are going to *Qo'noS,* so I did a quick scan of—"

"Get to the point," McCoy growled.

The EMH nervously clutched his hands together. "Uh, the Klingon medical literature is full of descriptions of the effects of various venoms produced by indigenous life forms. The convulsions, bloody froth, and finally coma . . . in a Klingon, they would all be considered indications of an animal bite of some kind."

"Not insect?" McCoy asked, his professional interest piqued.

The EMH relaxed in response to McCoy's interest. "Most local insect venoms capable of producing fatal effects in a fully grown Klingon don't progress through symptoms so quickly, and there is characteristic skin mottling, which . . . seems absent in this case."

"What species of animal could do this?" Kirk asked, his pulse quickening. Finally, here was something he could work with. A way to attack the problem. Change what he could not accept.

The EMH replied promptly. "There are twenty-three in the Audubon catalogue for Klingon land and air life forms. Another eight in the sea-dwelling categories."

"Check the computers again," Kirk said. "Have any of those animals been transplanted to Chal?"

The EMH looked to the side, accessing the ship's main medical library again, then shook his head. "Not officially." He frowned. "And they're certainly disagreeable enough that no one would want to bring them along as a pet."

"You obviously don't know Klingons," Kirk said.

"Can you put the toxicology data about the animal venoms on my padd?" McCoy asked.

"Of course."

"And cross match them with Teilani's blood and tissue analyses?"

The EMH nodded happily. "This is what I was created for. A genuine medical emergency. The use of all my skills as a computer-based intelligence to interact in a completely familiar way with the humans I serve!"

"We don't need a diagnostic report," McCoy said drily. "Just your medical expertise."

The EMH looked around, then picked up a large medical padd from a work counter. "Everything you need is . . ."—Kirk saw the padd's screen light up with a text display—". . . right here." The hologram handed the padd to McCoy, then folded his hands behind his back. For an instant, Kirk recognized the EMH's expression of self-satisfaction—just the sort of attitude McCoy had been known to display. But then, there was a little bit of Dr. McCoy in every EMH, even the Mark I.

Another question suddenly occurred to Kirk. "The types of animals in the records, what's their size range?"

"At one end of the scale, the female tree-dwelling firespitter attains a length of 4 meters and a mass of 220 kilograms. At the other end, the burrowing crested ratifer usually grows no larger than 400 centimeters, with an upper mass of 6 kilograms."

Kirk frowned. "You're certain?"

"I assure you that a Level Two Diagnostic procedure is constantly running in my background."

"What is it, Jim?"

"Bones, the ratifer is the size of a domestic cat or small dog. We should have seen something like that running around. Teilani would certainly have reacted if something that size bit her."

"Slow down," McCoy said. "There's still no evidence of an animal bite. That's why I keep thinking an insect might have been involved. It's possible I could have missed a small stinger or puncture wound on a physical scan, so I'm going to set up the sensors for a microscopic sweep of her skin."

Instinctively, Kirk inwardly flinched at the thought of his beloved's body becoming the subject of study of Starfleet's machines.

"I know," McCoy said, as if he shared Kirk's thoughts. "It can seem impersonal. That's why I stay with Starfleet, trying to get it through their thick heads and pointed ears that medicine is more than chemistry and engineering. But sometimes, even I have to trust in the technology."

Kirk nodded. How long had it taken him to learn what his friend had always known? That there must be a balance in all things.

Once, he himself had been a creature of technology, enraptured by his starship and her machineries of speed and power. But that was before he had embraced only what he could construct with his own two hands, using materials freely gathered from nature.

It had been Teilani who had pointed him in the right direction, encouraging him to find the right balance. And wisely allowed him to discover the lesson for himself.

How could she leave him now, when there was so much more for them to discover together?

How could he continue his journey alone, without her wisdom and her love?

"I trust the technology, Bones," he said. "I just . . . I

just have to *do* something. You can't know what it's like to see someone you love trapped like that and be so helpless."

Instantly, Kirk regretted his words as he saw the shadow of pain touch McCoy's face. "Bones, I'm sorry." In the midst of his own sorrow, he had forgotten his friend's. McCoy's father had contracted a terrible disease when Leonard McCoy was a very young physician. There'd been nothing the son could do for the father, except watch the progress of the ravaging disease. Until the day that his father's entreaties grew so insistent, when McCoy purposefully stopped the medical support keeping his father alive.

Whatever private hell that act had forced McCoy into, its depths had been increased by the discovery of a cure for that disease only a short while later.

"Of course you know," Kirk said. "Sometimes I speak before I realize what I'm saying."

McCoy nodded. "You know, hearing you say that almost makes the past 149 years worthwhile. Almost."

"I need to help her, Bones."

The doctor shrugged. "There's really nothing you can do right now. Maybe look at the pictures of the Klingon animals, see if you might have seen—"

"Pictures!" Kirk said. "Everyone was taking pictures at the wedding. There were holocameras and visual sensors and imaging glasses . . ."

"That's just the thing," McCoy said. His own despair clearly melted like Kirk's in the sudden knowledge that there might be something more they could do, no matter how slim their chance of success. Kirk knew it was one way in which he and the doctor had always been alike.

McCoy's voice had new energy. "We need all of them

collected and analyzed. Every image has to be scanned in detail."

Kirk looked back at the EMH. "I think we can do better than that. I have an idea."

The EMH looked at McCoy. "The way he says that, should I be worried?"

McCoy nodded. "I usually am," he said.

TWELVE

---- ☆ ----

Kirk opened his eyes to see Teilani before him, resplendent in her red-leather wedding dress.

The fusion bubbles suspended above the clearing cast soft radiance around her. The glittering firesprite cloud was a frozen veil of light behind her.

Kirk wanted to reach out to her, to hold her hand, trace her scar with his finger. But he knew his hands would feel nothing. And he knew there was nothing to feel.

"She really is quite beautiful," the EMH said.

For some reason, when the time had come for them to meet here, the EMH had taken form not in his duty outfit but in a dress uniform. The hologram looked like one of the guests in this reconstruction of the wedding. Kirk wondered if the change of garb meant that it was somehow important to the EMH, an artificial being, to fit in.

"What do you know about beauty?" Kirk asked the hologram.

"Not a great deal, I'm afraid. But I know how much she means to you. I was aware of all the changes in your heart rate, respiration, and blood pressure during our session with Dr. McCoy in sickbay. And I know that beauty is something that can have a powerful emotional effect on people. Since you presented all the physiological symptoms of someone experiencing emotional turmoil, and are doing so right now, it seems likely that her beauty is one of the reasons she has such an effect on you. And because of the strength of that effect," the EMH concluded, "I believe that she really is quite beautiful. Am I correct?"

"Yes," Kirk said. It was both a wonder and a concern to him that the computer-based intelligence programs of this era were becoming so capable of understanding—and discussing—abstract concepts. Though there was much he would like to consider in the ramifications of those advances, he and the EMH were here on the holodeck to take action, not talk, if they were to save Teilani.

Suddenly, a section of the dark forest ringing the clearing brightened as the holodeck's entrance arch materialized.

"Is that part of the forest?" the EMH asked, apprehensive.

Kirk began walking toward the arch. "It's the holodeck entrance."

Then Spock stepped through the arch. Like Kirk, he had changed into a Starfleet uniform. After the events in the Goldin Discontinuity, both had elected to maintain their reserve status with the fleet.

The EMH rushed past Kirk to the edge of the arch. "Is that . . . the *ship?*" he said as he peered past Spock.

In the corridor outside the holodeck, two crew members walked by the entrance opening. The EMH waved at them excitedly. "Lieutenant Strieber! Ensign Hopkins! It is I! Your Emergency Medical Hologram!"

Kirk saw the lieutenant and the ensign hesitantly return the wave, obviously unused to being accosted by the hologram outside of sickbay.

"Computer, resume program," Spock said.

The EMH stumbled backward, waving his arms as if to keep his balance as the arch disappeared and was replaced once again by the dark encircling forest of Chal.

"That was certainly exciting," the hologram said breathlessly. "I've only ever seen the corridor outside sickbay. This one was different. Wider. A slightly darker hue to the friction carpet. Did you notice?"

"Spock, can't we do this on our own?" Kirk didn't want to waste any more time with the EMH if he didn't have to.

"By being present in the holodeck, the EMH will be a much more efficient interface to the imaging systems we require," Spock said. He looked around the clearing. The reconstruction of Teilani remained frozen in midstride.

Well to the side, Kirk now saw a version of himself with Scotty by a banquet table. Almost all the guests were present as well, though eerily, some of them had blurred faces and indistinct clothing, as if they had partially melted.

"The reconstruction is still ongoing," Spock explained. "The authorities on Chal have been quite efficient in locating all the guests who recorded images from the ceremony and the celebration. All those images have been uploaded to the holodeck's main computer core. However, since the majority of the images were three-dimensional still shots, movements will be discontinuous over time. We will need an intuitive interface to create fill-in sequences."

Apparently insulted, the EMH sniffed. "I'll have you know I am much more than an intuitive interface."

"That's the problem," Kirk said impatiently. "How about if you just don't say anything until we ask for something."

The EMH opened his mouth to protest, but Kirk held up a warning finger.

The hologram harrumphed instead.

"Better," Kirk said. "All right, Spock, how do we do this?"

Kirk followed Spock as he walked across the clearing to the small raised platform where the string quartet was locked in place. The distance was only about 10 meters—a holographic illusion, Kirk knew, made possible by the act of walking on a force field that moved backward with each step like a treadmill while the holoemitters altered the scenery to make it appear he was actually walking forward.

Even as he walked behind Spock, and the silent hologram followed him, Kirk felt the simulated ground change beneath his feet from the flatness of a starship's deck to the slightly rough surface of the more or less level clearing. By the time they came to a stop by the quartet, Kirk was able to feel the slight springiness of the grass in the clearing beneath his boots.

"It feels like we're getting down to the final details," Kirk said.

"Doctor," Spock formally addressed the EMH, "please report on the status of the image processing."

The hologram's voice was perceptibly sulky, but he

complied at once. "One hundred percent of 627 individual shots and 810,917 moving-image frame captures have been enhanced for 360-degree holodisplay. The processing engines are now extrapolating forward and backward according to the time codes in order to assemble a complete model of the clearing. The model will include all elements that remained unchanged throughout the 4-hour-and-22-minute time frame covered by those images." Then the hologram pressed his lips together tightly as if he wanted to speak but was pointedly waiting for permission to do so.

"Is there something more you wish to add?" Spock asked mildly.

"The computers want to know what music was playing."

"Music won't be necessary," Kirk said.

"It's so the movements of the musicians and the dancers can be extrapolated in more detail," the EMH added.

"Not required," Kirk said abruptly. "All I want to see is a reconstruction of Teilani's movements throughout the evening."

Suddenly, the fusion bubbles overhead started in motion and Kirk felt the soft touch of a gentle breeze on his face. The firesprites circled through the trees. Individual leaves on the trees moved as the lights passed over them.

"The clearing model is complete," the EMH announced.

"Begin with time code one," Spock said.

Instantly, the sky above Kirk was a deep indigo. It was just after sunset. Only three fusion bubbles were aloft and the firesprites were gone, not to be released until a time code after the ceremony.

No guests were present. Kirk looked around and saw the caterers setting up the low banquet tables. Just where the main path broke through the clearing, he saw the magistrate on his *ordover,* captured in midcanter. Kirk realized these images from before the start of the festivities must have been captured by Teilani's Aunt Elanea. She had arrived early with several of Teilani's friends to help the bride dress and to oversee all details of the celebration.

Kirk turned to the other side of the clearing. He and Teilani had been in their half-built house when the magistrate had arrived, laughing at some of the more risqué wedding gifts Teilani's teacher friends had brought with them.

"Jim . . . ?" Spock said gently. "We should proceed."

Kirk knew Spock was right. "How long is the full sequence?" he asked the hologram.

The EMH reeled off the statistics of Teilani's last day of life. "Over the four hours twenty-two minutes of the covered event, the imaging engines can present one hour eighteen minutes of full motion, with a total accuracy assurance of ninety percent or greater. Sequences re-created from still images will take an additional seventeen minutes to present, with an image-accuracy assurance of eighty percent or greater and a movement accuracy assurance of less than twenty-five percent."

One hour and thirty-five minutes, Kirk thought. He didn't know if he could relive those moments, knowing how it would all end.

Spock came to his rescue.

173

"Doctor," Spock said, "how long would it take *you* to review the reconstruction at your maximum sensory input settings?"

The EMH paused for a moment. "Twelve point three two seconds."

Kirk sighed, relieved. *Of course. Trust the technology.* McCoy would approve.

"Then please review the reconstruction at your maximum speed," Spock instructed. "I would ask you to pay close attention to any animal or insect—"

"—or person," Kirk added without thinking. It made sense to cover all possibilities, no matter how unlikely.

"—or person," Spock agreed, "who makes physical contact with Teilani."

"That's it?" the EMH said.

"Please comply," Spock said.

The EMH grimaced. "If you insist."

The clearing shimmered around Kirk and Spock and the Mark II hologram dissolved into a blur of color. Then, as the reconstruction played out at a hyperaccelerated speed, flashes of light and shadow raced past and the stars overhead swept across the night sky.

Precisely 12.32 seconds later, the blur of motion stopped and the EMH streaked to a stop beside Kirk and Spock.

It was the end of the evening. At the final time code, the clearing was blindingly lit by an overhead searchlight that shone down from a hovering shuttlecraft. A Starfleet security team was scanning the porch with tricorders. Other Starfleet officers who had beamed down from the *Sovereign* were talking with guests by the firepit. Unsurprised, Kirk saw that he and Teilani and Spock, McCoy, and Scotty were missing. Within two minutes of Teilani's going into convulsions, he and the others had transported up to the *Sovereign.*

By the time this final image of the evening had been recorded—15 minutes after their transport—McCoy had already made his preliminary diagnosis, the EMH was preparing the stasis chamber, and the *Sovereign* was a sixteenth of a light-year away, traveling at warp factor 9 and accelerating toward the Klingon homeworld.

What did surprise Kirk was the number of Starfleet personnel who were present. When he had shouted for McCoy, he had seen only a handful come crashing out of the forest. Where had all these other ones come from so quickly, and why were they so well organized?

Reporting on the reconstruction of the wedding he had just observed, the EMH concluded: "There was a great deal of hugging and kissing; no insects at the resolution I could see; and contact with eight animals."

"What kind?" Kirk asked sharply.

"The magistrate's *ordover.* Your horse. Your two dogs. And four dogs belonging to guests. The shaggy one licked your wife's face quite thoroughly. As an Emergency Medical Hologram, I must say the face licking was most unhygienic."

"But not an attack," Spock said.

Kirk had lost interest in looking for wild animals. His interest had shifted to the Starfleet security team. "Spock, look at the size of the security force. *Forty-two* personnel deployed in under twenty minutes."

Spock raised an eyebrow, understanding. "That is a valid point."

"What is?" the EMH said.

"Starfleet was expecting trouble," Kirk said. He felt anger mobilizing within him. Up till now, Teilani's fate had been a terrible, accidental tragedy. But the more he puzzled over how extensive Starfleet's security arrangements had been, the more enraged he became that no one from the fleet had informed him that Admiral Nechayev was providing more than just a few guards as a courtesy. And what that omission meant. "Spock, they knew. Those bastards in command *knew* something might happen."

"It is a logical inference," Spock said, "but not yet proven."

"Not yet proven . . . Forty-two security officers. That's proof. We're not looking for an animal." He pointed an accusatory finger at the EMH. "Did they upload a guest list to you?"

The EMH nodded anxiously. "Yes."

"Can you match the names to the people recorded here?"

The Mark II hologram nodded again.

"Good. Do you have images of people whom you can't match to names on the guest list?"

The EMH looked off to the side. "Almost all the Starfleet security personnel."

"No, don't pay any attention to people who were recorded after Teilani went into convulsions. Only those who were here before and who weren't on the list."

The EMH replied at once. "Twenty-six people."

Kirk stepped back and pointed to the ground. "I want to see them. All twenty-six. Standing right here."

"Extrapolating," the EMH said. Then 26 holographic figures formed in a line before Kirk.

Kirk rapidly assessed each of them. "Delete the ones I point to," he said. He chose Memlon first—the child was part of the family, and no invitation had gone out because it was just assumed he'd be there with his parents. Then Kirk pointed to the magistrate and the three women who handled the catering and the four members of the string quartet. Fourteen more figures disappeared as Kirk recognized the two men who had operated the fusion bubbles, the four drink servers, and the eight caterers' assistants.

That left three uninvited guests.

"Remarkable," Spock said.

Kirk thought so, too.

Each of the three was a child. Two boys, one girl, slightly older than Memlon, perhaps 10 years old.

"Teilani's students?" Spock asked.

"No. I know most of them." Kirk studied the children intently, certain he had never seen them before. But they did look vaguely familiar. "Doctor," he said, "did any of these children have contact with Teilani?"

"The shorter boy. The other two never came close to her."

Kirk walked around the simulations. All three children were attired in typical clothing for the world and the season—loose white pants and tunics. But instead of sandals, they wore boots. That was unusual for Chal.

"Show me how the boy and Teilani interacted."

The EMH pointed over to the house. "It was on the porch. Time code four hours and two minutes."

Only minutes before Teilani had collapsed.

As one, Kirk and Spock moved toward the house. "Replay now," Kirk said.

Then he stepped to the side to avoid colliding with himself.

There he was, in his jeans and T-shirt, walking along the path beside the tree stump.

And there Teilani was, sitting on the porch in the midst of her friends.

And the children.

Kirk saw the three small white-clad figures, moving in sudden, discrete jumps where the computers didn't have enough visual information to accurately reconstruct their exact movements.

Then the shorter boy was on the porch stairs, looking up as if he had been saying something to Teilani. Two of Teilani's friends moved out of the way so the boy could rush up the steps.

Now he was before Teilani, and she opened her arms and he leaned in close and—

"Freeze program," Kirk said grimly.

He walked past himself to the porch, where Teilani was locked in an embrace with the child. Kirk saw that two of the women on the porch were holding up holo-imagers, which accounted for the completeness of the visual information here. One of them seemed to be recording Teilani during her encounter with the boy.

Kirk and Spock stepped around the women to stand beside Teilani and the wooden chair she sat in. Kirk had made that chair. It was rough and unfinished, his hands were not yet up to detail work, but Teilani had declared it perfect.

"There," Spock said. He pointed to the back of Teilani's neck, just above her hairline. The boy's hand was poised above it, clenched in a fist with only his index finger extended. "Reverse five seconds," Spock said.

The boy's hand moved away as Teilani sat back in reverse. Then the two simulated figures were motionless again. "Continue playback, one-quarter speed," Spock said.

The EMH walked up the stairs of the porch, as if wishing to see for himself what Kirk and Spock found so compelling.

Slowly moving forward in time, the reconstructed figures came back to life. Teilani leaning down to wrap her arms around the boy in a hug. His hand moving down, index finger extended.

"Watch his nail," Spock said. The nail of the boy's index finger was slightly blurred, as if there had not been close enough imagery of it.

Then Kirk saw Teilani flinch. Just a slight, reflexive bunching of her shoulders as the nail of the boy's index finger made contact with her neck.

"Damn them . . ." Kirk whispered. He tapped his communicator. "Kirk to McCoy."

McCoy answered at once from sickbay.

"Check your sensor scans of Teilani's skin," Kirk told him. "Back of the neck, over the spine, about two centimeters up past her hairline."

"What am I looking for?"

"If it's there, you'll know it when you see it."

"Give me a minute," McCoy said.

Kirk reached out to touch the shoulder of the holographic reconstruction of his bride, but stopped only centimeters away, unable to complete the movement, stricken by the realization that this might be the only way Teilani could appear to him now, forever, as a simulation. A memory destined to fade.

McCoy's voice interrupted his dark thoughts. The doctor didn't sound encouraged. "Jim, I'm seeing a very slight break in the skin. Almost as if she pricked herself with a hairpin. Is that what you mean?"

"It's a scratch, Bones. Deliberately inflicted."

"By what?"

"A ten-year-old boy. I'm going to guess there was a nerve toxin painted on his fingernail. I think you'll be able to find traces of it near the wound."

"Spock?" McCoy said.

Spock replied. "I am here, Doctor. It is a logical conclusion based on the evidence before us."

"Jim, are you sure you want me to do this?" McCoy asked. "To examine the wound, I'm going to have to take her out of stasis, and at this stage, every minute out is going to cut at least two hours off the time she'll be able to survive in there."

Kirk looked at Spock for confirmation.

"We're still four days from *Qo'noS*," the Vulcan said. "Once we arrive, the Klingon specialists will have less than fifty hours to treat her. Breaking the stasis field now will decrease the amount of time available to them."

"But if we identify the toxin," Kirk said, "they'll have four days to prepare a counteragent for it."

"If it *is* a toxin," McCoy's voice added.

Spock folded his hands behind his back. "This is a decision only you can make."

Kirk stared at the reconstruction before him. He knew he could count on Spock for the logic of the situation, on McCoy for the medical realities of what should be done, but his own instincts left him no choice.

"Take her out, Bones. As fast as you can. But find that toxin."

"If the EMH is down there, I could use a second pair of hands."

"At last, someone who appreciates me," the hologram said. He faded out at once.

Kirk turned his back on the reconstruction. "Let's go, Spock." He ran down the porch stairs to the path.

Spock was right behind him. "Where, exactly?"

"The bridge."

"To do what?"

Kirk strode past himself on the path again, without a glance. "End program," he said.

The clearing and the guests flickered, then winked from sight, leaving only a large room with bright yellow gridlines painted on dark emitter panels.

"Put your logic to work on this," Kirk said as he sprinted toward the holodeck arch. "We only have two facts. One: Starfleet suspected somebody might try to do something like this. Two: That means Starfleet knows the monster who sent a child to kill Teilani."

Spock hurried after Kirk into the corridor and toward the closest turbolift.

"That is not enough information from which to draw a logical, reliable conclusion."

"Forget logic," Kirk said fiercely. "I already know the conclusion." They stopped by the turbolift alcove, waited for the doors to open. "And so do you. If not through your logic, then in your heart."

The two lifelong friends looked at each other, until Spock nodded, reluctantly acknowledging the only answer there could be.

"Tiberius," Spock said.

The doors opened.

There was only one place to go.

THIRTEEN

☆

The captain of the *Sovereign* looked back from the main communications console and smiled apologetically at Kirk. "I'm sorry, but, here—you can see for yourself. There is no record of a Captain Hu-Lin Radisson, as part of Starfleet, or any other fleet we have records for."

Kirk wanted to drive his fist through the communications console and physically pull out the information he needed. But more than that, he wanted to keep this captain's cooperation, even if he did look as if he were a teenager. Was Starfleet accepting cadets out of primary school these days?

"Captain Randle," Kirk said as calmly as he could. "I was on her ship. I spoke to her. So did Spock and McCoy and Captain Scott."

"About that ship . . . the whole science convoy, actually—"

Spock didn't let Captain Randle finish. "There are no records for those vessels, either."

The young captain looked relieved that he hadn't had to deliver the bad news to his distinguished passenger himself.

"What do you mean, no records?" Kirk demanded of Spock.

"The *Heisenberg,* the *Schrödinger,* and the *Pauli.* If Captain Radisson does not exist within Starfleet's records, then it is logical to assume that her convoy of science vessels has no accessible records, either."

"For whatever it's worth," Captain Randle said diffidently, "the *U.S.S. Venture* has a shuttlecraft called the *Pauli.*"

"Excuse us for a moment," Kirk said. "Spock, over here."

Kirk led Spock to the alcove by the port turbolift doors. He kept his voice low. "What else does your logic tell you?"

Sometimes Kirk envied Spock his superb composure. Right now, Spock evinced not the slightest trace of the emotions coursing through Kirk. Going by his Vulcan friend's face, the two of them might have been discussing the weather on Earth—or some other equally boring topic.

"That Captain Radisson's Project Sign is indeed highly classified," Spock said. "You and I are both aware that there have always been certain Starfleet vessels whose existence remained unacknowledged. But with few exceptions, these were test vehicles, or proof-of-concept designs. Not fully staffed and operational to the extent we saw on the *Heisenberg.*"

Kirk nodded, looking past Spock to the rest of the *Sovereign*'s bridge. It was almost identical to Picard's bridge on the *Enterprise*-E, except here the finishes tended toward the silver-blue range, not the copper-bronze. And there wasn't a central captain's chair. Instead, like the *Voyager,* there was a command bench, with room for the captain and his senior officers. *Another ship flown by committee,* Kirk thought in dismay.

"I remember at the time," he said, "you felt the *Heisenberg* was a prototype."

"She had many advanced features. The holographic bridge displays."

"Holographic crew members," Kirk added, remembering Radisson's security officer. "Not just an EMH. And they had full run of the ship, too."

Spock suddenly frowned. It was subtle, but to Kirk, it was as striking an expression of emotion as if Spock had snapped his fingers and cried out, "Eureka!"

"What is it?" he asked.

"Jim, it is entirely possible that *none* of what we saw onboard the *Heisenberg* was real."

"I beg your pardon."

"Given your description of the holographic capabilities of Captain Radisson's ready room, and the presence of at least two holographic crew members, we cannot be certain that anything else we saw was not another level of illusion."

"But why, Spock?"

Spock raised both eyebrows, as if he were stating the obvious. "To keep the truth hidden."

"The truth about what?"

"Project Sign. The real reason why Captain Radisson attempted to convince you that Tiberius had died. How the convoy managed to—"

"Wait a minute—*you* knew she was lying, too?"

In his restrained Vulcan way, Spock seemed surprised by the question. "Are you saying that *you* were also aware she presented false evidence to us?"

Kirk couldn't believe that neither one of them had

dared discuss this secret in the past eight months. "The helmet. I *knew* it was a fake. The faceplate wasn't shattered in enough pieces."

"Very observant," Spock said carefully, in such a way that Kirk knew the faceplate wasn't the reason Spock had detected Radisson's deceit.

"How did *you* know?"

Spock's chin lifted slightly. "At the time I didn't. Dr. McCoy told me . . . later."

Kirk's mouth opened in disbelief. *"Bones* knew?"

"The blood, bone, and tissue on the helmet was an exact genetic match for yours. But because the ship had proven to have such extensive medical facilities, including a full cloning lab, the good doctor also scanned for nutrient solution, the kind used to bathe cloned organs grown *in vitro.* Detecting it led him to conclude that the evidence had been manufactured onboard the ship."

"I thought they'd reprogrammed his tricorder to give false results," Kirk said. "How else would they have convinced Bones that the tissue had the quantum signature of the mirror universe?"

Spock had a quick answer, and Kirk realized the Vulcan diplomat had given the matter careful thought. "It seems the entire labor camp on the asteroid was constructed and supplied with components from the mirror universe. Some of those components could have been the source of the raw matter processed through the *Heisenberg*'s replicators that produced the necessary nutrient solutions and thus the tissue with the appropriate quantum signature." Spock looked closely at Kirk. "Why did you never tell me you knew Captain Radisson was attempting to deceive us?"

Kirk wasn't about to be put on the defensive here. Not

when there was enough guilt to go around. "Why didn't you and Bones tell *me?*"

"And Captain Scott as well."

Kirk threw up his hands in frustration. "All right. All three of you. Why keep me in the dark?"

Spock looked contrite. "We assumed that since Starfleet was going to so much trouble to convince you not to pursue Tiberius, they must have a good reason. We thought it would be best for you if you returned to Chal with Teilani and got on with your life."

"You thought it would be best for *me?"*

Spock handily deflected the question. "Why did you not tell us about your suspicions?"

Kirk took an indignant breath, hesitated, realized he was in the same shuttle as his friends. "I . . . thought it would be best if you were all able to get on with your lives, without getting caught up in another one of my . . ."

" 'Harebrained schemes,' I believe Dr. McCoy calls them."

Kirk screwed up his face as he tried to comprehend his friends' actions. "Do you three just get together to talk about me when I'm not around?"

Spock nodded. "Yes."

Kirk sighed. "Is there anything else you've been keeping from me?"

"Is there anything else you've been keeping from us?"

Kirk saw Captain Randle looking over at them as they continued to engage in their whispered conversation at the side of his bridge. Kirk waved at him, then leaned closer to Spock. He dropped his voice even lower.

"Project Sign is a lot bigger than just three nonexistent ships and an unusual captain."

"Indeed?"

"After what happened, and I got back to Chal, for the first few weeks with my new lungs, and . . ."—Kirk held up his hands—". . . *these,* I couldn't really do anything. So I requisitioned a Starfleet data terminal. Told the quartermaster I was thinking about writing my memoirs."

Spock raised an eyebrow.

"But what I did was, I tried to see if I could find out if Radisson had been telling the truth about anything she said to us. Especially about the mirror-universe duplicates replacing a hundred Starfleet officers."

"And . . . ?"

Kirk felt uncomfortable even discussing anything as outlandish as he was about to say next. "I found references to twenty-three senior command staff who had held desk positions at Headquarters, who suddenly requested assignment to the front lines in the war with the Dominion, then all conveniently died, no bodies recovered, in the loss of only four ships."

"Casualties have been high. The Jem'Hadar are not known for taking prisoners."

"Spock," Kirk hissed, "why would *one* scoutship have two admirals, a fleet admiral, and a fleet captain onboard? Unless Starfleet needed people to disappear, so they selected ships that had already been destroyed and changed the records to add the officers they needed taken from the record."

At last Spock showed some sign of alarm. He raised one eyebrow. "Jim, are you suggesting Starfleet murdered mirror-universe counterparts?"

"Of course not. But what I am suggesting is that Starfleet caught some counterparts—those twenty-three officers, for instance—and has them locked up some-place. So to explain their sudden absence, someone in Records makes the appropriate changes to show they lost their lives in battle. I guess in a sense, they did."

Spock held his hands together in concentrated thought. "The real Admiral Nechayev was being held in the labor camp, so no such cover story was necessary to explain her absence. After her rescue, she simply re-turned to duty with few people knowing what had happened."

"And some officers weren't so fortunate," Kirk mut-tered darkly.

"If Project Sign is able to wield that much influence, to obscure records, hide ships . . ."

"Threaten us. I still can't believe we all acquiesced so easily."

Spock nodded. "Teilani said much the same thing to us before the wedding."

Kirk's heart stopped for a beat as he pictured his beloved. *"She* knew about all this?"

"No," Spock said. "Not in detail. But she was suffi-ciently attuned to you to know that your emotional outlook had changed since returning from the disconti-nuity. She was troubled by the fact that you had a Starfleet terminal installed."

Kirk ached for his lover and her comforting wisdom. "She . . . never told me."

"As it was with us," Spock said, "she did not wish to cause you further pain."

"And what did it get her?" Kirk said bitterly. "Or us? We all kept secrets from each other. We tried to pretend that what had happened never happened. And in the end . . ."—his voice suddenly failed him—". . . it may have cost Teilani her life."

"Not yet," Spock said. "There may still be time to take action."

Kirk shook his head, momentarily overcome by despair. "On a starship to *Qo'noS*? With no way of contacting Radisson or whoever's in charge of Project Sign?"

"Between the two of us, Jim, I believe we have the influence to contact anyone in the Federation." Spock glanced around the bridge. "Starfleet provided this ship merely to transport one patient. That should be a sign of what we might be able to accomplish in the next four days."

Kirk nodded, despair again diminishing with the knowledge that there was something more he could do. That *they* could do. "You're right. We know enough people at Headquarters. We could start asking the right questions. We could ask them loudly enough. Mention Project Sign and Radisson over nonsecure channels. That might get their attention."

"It might also earn us a berth on a prison asteroid."

Despite their situation, Kirk felt a smile break out on his face. "Then let me do the talking, and you and Bones and Scotty can break me out later."

In his way, Spock returned that smile. "If we are to have learned anything from these events, it is that we are stronger together than apart."

Kirk agreed. There was nothing he and his friends could not accomplish, provided they stayed united.

Hu-Lin Radisson, through whatever subtle means, had almost succeeded in forcing them apart.

Almost.

"Let's go ask Captain Randle if we can borrow the communications console," Kirk said. He led the way from the alcove to speak to the impossibly young captain now seated on his command bench.

Unexpectedly, Randle leapt to his feet. He seemed to Kirk to be even more nervous than he had been only five minutes ago. "Um, Dr. McCoy called up from sickbay while you were in conference," he said. "He wanted you to know that your wife is back in stasis, and he is running the spectral analyses now and should have results in another ten minutes."

"Good," Kirk said. "Thank you. Now, what we'd like to do is make some personal calls to Starfleet Command, and we'd like your communications officer to set up a station where we can do so in private."

"I would truly like to oblige you, Captain Kirk, Ambassador Spock. But unfortunately, we are under a communications blackout."

"Since when?" Kirk asked in surprise.

"About . . . five minutes ago. Direct orders from Command." Randle reached down to turn his captain's display around. Kirk saw the insignia of Starfleet Headquarters on an order-transmission screen.

"Very well," Spock said gravely. "I would like to invoke my diplomatic status to contact my embassy on Earth."

Randle swallowed hard. "Ambassador, I really am sorry, but . . . this is a Class-Four communications embargo. No exceptions."

Kirk could feel his self-control beginning to slip away. "Class Four is a war zone rating. We're nowhere near the Cardassian border."

"Captain Kirk, my orders are explicit. We cannot initiate any contact with anyone. And we cannot respond to any contact unless the proper Class-Four codes are used."

Deep down, Kirk knew it wasn't Randle's fault. But he immediately wondered if any of Scotty's remote controls were still installed on this ship. If he could take control of her again, long enough to make contact with the right people at Headquarters . . .

Then the *Sovereign*'s Bolian security officer called out urgently enough that he caught the attention of everyone on the bridge. "Captain Randle, we are receiving a Class-Four communications."

Randle turned to Kirk. "If it's Command, I'll ask if you can have an exemption."

"If it's Command, I'll ask them myself," Kirk said flatly.

Randle glanced anxiously over at his blue-skinned security chief, then back to Kirk. "Um, actually, regulations don't permit passengers to remain on the bridge during the receipt of Class-Four communications."

Kirk didn't reply. He just stared at Randle, letting the young captain know that the only way he was leaving this bridge was stunned by phaser. He saw Randle's almost pleading look at Spock.

"Given the unusual circumstances of your current mission," Spock said blandly, "logic suggests that this communications will involve Captain Kirk in some way."

Randle nodded in relief. "Well, I'm certainly not going to argue logic with a Vulcan."

"Commendable," Spock said.

"Onscreen," Randle ordered.

191

Kirk turned to the main viewscreen in time to see the moving stars of warp 9.3 wink out as they were replaced by—

"This is Captain Picard of the *U.S.S. Enterprise.* I have an urgent message for—ah, Captain Kirk—I hadn't expected to see you on the bridge."

Randle nervously stepped forward. "If this doesn't involve them, they were just getting ready to—"

"Oh, but it does. Captain Kirk, Ambassador Spock, I bear a message from a mutual friend."

"Hu-Lin Radisson," Kirk said.

Picard nodded, and even Kirk could sense his discomfit.

"The *Enterprise* will be in transporter range within five minutes. Please stand by to join me."

"Sorry, Jean-Luc," Kirk said. "I have no intention of leaving Teilani."

"Even if by doing so, you could save her life?"

"I'll be with you in five minutes," Kirk said.

FOURTEEN

☆

Picard watched Kirk watching the main viewscreen in the observation lounge of the *Enterprise*-E. He was surprised that Kirk wasn't showing any surprise.

"When was this recorded?" Kirk asked.

"Three months ago."

As the recording looped back to the beginning, Picard saw Kirk turn away from the screen to look across the conference table at the display cabinet where all the replicas of the starships *Enterprise* were displayed. Picard had no way to tell what the man was thinking or feeling, any more than he could for Spock, who sat to his captain's side.

"I was on Chal then," Kirk said.

"Oh, yes, we know."

"We?" Kirk asked. His smile looked brittle to Picard.

"Starfleet," Picard said in clarification.

"Not Project Sign?"

Picard sighed. Kirk had always been a rebel during his career. Constantly questioning orders or making up new ones whenever he was out of range of Command. And now, with so much at stake for him personally, any restraint on Kirk's part against disobeying Starfleet directives was likely nonexistent.

"I must state for the record that we have been expressly ordered never to discuss that matter."

"For the record? You're recording this meeting?" Kirk asked.

"Standard procedure," Picard said.

Kirk was already looking searchingly around the observation lounge as if trying to locate its hidden visual-sensor lenses. "Project Sign, Project Sign, Project Sign."

Picard rubbed the back of his neck. *So he's going to be like that.*

"Did you know Captain Radisson does not exist?" Kirk said in a challenging tone. "And her ship, with all its wonderful holographic wizardry . . . no records. Never built. None of her convoy."

"Captain . . . *Jim* . . . this is a serious matter."

Kirk's fist hammered down on the conference table with enough force to make Picard react to the bang it made. "You think I don't know that?" he said in a deceptively calm tone. Then he gestured at the screen. "Do you think I'm surprised by what you're showing me?"

"I certainly would be," Picard said. And it was true.

On the screen, the recording now playing had been made by a security scanner at the Starfleet Archives Annex on Pluto. The tiny planet was, perhaps, one of the most secure locations in the Earth system for the long-term storage of historical data. Pluto had a frozen core, which meant it had no geological activity. And even eons from now, when Earth's sun at last ballooned into a red giant, the dying star would expand only as far out as the orbit of Mars.

In that future time, all traces of humanity's existence, and all traces of life, would be scorched from the surface of Earth and the inner planets and moons. But deep within the caves of Pluto, the records of that life would remain unharmed. Whether those records would inform humanity's descendants of where they had come from billions of years in the past or merely serve as amusing artifacts to a younger race of starfaring archeologists to whom humans would be a long-vanished mystery was yet to be known.

But the mystery of today was how, on Pluto, James T. Kirk had passed through Starfleet's most stringent genetic identification techniques to gain access to his personal logs, while hundreds of light-years away, James T. Kirk was building a wooden home on Chal.

"Of course it's Tiberius," Kirk said with passion in his voice. "Radisson was lying when she said he had died. She manufactured false evidence."

Picard was astounded that Kirk had learned the truth. During his own classified meeting with Radisson, Picard had concluded that Radisson's story was too pat, and that critical information was being withheld from them about Tiberius's fate. But then, Picard admitted to himself, he had had the benefit of analyzing the debriefing procedure for his entire crew and then discussing it with his command staff. He knew Kirk had had no such advantage.

But, Picard reminded himself, his own presence here was because of a Starfleet mission. And Kirk could not be allowed to take part. His involvement would be too personal, and thus too dangerously unpredictable.

"Although I don't entirely agree with Captain Radisson's methods," Picard said firmly, "I do understand why she resorted to them."

"Enlighten me," Kirk said.

"Starfleet's investigation of the mirror universe is one of its most critical and most important operations. Counterparts could be anywhere. All information must be tightly constrained or—"

"Innocent people might die?" Kirk asked.

Stung by the bitterness of Kirk's voice, Picard spoke from the heart. "Jim, please, I can't tell you how sorry I am about what happened to Teilani. It's true Project Sign had concerns that Tiberius might be going to Chal, but in all honesty, their chief fear was that he would replace *you*. That's why all the security forces were deployed to your wedding. To prevent your disappearance. Not an attack on your bride."

"That is not logical," Spock said.

Picard was startled by the Vulcan's bluntness. "Ambassador Spock, with utmost respect, I beg to differ. Captain Kirk enjoys an unprecedented level of access to all levels of Starfleet Command. I doubt there is a senior officer—or *any* officer—who would not grant him any request, supply almost any information. If Tiberius were to take Jim's place, the repercussions could be most grave indeed."

"Everything you say is true," Spock agreed.

Picard didn't follow the ambassador's reasoning. "Then I do not understand your objection."

"If Tiberius were to replace Jim, then who is more likely to notice the substitution than his wife? If I were planning the operation, I would be certain to remove that possibility first, by arranging for her death."

Picard hesitated as he saw the flash of anguish that tightened Kirk's face. Spock was correct. He wondered why Starfleet had not taken that into account. "I can only tell you what Radisson told me in my briefing," he said slowly as he thought the matter over.

Kirk shoved his chair back as he stood up and began to pace the length of the observation lounge. Even at the best of times, Picard knew, Kirk had never been one to endure long periods of talk and inaction. "I'm not here to argue with you, Jean-Luc," Kirk said. "You told me I could help save Teilani. What do you know?"

Picard pointed to the screen where Tiberius, impersonating Kirk, passed through the identification station again. "Tiberius is after something in this universe."

"The *Enterprise,* as I recall." Kirk paused before the display case.

Picard shook his head. "Captain Scott has done a thorough job of arguing his case. The thinking at Headquarters is that a transporter that large cannot be built. The purpose of that device is still unknown."

Spock's next words made Picard decide to take a chance at doing something that was not strictly according to regulations.

"I did detect a transporter effect in the moments before the device was neutralized," Spock said.

"Computer, suspend recording of this meeting. Authorization, Picard."

"Recording suspended," the computer voice announced.

"Jim, I think you're a bad influence on me," Picard said half seriously, "but I feel I should share something with you."

"Something you've been asked not to share?"

Picard rocked his hand back and forth a few times. "A general prohibition against talking about Project Sign and my crew's debriefing. But this is . . . you knew the *Enterprise* was severely damaged by what that device did to her?"

Kirk nodded as he turned away from the display case. "Scotty had heard something about it, but he couldn't get any details."

Picard didn't enjoy thinking back on what he had seen that day. The horrible gaping holes in his ship, the ignominy of being towed from the Goldin Discontinuity by tugs, all the way back to the San Francisco Yards. "Powerful transporters were used to remove critical components from the ship. Main computer junctions, one of the primary memory cores, medical equipment, complete warp assemblies from two of our shuttles, quantum torpedoes . . . my chair."

"That would explain my sensor readings," Spock said.

Kirk walked forward to stand in front of one of the viewports and looked out at the moving stars. "Sounds like Tiberius built a ship on the other side and needed to outfit it."

Picard stood up from the conference table. "That is the likely explanation," he said, straightening his uniform jacket. "We know the mirror universe lags significantly behind our own in most areas of industrial development. A result of their constant wartime footing. The components removed from the *Enterprise* were among its most advanced." He still felt violated by the mutilation of his ship, but he could hear in Kirk's voice that Kirk wasn't too interested in machinery.

"Any idea what Tiberius is after now?" Kirk asked, without turning around.

Picard walked around the table to join him at the viewport. "Information. About you."

Kirk wheeled sharply to face him. *Now* he was interested.

"Specifically," Picard said, "something to do with your early career. The files he accessed on Pluto, they were your personal logs from your first five-year mission."

Kirk's brow knit in concentration. "I . . . really have no idea what could be of interest in them. Anything technical would have been in Spock's science logs, or Scotty's engineering records. And a century ago, our two universes were much more similar. Our science and engineering were equal. So . . . I doubt if there's any vital component from those days that didn't already exist in the mirror universe as well."

The two captains stood side by side by the viewport. "That's exactly what Captain Radisson has concluded," Picard told him. "That's why we need your help."

"Captain Radisson should have thought of that eight months ago, when I offered to help."

"She regrets that decision, as do I," Picard said. "This is your chance—and *her* chance—to try to make things right."

"What can I do?" Kirk asked simply. "And how will it help Teilani?"

Picard had been hoping Kirk would have held that second question to the end, but he pressed on as Radisson had instructed him.

"Project Sign has been tracking Tiberius's movements

in our universe for the past six months, but always after the fact. There seems to be no pattern behind his appearances or his actions."

"What actions?"

"That's where we need your help. His actions always seem to have something to do with you. We need you to analyze his movements to see if you can see the pattern. And if you can, then maybe you'll be able to predict where he'll show up next, and . . . we'll have him."

Kirk remained as inscrutable as a Vulcan, giving Picard no hint as to whether he was considering or dismissing his plea. "And Teilani?"

"Well . . . once we have Tiberius, we can find out what he did to her, and that will give us a starting point for reversing it." Picard glanced hopefully at Kirk. "It's a wonderful opportunity."

"For a starting point," Kirk said, turning back to the stars, "Teilani has five days at most. Six at the outside. Then it doesn't matter if Tiberius gives us the cure with instructions."

"But . . . she's in medical stasis, isn't she? That should stabilize her for months."

Kirk shook his head as if he didn't trust himself to say anything more.

Spock rose from the table. "Teilani has a unique physiology," he explained. "It resists stasis."

"I . . . I didn't know," Picard said, appalled. "I'm sure Captain Radisson didn't know, either."

"Yes, she did," Kirk said. He tapped a knuckle against the viewport. "Jean-Luc, how is Tiberius able to travel around without people thinking they're seeing me every place along the way?"

Picard knew the answer, knew that the computer recording was still suspended. "Completely off the record," he said. He saw Kirk glance at Spock.

"Who would I tell?" Kirk asked as he turned back to Picard.

Picard took that question to be Kirk's way of saying their discussion would be kept confidential. "Through the crossover events at Deep Space 9," he began, "we have learned that the Alliance has developed a multidimensional transporter device. It is capable of retuning a Federation transporter to re-create the crossover effect you first discovered on Halkan. We believe that Tiberius travels to a particular location within the mirror universe, uses the device to beam over to our universe, conducts his business, then returns to his own universe in the same way."

Kirk nodded, strangely unemotional still. "That's how Intendant Spock and Kate Janeway moved me around the Moon when we were being chased by Alliance soldiers. They didn't have that device, though."

"Neither do we. Though we're closing in on how it must work and we're confident we'll be able to duplicate it."

Picard met Kirk's long questioning look directly.

"The way you keep saying 'we'll' do this, 'we' can do that—are you part of it now?" Kirk asked. "Project Sign?"

Picard shook his head. "I'm just a messenger."

"So you really don't know what's going on?"

Picard recognized that Kirk was troubled. He recognized the pain the man must be feeling, facing the loss of someone so dear to him. And he tried to take that into account. But he had his orders. "Jim, what I'm about to do now isn't a gray area subject to interpretation. It is a direct violation of my orders. But in my judgment, it is a necessary violation." He couldn't help himself. He threw his shoulders back, tugged down on his jacket, his voice adopting a much more formal tone. "If you do not agree to cooperate with the project, then you will be placed in protective custody until Tiberius is captured or known to be dead."

But he'd forgotten that Spock had always been able to outdo him in terms of formal severity. "That is a flagrant violation of the Federation's guarantees of personal rights and freedoms. It will never withstand the legal challenges I shall bring to bear against it."

"I've already made that argument to Captain Radisson," Picard said defensively. "She assures me that by remaining free and subject to replacement by Tiberius, Jim represents a significant threat to the security of the Federation. It will be a lawful detention."

And with that came the moment he had dreaded would come. He addressed himself to Kirk. "I need your answer, Captain. Yes or no?"

Kirk studied him, as if waiting for something more. "But those aren't the only options."

Why am I not surprised he said that? Picard thought. But there was no way out for Kirk this time. "Unfortunately, as far as Starfleet is concerned, they are."

Kirk didn't appear to realize the seriousness of the response he was inviting. Picard listened, nonplussed, as Kirk issued a challenge of his own.

"You tell whoever it is you answer to at Project Sign that I *can* stop Tiberius for them. I can secure the Federation. But for me to do that, the project is going to have to accept *my* terms. And you tell them that there is nothing they can say or do to threaten me, because they've already done their worst.

"You tell them that if Teilani dies because of their inaction, I'll join Tiberius, and I'll tear down the Federation myself.

"You tell them that *I* want *their* answer. Yes. Or no."

FIFTEEN

"Dr. M'Benga, I presume?"

M'Benga looked up from her desk in the infirmary to give whoever it was using that tired old line on her the tired old smile it deserved.

She blinked in surprise and her smile became genuine. "Captain Kirk?!"

James T. Kirk held a finger to his lips. "I'm undercover," he said in a low voice, and as if to prove his statement, he opened one side of his Vulcan traveler's cape, complete with hood, to show his pale gray civilian clothes.

M'Benga didn't know what to make of Kirk's sudden appearance and unlikely outfit. But she was still delighted to see him. It had been at least two years since they had met on Chal. She whispered conspiratorially, "Do you need to hide out in the surgery?"

"I think I'll be safe here." Kirk glanced around the infirmary as though looking for something specific. "I was surprised to see you'd been posted to DS9."

M'Benga straightened up the padds on her desk, still flustered by the unexpectedness of this visit. "Well, the whole crew, Barc, Pini, everyone . . . we were fairly certain the court-martial would rule in Christine's favor. So, we all opted for nonship duty so we'd be available for recall when she got her new command."

Whatever his purpose, Kirk had finished his visual examination of the infirmary and now he was looking at her as if she were a long-lost daughter. "She blew up the *Tobias*. I know how much she loved that ship."

M'Benga nodded. "The only reason the Jem'Hadar didn't blow us out of space was because they were convinced we'd recovered a Borg artifact, and they wanted it. They had us englobed and we'd really taken a beating from them. Our shields were failing, warp core ejected."

"You *got away* from the Jem'Hadar?" Kirk sounded truly impressed. He sat down on the corner of her desk as if he were settling in for a good long chat with her.

"Captain MacDonald got us away. She actually negotiated with them. I think there was probably a Vorta onboard one of their ships. I'm sure that's why negotiation was possible."

M'Benga paused, but Kirk looked so interested that she found herself babbling on. "Anyway, Christine managed to talk them into letting the crew beam down to safety and take the shuttles. The Jem'Hadar probably thought they could pick us off later. And then," M'Benga smiled at the memory of her captain's audacity, "she completely dropped the shields, moved into docking range so they could get their cargo shuttles into our hangar bay, and, well, when the boarding party arrived . . ."—M'Benga chuckled at the absurdity of telling this story to James T. Kirk, of all people—". . . they were all by themselves. Christine had already beamed down directly from the bridge and there were ten seconds left in the self-destruct countdown."

"She cut it fine," Kirk said, and M'Benga could hear more than a hint of admiration in his voice. "What happened next?"

"When the *Tobias* exploded, she took out five Jem'Hadar attack ships and one warship." M'Benga fell silent for a moment. It was hard to believe almost a year had passed since that day. Though the story had a happy ending, at the time she and everyone else in the crew had been certain their time was up. But once again, their captain had pulled them through, just as all good starship captains were supposed to—but didn't always. "I think Starfleet's actually going to give her a medal."

"She'd rather have a starship."

"She'll get one of those, too." M'Benga studied Kirk and his strange outfit. "At the risk of being rude or . . . or exposing your undercover mission, whatever it is, what *are* you doing here?"

Kirk moved off her desk, looking serious. "It is a mission, Doctor. And . . . I am in need of medical assistance."

Like a computer program coming online, M'Benga felt herself suddenly switch into professional mode. "Of course. What can I do for you? Shall I call Dr. Bashir?"

"No, Dr. Bashir is off the station."

M'Benga's attention sharpened. Julian was taking a day off. She knew he had booked a holosuite with Major Kira and the O'Briens. "Actually I believe he's just across the Promenade in Quark's."

"No," Kirk disagreed, his tone leaving no room for argument. "He's responding to a sudden but minor medical emergency on Bajor. It's best he not know I'm here."

M'Benga wasn't comfortable with that. "With respect, Captain, he is my senior officer and I do have to report all medical activities that take place in the infirmary. And you did say that's why you're here, correct?"

"That's right. I'll need a complete somatic scan, at the molecular level, encoded to a time-sensitive transporter ID trace."

M'Benga took a few seconds to speculate about why Kirk would require such a test.

"It is an unusual request, isn't it?" Kirk said.

"May I ask what the purpose is?"

"Identification," a new voice offered.

Three more civilians had just walked into the infirmary. Two men, one woman, all in Vulcan cloaks like Kirk's.

Then the man who spoke folded back his hood, and once more M'Benga blinked in disbelief. "Captain *Picard?*"

Picard held up his finger to indicate silence, but Kirk said, "I've already told her."

M'Benga stared at the four of them. "You're *all* undercover?"

"Correct," Picard said. "I admit this is most unusual. But Captain Kirk has spoken very highly of you, and we would like to recruit you into our little venture."

M'Benga felt a warning twinge in her stomach. "A Starfleet venture, I trust?"

"Absolutely," Picard said convincingly. "We have the proper command protocols for you to confirm our authority."

M'Benga knew this was the time that she was supposed to say, *No, that's all right; of course I trust the two greatest captains in Starfleet's history.* But she didn't. The mantra of life near Bajor replayed in her mind: *There is a war on. The Founders are shape-shifters. Trust no being.*

"Thank you," she said. "Under current circumstances, that will be necessary."

M'Benga saw Picard and Kirk exchange a quick glance, but she was utterly unable to gauge its significance.

Until Picard smiled and said, "The captain told me you were someone we could count on. I'm glad to know his trust in you is well placed."

M'Benga experienced a flash of insight telling her that even after she followed the command protocols and performed Kirk's somatic scan and whatever else the two captains had in mind, she wasn't going to have a clue about what they were really up to.

Now the man and the woman accompanying Picard pulled back their hoods. M'Benga recognized the *Enterprise*'s counselor, Deanna Troi. But not the rail-thin black commander at Troi's side.

Picard made the introductions. "Dr. Andrea M'Benga, I think you remember Counselor Troi, and may I introduce Commander Sloane, chief security officer for the *Enterprise.*"

M'Benga stood up to shake hands with both of them. "The Sloanes of Alpha Centauri?" she asked the commander in some awe. He nodded as if he were asked that question a dozen times each day. But then, his was one of the most famous names in the history of warp propulsion.

M'Benga cleared her throat. "Better give me those protocols," she said, "and then you can tell me what's going on."

Picard pulled an isolinear chip from his cloak and handed it to her. As she carried it over to a communications console, she couldn't help noticing that Commander Sloane was scanning her infirmary with a tricorder that looked twice the size of anything she had seen before. One whole side of it glowed with a warm amber shade.

Picard caught her side glance and hurried to explain. "A standard security scan, Doctor. Nothing to be concerned about."

"Oh," M'Benga said, feeling just the opposite of his assurance. She slipped the isolinear into a reader, then entered her personal encryption code. That was enough to open the first level of the chip's security, which told her that the chip, at least, had a Starfleet origin.

Sloane, meanwhile, now seemed interested in the overhead surgical palette in the examination alcove.

"Is anything wrong, Commander?" she asked.

"Do you have any problems with theft of infirmary items?" Sloane asked, his manner suggesting his question was only an idle inquiry, which of course it was not.

"Not really. We had a minor break-in a few days ago. Nothing serious, though. Why?"

"No reason." Sloane turned away from her and walked over to Picard. From her position at the communications console, M'Benga clearly heard the commander tell Picard he was going to talk with the station's chief of security.

"That's Constable Odo," M'Benga called out from her console, without being asked.

"Yes, I know," Sloane said as he walked out of the infirmary.

M'Benga spent the next five minutes in subspace communications with Starbase 210 and was able to confirm to her satisfaction that Picard, at least, was operating under the express orders of Admiral Phillip Tenn. M'Benga's specific orders from the admiral, appended to Picard's, included the admonition that she was not to reveal her involvement with Picard and his party to anyone on DS9, including Dr. Bashir and Captain Sisko, unless the safety of the station and/or its personnel became an issue.

M'Benga logged off the encrypted channel, then returned to Kirk and Picard. "Whatever you're up to, it seems serious."

"Very," Picard said, but nothing more.

M'Benga gazed long and hard at both captains. "You two are not going to be volunteering a lot of information, are you?"

Kirk and Picard both shook their heads.

M'Benga folded her arms against her chest, letting them know that she was ready to play the game at whatever level they chose. "A full somatic scan can take two hours," she announced, "and it *can* be extremely invasive, if you take my meaning." She paused to let Captain Kirk consider the full ramifications of that unpleasant possibility.

M'Benga saw Counselor Troi unsuccessfully hide a smile as if she had just detected a highly amusing emotion in Captain Kirk.

"On the other hand," M'Benga said, "if I know the purpose of the scan, perhaps I can make some, shall we say, adjustments to the procedure, to make it more pleasant for everyone concerned."

Kirk blurted out his reply to her challenge. "I'm going to be taking a trip."

"Careful, Jim," Picard warned.

"It's all right," Kirk said. He continued. "And when I come back, Captain Picard wants to be sure that . . . I'm still me."

"I see." Kirk's situation was suddenly clear to M'Benga. "But there are simpler ways to detect a Founder impostor. Extracting a blood sample. Setting a phaser to three point five."

The blank stares she was getting from Kirk, Picard, and Troi informed M'Benga she was well off the mark. "So we're not looking for Founder impostors?"

Kirk shook his head. "But please don't ask anything more."

"Fine with me," M'Benga said briskly. She pointed over to the examination alcove. "Onto the table."

Kirk paused awkwardly. "Do I . . . have to take anything off?"

"That all depends on how cooperative a patient you are."

Kirk acknowledged that comment as the implied threat it was and quickly went into the alcove.

"If you'd like something to eat, there's a replicator over there," M'Benga told Picard and Troi. "It's Cardassian, so don't get your hopes up."

"We'll be fine," Picard said. "I don't suppose you could close the infirmary?"

But M'Benga had a very clearly defined line she would not cross. She was a doctor, and out there in the station were more than a thousand potential patients. "Not a chance. But if you don't want to be seen, you can wait in surgery, and I'll draw the privacy screen around the examination table."

"That will be acceptable," Picard said.

M'Benga started for the alcove, then looked back. "Captain, Counselor, does anyone know you're here, except for me?"

"No," Picard said. "But not for the reasons you think. This has nothing to do with the Dominion. And . . . that's really all I can tell you."

M'Benga knew she probably wasn't even entitled to know that much, so she accepted Picard's minimal explanation. "I'll be in to see you in a few minutes to let you know how long the scan will take."

Picard thanked her, then headed into the surgical suite with Troi.

M'Benga looked across the infirmary to see James T. Kirk sitting on the table, watching her warily.

Better not keep the patient waiting, she told herself.

But as she went to the supply cupboard to get the instruments she'd need to start the somatic scan, M'Benga couldn't help wondering who it was Kirk and Picard were trying to hide from. If they weren't concerned about Dominion spies on DS9, then who else was there here to be worried about?

And why did I accept their incomplete explanations with so little complaint? she thought.

It was almost as if she were used to taking orders without asking questions. And M'Benga knew that kind of behavior wasn't like her at all.

At least she thought it wasn't.

* * *

"So, was it a Borg artifact?" Kirk asked.

It was a few seconds before Dr. M'Benga looked up from her medical tricorder. "Hmm? I'm sorry?"

Kirk concentrated on not moving, though M'Benga had told him he could talk without disturbing the scan. "What the Jem'Hadar were after on the *Tobias.* You said they thought it was a Borg artifact, and I was wondering if it was."

"Oh, that, no. Not Borg. We sent the sensor logs to Starbase 324. It turned out to be some Pakled contraption, cobbled-together junk. Too bad the Jem'Hadar didn't get it."

Kirk watched as M'Benga went back to her instruments, making adjustments, frowning at her tricorder as if it were a misbehaving child.

"You remind me of your great-grandfather," Kirk said. "He could turn himself off and on like that. Total concentration. I thought it had something to do with his Vulcan training. But I suppose it was just him."

M'Benga looked up again. "Hmm?"

Kirk sighed and shook his head. "Later."

M'Benga admonished him. "Talking, yes. Moving your head, no."

"Whatever you say, Bones."

That got her attention. She smiled. "No one here calls me that. Dr. Bashir . . . he's very serious. Very proper."

"Very boring?"

M'Benga searched for the correct word. "Sincere. That's the polite way to put it. But a remarkable healer."

Kirk just remembered in time not to move his head by nodding agreement. "Three years ago, he saved my life."

"As I heard the story, he had a bit of help from Admiral McCoy."

"A bit."

"How is he?"

"I believe Dr. McCoy hit the maximum age for humans about ten years ago. Now he gets younger each year. Either that or there're no original parts left."

M'Benga laughed appreciatively. "He's an inspiration to us all. And speaking of original parts, when did you have your lungs done?"

"You can tell?" Kirk asked, chagrined. He couldn't anymore, unless he significantly overexerted himself.

"They're artificial tissue, so that stands out. I'd say you had them done a year, a year and a half ago?"

"Almost eight months, actually."

M'Benga whistled as she reached up to make an adjustment to the controls on the overhead palette. Kirk couldn't tell what she was doing. The multitude of Cardassian interfaces and displays was confusing. One or two he could handle. But a whole room of them was pushing it.

"You healed exceptionally fast," the doctor said. "Where was it done?"

Kirk thought about the real answer to her question, decided he couldn't give it. "An experimental clinic. Same place I had my hands replaced."

M'benga lowered her tricorder and stared at him. "Your hands *replaced?*"

Obedient to her directive, Kirk didn't lift them for inspection now, but he said, "Both of them. I . . . had an accident. They were badly burned. Enough so they couldn't be reconstructed." He stopped as he watched M'Benga become completely consumed by the act of examining his closer hand. She held her tricorder over it. "I'll be damned," she marveled. "I didn't even notice." She looked up at him. "May I?"

"Please." Kirk watched as she gently lifted his hand with hers and manipulated his fingers and his wrist. He could tell she was startled and impressed.

"I've never seen work like this. Obviously, your hands were amputated and buds implanted in the same procedure?"

"It was all done in the same day, I know."

"What clinic was it? It's really spectacular work."

Kirk smiled apologetically. "I hate to say it, but I really can't tell you."

M'Benga's eyes bored into him, as if he had issued a challenge to her medical authority. "Something to do with what you're involved with today?"

"That's right." Kirk thought about how much he liked M'Benga. As a person, and as the *kind* of doctor she was. A definite throwback to the days of Dr. McCoy and a different, personal way of conducting medical care. He wished he could tell her about the *Heisenberg* and its advanced medical facilities and its EMH with an attitude. He didn't blame M'Benga for resenting his silence.

But she was a good Starfleet officer as well as a doctor, and she moved on, if grudgingly. "So . . . changing the subject, how's Teilani? You two married yet?"

Kirk closed his eyes.

"What the blazes?" he heard M'Benga exclaim. "Your blood pressure just . . . oh, Captain Kirk. I'm sorry. What happened? Is she all right?"

Kirk felt the desperation roll over him again, the same desperation he had been fighting for the past two days, ever since he had given his ultimatum to Captain Picard to deliver to the secret masters of Project Sign. An ultimatum that, to Kirk's honest surprise, they had accepted.

According to Picard, Captain Hu-Lin Radisson—the captain who did not exist—had personally authorized Kirk's "request" to go after Tiberius himself. Though she had added a few conditions of her own, which Kirk was invited either to accept or to decline. But if he chose the latter option, he was to prepare for a long period of incarceration.

"She's dying," Kirk said quietly as he opened his eyes.

He could tell M'Benga truly was affected by the news. And sharing his sorrow with someone who cared only made it even more unbearable.

"May I ask . . . what happened?"

Kirk didn't see how the broad details could be part of Radisson's security requirements. He at least could tell M'Benga about Teilani, if nothing else.

"An assassination attempt," Kirk said tersely. "She was exposed to a nerve toxin."

The doctor in the M'Benga was never far from the surface. "What kind?"

"They're not sure. Something related to a class of naturally occurring toxins on *Qo'noS*. That's where she's going now. There's a specialized poison clinic that's ready to treat her—try to treat her."

"She's in stasis?"

"Dr. McCoy is with her. But she's resisting the stasis. He thinks she has only a few days."

M'Benga put her hand on Kirk's. "I am sorry. She was . . . she *is* a wonderful person. She did so much for her world, and . . . for you, I know."

Kirk nodded, not wanting to say any more.

"Is what you're doing here, with Captain Picard, connected to what happened to Teilani? With your accident . . . ?"

Kirk nodded, just a slight movement, not enough to disturb M'Benga's scan.

"Are you trying to find the people responsible?"

He nodded again.

"If there's . . . anything I can do, any way we can talk about it without compromising whatever secrecy arrangements apply . . ." She gave his hand a squeeze, and he could feel it, just slightly. "This scan is going to take another ninety minutes or so. We have lots of time to talk."

In the midst of his misery, Kirk found himself contemplating her offer. Maybe there was a way. "Are you familiar with nerve toxins?" he asked.

"Animal based? Sure. I saw enough of them on the *Tobias.*"

Kirk took a deep breath before he asked his next question. "Ever hear of any that can be delivered by a scratch?"

M'Benga tapped her tricorder against her palm. "A great many toxins are delivered that way. Some by poison sacs in the mouth, some by stingers, some by poison glands under an animal's claws."

"No, not like that," Kirk said quickly. "This was a toxin that was painted on the fingernail of a child. A ten-year-old boy who gave Teilani a hug and . . . gave her a scratch on her scalp." Kirk had to take another breath to steady himself. He had been right there. He saw the moment again in his mind's eye. While he himself had been standing by the stump on the path, the boy had been on the porch.

If he had just kept going, forgotten the damn stump, gone to Teilani's side where he was supposed to be, the boy wouldn't have been able to . . . *No. The child would have found another opportunity. If not that night, then another.*

He could not afford to indulge himself in futile self-recrimination. It was simpler to remember that Tiberius had done this. That Tiberius would pay.

And then he realized that Dr. M'Benga had fallen silent.

"Doctor?" he prompted.

"Hmm? I'm sorry?"

"The toxin," Kirk said urgently, puzzled by her sudden disinterest. "Painted on a child's fingernail. Delivered by a scratch. Have you ever heard of anything like it?"

M'Benga's voice was unsteady. "A . . . child . . . ?"

Kirk peered at her closely, wondering what was wrong. "A ten-year-old boy. McCoy found traces of the—Doctor!"

Kirk pushed himself up and off the examination table. M'Benga had collapsed on the deck.

He knelt down to be sure the doctor was still breathing. She was. He charged across the infirmary toward the surgical suite, to get Picard and Troi. They were at M'Benga's side in seconds.

Kirk and Picard hoisted the unconscious doctor onto the examination table. At once, Troi employed the medical tricorder to confirm that M'Benga had suffered no internal injuries. "It seems she simply fainted," the counsellor said.

"Any idea why?" Picard asked.

"No, we were just talking," Kirk said. "She was making adjustments, running the scan."

"I'm going to have to ask Beverly to complete the scan," Picard said.

Kirk realized that the time pressure they were under was getting to Picard. "You told me Radisson insisted that the scan not be done with Starfleet equipment. Just in case there was any sort of hidden program that could overwrite the results with a second set of data later on."

"I'll have Dr. Crusher do the scan on this equipment," Picard countered. "She can be here by shuttle within the hour."

To Kirk, right now, an hour was an eternity. The *Enterprise* was stationkeeping in the Oort cloud of Bajor's system, tens of millions of kilometers away, so no record of her presence here could be made. "Wouldn't Dr. Bashir be a better choice? He won't have reached Bajor yet."

"Absolutely not," Picard said. "Dr. Bashir has a mirror universe counterpart. Many of the people on the station do. And according to Captain Sisko's reports, crossovers in this region have become an almost regular occurrence. Radisson specifically ordered us to refrain from all contact with any person in either universe who is involved with ongoing crossover events. If word leaks out to Tiberius . . ."

"She's waking," Troi warned, giving them both notice that any discussion of the mirror universe would have to be postponed.

"Dr. M'Benga," Kirk said, "do you know where you are?"

M'Benga rubbed her face, looked around in confusion. "Was the commodore here?"

"No commodores," Picard said. "Just captains."

M'Benga recognized Kirk, then Picard and Troi. "What am *I* doing on the table?"

"You fainted," Troi said.

M'Benga sat up. "I don't faint." She started feeling around the table for something until Troi handed her the tricorder. M'Benga quickly used it on herself, made an odd sound in her throat.

"Diagnosis?" Picard asked.

"Maybe I did faint," the doctor allowed. She smiled weakly at Picard. "What did I say about eating from those Cardassian replicators?" She swung her legs off the table, planting her feet gingerly on the deck before she stood up fully.

"Dr. M'Benga," Kirk asked, "do you remember what we were talking about?"

M'Benga leaned back against the examination table for support. "Christine? The Pakled artifact we found?"

Kirk decided to wait until he and the doctor were alone again before he would try to refresh her memory. There was no sense in provoking Picard unnecessarily. "Shall we start again?" he asked instead.

"Or should you take something?" Picard still looked concerned. "Maybe a rest break?"

"I'm fine, really," the doctor insisted. "While the scan's underway, I'll run a few tests on myself, but I'm sure I . . . I . . ."

Like Picard and Troi, Kirk turned to see who had startled M'Benga by merely stepping through the infirmary's entrance.

They were two of Radisson's "conditions."

Kirk wondered how Picard was going to explain away

this one while staying within the letter of Radisson's orders.

"Greetings, Dr. M'Benga," Spock said as he pulled down the hood of his cloak. "It is good to meet with you again."

But M'Benga didn't say anything in reply. She was too busy staring at the second visitor.

The second Spock pulled down his hood as well. "Dr. M'Benga, I am pleased to meet with you for the first time."

"Two Ambassador Spocks?" M'Benga said in a tone of disbelief.

"Actually, only I am an ambassador," Spock said.

"While I am an intendant," the mirror Spock said in qualification.

M'Benga turned to Kirk, and he saw the understanding in her eyes. "That trip you're taking . . . you're going through the Looking Glass. . . ."

SIXTEEN

☆

Captain Picard didn't know what he was going to do with Captain Kirk. The man had written most of the rules when it came to being a starship captain. But now he seemed determined to rewrite them all again. And that was unacceptable in the Starfleet of today.

"Coming up on coordinates," Data announced from the conn.

"Relative stop," Picard ordered. He shifted uncomfortably in his new chair. It was eight months since he had had it replaced, after the *Enterprise* had been gutted in the Goldin Discontinuity. Most of the repairs and replacements resulting from that incident had been definite improvements, including the new permanent viewscreen. But this chair . . . it still wasn't right. And Picard was reluctant to go back to Engineering and ask La Forge to replicate yet another one.

"We are at relative stop," Data announced.

The viewscreen was awash in billows of glowing plasma storms, roiling for millions of kilometers. Though the ship was in the Badlands, this area of space seemed to Picard to be almost identical in appearance to the Goldin Discontinuity.

But then, that's why he and his crew were here.

"Any sign of our hosts?" Picard asked.

Zefram Sloane responded from his security station at the side of the bridge. "No, sir. Sensors show no other ships within range."

"That's surprising," Riker said. He leaned forward in his chair beside Picard and tapped into the main sensor display on his small tactical screen. Sensors were severely restricted in this region, but the ships they were waiting to contact were supposed to be transmitting hailing frequencies. "If they're not within range by now, it'll take them at least another two hours to get here."

Picard reached behind the small of his back and tried once again to flatten the annoying lumbar bulge in the back of his chair. "Our guest will be wearing a path in his carpet," he said with a sigh.

"Which one?" Riker asked.

Picard knew his executive officer had a point. He didn't think the *Enterprise*—D *or* E—had ever carried such a tense collection of passengers.

Picard could understand Captain Kirk's distress, up to a point. Kirk was faced with the loss of his wife and his unborn child. And in a desperate attempt to try to find a cure for Teilani, he had left her side. Picard had faced the tragic loss of family members and remembered all too well the pain and remorse he had suffered. That was the only reason he had not abandoned Kirk when the man had behaved so recklessly on Deep Space 9.

"Should I check in on them?" Riker asked.

Much as he enjoyed the calm of his bridge and the quiet professionalism of his own crew, Picard nodded. "Invite them to the observation lounge." It was better to offer an invitation to Kirk and the others than to have them work themselves into such a state that they started making demands again.

"Before they start kicking down the doors and demanding to be let in?" Riker said.

"Exactly."

"Riker to . . . Ambassador Spock."

Intrigued, Picard wondered why the commander had not chosen to speak to Kirk.

"Spock here."

"Captain Picard would like to invite you and your party to the observation lounge. The view is staggering."

"Has the convoy arrived?"

"No sign of it yet," Riker said. "But our sensors could be compromised by the storms."

"Understood, Commander. We shall be there momentarily. Spock out."

The viewscreen flickered with the intensity of a nearby plasma coil, lighting up the bridge as if a lightning storm were in progress. A slight variation in the constant vibration through the deck told Picard that the force-field generators were stepping up their efforts.

Properly responding to his captain's concentration on the ship's status, Riker looked at him reassuringly. "Nothing we can't handle, sir."

"It's not the storms that have me concerned, Number One."

Riker lowered his voice, to make their conversation private. "You don't seem to hold out much hope for this mission."

Picard knew better than to keep his doubts from Riker. He was a good officer and often came up with a new approach to challenges they faced. "To tell the truth, Will, I don't know what to hope for. I know Captain Radisson is not keeping me fully apprised of the goals and intentions of Project Sign. And Captain Kirk is equally reticent to discuss his plans with me."

"You can't really blame him. You did tear into him on Deep Space 9."

Picard stiffened. Offering advice was one thing, but questioning his decisions was quite another. It wouldn't do to have Riker start following Kirk's example and start overstepping his authority.

"Captain Kirk threatened the mission by revealing so much of it to Dr. M'Benga. In direct violation of his orders, Commander Riker."

"Not to be the devil's advocate, sir," Riker said noncommittally, "but the real revelations didn't begin until the two Spocks arrived. They were considerably ahead of schedule, and that wasn't Kirk's fault."

"He still told her too much," Picard insisted. "Orders are not something one can pick and choose from, as seems to be the captain's style."

"I've always thought that's one of the reasons we're out here," Riker said, "instead of some fleet of automated ships like Radisson's, staffed by holograms and artificial intelligences."

Picard wasn't certain of the point Riker was trying to make, but he appreciated Riker's light tone. His first officer appeared determined to be nonconfrontational, as if to make certain that their discussion could not escalate into an argument.

"So we can pick and choose," the commander continued. "Rules are rules and orders are orders, but out here, where there's so much that's new . . . we do have to be flexible."

"There's a difference between flexibility and insubordination," Picard said.

"I agree, sir. But one thing I've noticed is that whenever Kirk crosses paths with you, it's as if you forget how flexible you are yourself. Suddenly, you're like some stern father figure trying to set a good example for your wayward son." Riker smiled to take the sting out of his comment.

Picard shifted in his ill-fitting chair. "I should hope that given the fact Captain Kirk is a century older than I, it would be the other way around."

Riker kept his eyes expectantly on Picard but didn't say anything.

Picard couldn't help smiling at him. "Is there something else you'd care to add before I put you in leg irons for general insolence?"

At that, Riker laughed. "I was just thinking, Jean-Luc . . . after everything that happened in the Briar Patch, you would have been quite at home in Kirk's era. If you had been cut off from Command as often as he was in his day, I think you would have demonstrated how 'flexible' you could be when it came to orders, and the Prime Directive. I even think you'd have enjoyed it, too."

Rather pleased by Riker's description, Picard feigned indignation. "Are you somehow suggesting that I might be *jealous* of Captain Kirk?"

Unexpectedly, his efforts to turn the conversation to banter were not picked up on by Riker. "Not of Kirk," Riker said seriously, "but of his time, yes. Things were different then. It was easier for one man to leave his mark on history. Today, there are more starships, and many more captains. Competition is tough."

Picard allowed Riker to make his point. To a certain extent, after all, it was true.

"And in a way," Riker went on, "I wouldn't be surprised to find out that Kirk was jealous, too. Not of you," he quickly added, "but of your time. When you look at Kirk's career, it was a constant fight for him to keep that chair."

Riker leaned forward, caught up in his thesis. "One five-year mission, and Kirk was promoted to the admiralty, where he might as well have disappeared. Then he got command again, almost by accident, when the V'Ger incident took place. That gave him another five-year mission, but then he was forced to take a teaching position at the Academy. He got the *Enterprise* back, he lost her again. He got her back, lost her. From year to year, Kirk never knew when or *if* he'd ever get another chance to command a ship—which is clearly what he loved to do most of all."

Riker looked keenly at Picard. "When it comes to the nuances of your approaches to command, you're both the products of your different eras, but in your hearts, where it matters most, you're both the same. Neither one of you holds back when you believe Starfleet is overstepping its authority. You just want to do what you love to do, and do it better than anyone else." He shrugged and sat back in his chair as if he hadn't intended to get so long-winded or philosophical.

"Will, I had no idea that you were such a scholar of Captain Kirk's career," Picard said. He tried to remember if he had ever told his first officer that he had had almost this identical conversation with Kirk the last time their paths had crossed.

Riker smiled. "We all are. You want to work on this bridge, it goes with the territory."

Picard heard the turbolift doors open behind him and glanced over his shoulder to see Kirk, both Spocks, and the final two team members requested by Captain Radisson—Kate Janeway and T'Val—step onto his bridge.

He stood up, wincing in discomfort as he straightened his spine. "Thank you, Commander; our discussion has been most enlightening. You have the conn. You know where I'll be."

As he escorted his passengers to the observation lounge, he decided that in one important way, he and his predecessor were actually considerably different.

Where Kirk had had the opportunity to experience both ages of Starfleet, he himself, thus far, had enjoyed the benefits only of its more mature stage. Picard took a moment to speculate about how he might have fared in the pioneering era, when everything had been so new and untried.

He could not deny that he missed the days when he and his crew had been explorers and adventurers, not, as seemed more and more the case, diplomats and spokespeople for the benefits of bigger and better interstellar business opportunities. It was to be hoped that those early days would somehow come back again, and soon.

There was always the chance, with Kirk's example to inspire the mission planners, that they might, he thought. But first, Picard knew, he and Kirk had to survive their next meeting.

* * *

"What do you mean, they're not here yet?" Kirk said as he paced back and forth past the viewports. Everyone else was sitting at the conference table in the observation lounge, but he had had enough of inaction. "We're three hours late as it is."

Picard was still sitting at the head of the table, ramrod straight, hands folded in front of him. "As I explained, Captain, we are not in direct communication with Captain Radisson. She gave us these coordinates and a rendezvous time. We're here as directed. All we can do is wait."

"I don't even know why we need them," Kirk said impatiently. As far as he could see, Radisson was going out of her way to make things more difficult for him. Maybe she was intentionally slowing him down. "I mean, how hard can it be to make one of those . . . multidimensional transporter devices?"

He was surprised when Intendant Spock answered. "It is not a straightforward matter," the frailer counterpart of Spock said. "When the Alliance in my universe became aware of the potential of crossovers from your universe, they enforced strict alterations in transporter technology. Those alterations were to prevent such accidents as took place at Halkan from ever recurring."

The intendant was referring to the first time that he and Kirk had met. More than a century ago, in the mirror universe. Kirk still feared that their chance encounter had set in motion the events that later led to the enslavement of humans and Vulcans and to the brutal tyranny of the Alliance in that world.

"In some ways," the intendant continued, "those changes spurred research into transporter technology beyond what your universe has achieved. I believe it is

229

one of the few areas in which we are actually more advanced than you."

Hearing a version of Spock's voice that sounded so much weaker than it should had a softening effect on the mood in the conference room. But Kirk knew that Intendant Spock, the leader of the Vulcan Resistance in the mirror universe, not only looked much healthier than he once had, he *was* much healthier than he had been eight months ago.

Seeing him then, for the first time in nearly a century, Kirk had been shocked by the change in Spock's counterpart. The mirror Vulcan's hair, still in the traditional style, had turned snowy white, as had his goatee. His dark eyes were hooded, deeply sunken, his lips dry and cracked. His thin, transparent skin, mottled by faint green spiderwebs of broken capillaries, was drawn tight over gaunt cheeks that were filigreed with wrinkles.

Even more alarming, his movements had been unsteady and his left hand trembled. Poor nutrition, stress, and wounds from untold battles had resulted in premature Bendii syndrome, a condition unseen among the Vulcans in Kirk's universe for generations. Intendant Spock had seemed at least another century older than Spock, who was a sound 146 years old—Vulcan middle age.

But now, after months of rest, recuperation, and the best treatment the Vulcans of Kirk's universe could provide, the intendant had put on much-needed weight. His gait was steadier, and even the trembling of his hand and arm was seldom noticeable. He was still slower in his movements than the Spock Kirk knew, and his hair and beard were still pure white, but he was renewed.

Still, Kirk didn't want to argue with him. He directed

his anger and impatience toward Picard. "Then why haven't we just stolen one of the devices?" Kirk said. "And so we don't offend Starfleet propriety or the Prime Directive, we can always give it back after we've replicated it."

But the Spock of this universe, not Picard, answered that question. "Captain, even if we possessed such a device, we would be unable to deploy it in the Badlands. To function properly, the device appears to require the existence of a co-located transporter. Within the same general vicinity in the other reality."

Kirk wanted no more of the endless excuses and qualifications, not even from Spock. "I've had enough of this."

"No, you haven't," Picard said.

Kirk bristled. The last thing he needed to hear was someone else telling him what his feelings were. "You're the captain of your ship and your crew," he said angrily. "Not of me."

"Captain Kirk, while you are on this ship, you are subject to my rules and my orders. And I am getting tired of your constant interference and complaints."

Spock stood up. "I believe this conversation can serve no useful purpose. You are both—"

"Sit down," Kirk and Picard said together.

Then they faced each other again.

"I'm not the one interfering here. It's you," Kirk said.

Picard got to his feet. Kirk welcomed the challenge. Anything was better than rule-bound apathy. "On the contrary." Picard said. "You made a promise to Captain Radisson, and you aren't following through."

"But *nothing's* happening, Jean-Luc! Don't you see? She wanted me out of the way. She threatened me. But I refused. I said I wanted to be involved. She said, 'All right, whatever you want.' And now it's been nothing but delays and confusion, which has given her exactly what she wanted in the first place. *I'm in the middle of nowhere on your miserable ship doing nothing!"*

"Captains," Spock said. "The stress of the situation is—"

But Kirk didn't need Spock to save him from Picard. "That's enough, Spock. This is between Picard and me." He took a step forward.

Picard remained at the head of the table. "No, Kirk. This is between you and Starfleet. I understand that battle. I've fought them myself when I felt circumstances warranted it. But I've never made that fight a personal vendetta the way you're doing now. You're not listening to reason; you're simply striking out in rage."

"Because of *you,* I trusted Starfleet to honor their commitment to me! To send me after Tiberius! To at least *try* to save Teilani's life, which is more than any of you are doing!"

Kirk found his new hands could make perfect fists now, as if all he had needed to redevelop his abilities had been the proper motivation. And right now, sending Picard flying over his conference table was just the motivation Kirk needed to feel he was back in control.

He took another step forward, certain Picard could read his intent.

He did.

"Picard to Security. Captain Kirk requires an escort to his quarters."

"You're doing it again," Kirk warned. "Exactly what Radisson wants you to do. Taking me out of the picture."

"You took yourself out, Kirk, a long time ago."

That was the final insult.

Kirk lunged at Picard, fist drawn back—

—only to be tackled by T'Val. In his anger, Kirk had forgotten that Kate Janeway and T'Val were even in the room.

Kirk hit the deck with a violent slam just as Commander Sloane rushed in.

Kirk tried to roll to his feet, but T'Val was astride him, her biomechanical hand a fist under his chin, crushing his uniform jacket, her other hand poised on his shoulder, just above the *katra* points that were the focus of the Vulcan nerve pinch.

"Give me an excuse," T'Val hissed at him, "and you won't wake up for a week."

Kirk clenched his fists at his side, but made no other outward move of resistance. There was a difference between bravery and stupidity, and he had crossed that line often enough in his life to know one from the other by now.

T'Val released him and jumped to her feet.

Kirk stood up slowly, his eyes on Commander Sloane standing in the open doorway of the lounge with one hand resting on his phaser.

"I will accept an apology," Picard said.

"So will I," Kirk answered.

"I am not your enemy, Captain."

"Then stop acting like one. At least acknowledge that Radisson is manipulating me, and she's using you to do it."

"Commander Sloane, show Captain Kirk to his quarters. He will be remaining there for the remainder of the mission."

"Until Teilani's dead, you mean," Kirk said bitterly.

Picard's eyes met his. Kirk didn't know which he saw more of in the man, anger or sorrow. But he didn't care which emotion moved Picard to act against him.

Kirk ripped his comm badge from his jacket. Once that symbol had belonged to his *Enterprise*. But now, as the symbol of Starfleet, it stood only for betrayal. "I told you, Picard, that if Teilani were to die, then I would help Tiberius destroy the Federation myself."

Kirk threw the communicator on the conference table, in front of Picard. "You *are* the enemy now. And so is everyone else who wears that. You tell Radisson that."

Then he pushed past Commander Sloane, out of the observation lounge, to find his own way to his quarters, where he could plot his escape from this nightmare of a ship.

He was halfway across the bridge when a voice called out to him.

"Captain Kirk. I'm so glad to see you're here."

Kirk stopped and looked up at the viewscreen to see someone he had never seen before, wearing a Starfleet uniform, smiling at him. "I'm Captain Mantell of the *U.S.S. Schrödinger*. The convoy's here and we're ready to proceed. Are you?"

SEVENTEEN

─────── ☆ ───────

Picard still felt unsettled after the confrontation in the observation lounge. Given the threats Kirk had made and the actions Picard had attempted, he was no longer certain he could allow the mission to proceed. The risks could be too great.

So, while Data and Riker made their preparations with Captain Mantell, Picard asked Spock to join him in his ready room.

He got to the point at once. "To be frank, Ambassador, I don't think Captain Kirk is up to this mission."

"I can understand why you might think so," Spock replied calmly. "But as someone who knows the captain perhaps as well as anyone else, I believe the best thing would be to allow the mission to proceed as planned, and as promised."

Picard had anticipated Spock's response. The Vulcan and Kirk were extremely close friends. But it was Picard's duty now to determine if Spock was speaking from loyalty or logic.

"You heard the threats he made," Picard said as he sat

235

back on the edge of his desk. "I find those difficult to discount. Given the stress he's under, they might even be a sign of instability."

"Captain Picard," Spock said, "if you want to know if Captain Kirk is capable of proceeding with the mission arranged by Captain Radisson, in my opinion, he is. I am certain that, on reflection, you will realize that he has said many things in the heat of passion, heightened by the tragedy he faces. But you must not forget that his frustration arose from being kept from taking an active role in saving Teilani. Give him that role now, and that frustration will be dealt with, and the words he said in the heat of the moment will be forgotten."

"It doesn't matter how well—or even *if*—I understand Kirk's frustration. I am responsible for the lives of everyone who is to go on Radisson's mission. For their safety, I cannot forget those words."

"If you allow Captain Kirk to continue his mission, I can guarantee his behavior. If you do not allow him to continue, then he will give you other reasons not to forget his words."

Picard stood away from his desk to face Spock. The new undercurrent that had just been added to their discussion seemed to call for it.

"That almost sounds like a threat. And surely that would be most illogical."

"Jim Kirk is my friend, Captain. And logic has little to do with that, or with what he is capable of if he loses the most important person in his life because of Starfleet's failure to act. Send him on the mission."

For long moments, the two men stood watching each other, like warriors in a duel, each waiting for his opponent to make the first move, and the first mistake.

"Spock, it almost sounds as if you want to add the words, 'or else,' to what you've said."

Although Spock's expression didn't change, and his voice remained even and unhurried, Picard detected what felt like the subtlest hint of warning in what the ambassador had said. "Your words, Captain. Not mine. And now, if you will excuse me, I believe I have said all that is required."

Picard watched Spock turn and leave.

For a few moments, he remained behind in his ready room. He looked down at his desk, letting his fingers lightly trace the outline of the ceramic Kurlan *naiskos* displayed there in its place of honor.

It had been given to Picard by his archeology professor, Richard Galen, on the eve of the professor's greatest discovery—the holographic message from an ancestral race, hidden in the genetic structure of diverse alien races.

Picard lifted the top of the squat figure to reveal the many small figurines inside, perfectly crafted 12,000 years ago.

That was the purpose of the *naiskos:* to remind those who saw it that each person is made up of a community of individuals.

Picard knew that was true of himself. One individual was the career officer who unfailingly supported Starfleet in all matters. But another was the career officer who had willingly chosen to throw away that career and stand up to Admiral Dougherty to defend the Ba'Ku.

And one was the lover, one the mourning uncle, one the rebellious son. Each of his many selves combined to form this outer shell that contained them all, sometimes allowing more of one than another to come to the fore, but always struggling to find the balance between the myriad hopes and desires, demons and angels that existed within him.

Picard looked to the closed doors of his ready room, thinking about what Spock had said.

He had no doubt that he had seen Jim Kirk's outer shell break today. He had seen a glimpse of the demons within the man.

But who didn't have such passions hidden inside?

And who could control them faced with what Kirk faced?

Picard carefully replaced the top portion of the *naiskos,* containing the community within, restoring the balance of the piece.

Spock was right.

He had to give Kirk the chance to do the same.

Or else Kirk's demons might rule him forever.

Kirk stayed on the bridge, watching and listening to the preparations being made to proceed with the mission.

He had seen Picard ask Spock into his ready room. He had seen Spock leave a few minutes later. But he would not ask what they had discussed. He was finished asking anyone for anything. All that was in his mind was getting off this ship, one way or another. Certainly stealing a shuttlecraft shouldn't be too difficult. And with the sensor distortions in this part of space, all he needed was a five-minute head start and he could disappear into the storm.

Then Picard finally returned to the bridge.

He walked over to Kirk. "I believe what you did in the observation lounge was wrong," Picard said.

I don't care what you believe, Kirk thought.

"But I understand why you did it."

No one could understand, Kirk thought.

"And if you are still willing," Picard continued, "I will fully support this mission, and your participation in it."

Whatever Spock said seemed to have worked. It just wasn't enough. Not now. "Before I accept," Kirk said, "what if it turns out there are two missions?"

"Explain," Picard said.

"The one Radisson says she sending me on, and the real one I suspect she's planned."

"To isolate you."

"That's it."

"I will promise you this," Picard said. "If Radisson *is* lying to you, then she is lying to me as well. And I will not accept that any more than you would."

"Even if it means going against Starfleet?"

Kirk didn't understand the odd smile that suddenly appeared on Picard. "Remind me to tell you what happened a few months ago in the Briar Patch." He put a hand on Kirk's shoulder. "Jim, I believe I have more faith in the wisdom of Starfleet than you do. But I will not tolerate the misuse of that faith. If I have to choose between Starfleet and doing what's right, you and I *will* be fighting on the same side."

Kirk heard the truth in Picard's voice and saw it in his eyes. *Maybe Jean-Luc does understand.* "Thank you. For Teilani's sake, especially."

Kirk noticed Picard glancing at his uniform jacket, knew what he was about to say next. "Should I see about getting you a new communicator?"

"Not where I'm going," Kirk said. He looked to the

viewscreen. The *Schrödinger*'s senior science officer, a young Vulcan commander, was on it, still transmitting warp calibration readings to Data on the bridge and La Forge in Engineering. "They'll be finished soon," Kirk said.

"Let's find out," Picard said. "After you, Captain."

Kirk shook his head. "No, after you."

Kirk remained on the sidelines for the next 10 minutes as Picard oversaw the operations of his ship. Clearly what they were about to attempt had never been tried before. At least in this universe.

Finally, though, La Forge announced that the warp core was tuned to the new output modulations. Everything that could be done had been done. Kirk found the moment oddly anticlimactic because it meant that the entire ship now had to return to its standby status.

"The *Enterprise* is fully ready to begin," Picard told the senior science officer. "We have only to wait for your arrival at these coordinates."

Kirk caught the Vulcan commander's almost unnoticeable expression of amusement as she said, "Captain Picard, we have been at these coordinates ever since we first made contact with you."

"Mr. Data?" Picard said.

"There are still no ships within sensor range," the android reported.

"Please switch to your forward view," the science officer said. Then she vanished from the viewscreen, to be replaced by the twisting lights and shadows of the Badlands.

"Monitor your sensors in the theta range," the science officer's voice suggested.

"Changing selectivity," Data acknowledged.

The science officer gave a final order. "Watch your screen."

A flurry of subspace static crackled over the viewscreen image, and suddenly, Kirk saw three starships in formation. At least he assumed they were starships. At the current magnification, they were little more than elongated white specks.

Picard was out of his chair at once. Kirk knew why. The idea that three ships could have moved that close to the *Enterprise* without being detected would be unnerving to any starship captain.

"Mr. Data, did you detect a tachyon pulse?" Picard asked.

"No, sir. I do not know how they managed to conceal themselves, but they were not cloaked. I am certain."

"Go to full magnification," Picard said, then added, "Commander T'thul, I am quite impressed by your capabilities."

The image on the viewscreen jumped as the magnification increased. Kirk scrutinized the three starships. They were clearly of Starfleet design, with a forward command hull, engineering hull, and two warp nacelles, but the ships had an odd half-melted look. It was as if a ship like the new *Enterprise* had been draped in fabric, creating a webbed effect between the various hulls, making them appear to flow smoothly into each other instead of the ship being composed of separate elements.

"I've never seen anything like those," Commander Riker said as he stood beside his captain.

Kirk saw Data turn around from the conn. "Captain, our sensor recording instruments are offline."

"Go to backups," Picard ordered.

"Sir, I mean *all* our sensor recorders are offline. We can see those ships, but we can't record any sensor returns from them."

The image of the strange starships was replaced by Captain Mantell of the *Schrödinger*. "Sorry, Captain Picard, that's our doing. Even the design of our ships is classified."

"I understand," Picard said. "But you could have instructed us to turn off our sensors for you. Is that how you hid in plain sight? By transmitting a false image directly to our viewscreen?"

Mantell shrugged off the question. "I'm not at liberty to say, Captain."

"Is Captain Radisson available?" Picard asked.

"Not at the moment, though she sends her regards. Are you ready to proceed?"

Kirk saw the frustration on Picard's face. *Good,* Kirk thought. *So he knows what it feels like to deal with these people, too.*

"Enterprise standing by," Picard said. Then he returned to his chair. Riker sat beside him. The turbolift doors opened and Kirk saw Counselor Troi enter the bridge and take her place on Picard's left.

Kirk looked for Spock. He was standing at the back of the bridge, near the unstaffed auxiliary life-support station. Intendant Spock, T'Val, and Kate Janeway had remained in the observation lounge. Kirk had the strong impression that they preferred not to be around him. "Do you think this is actually going to work?" Kirk asked.

"The moment for asking that question has long passed," Spock said. "However, as much as Captain

Radisson might be eager to rid herself of you, I sincerely
doubt she would be willing to destroy a Sovereign-class
vessel to do so."

"Let's hope she has as low an opinion of me as you
do."

"Indeed."

On the viewscreen, Captain Mantell was giving Picard
his final orders. "On my mark, Captain, go to one-tenth
impulse, bearing zero zero zero, mark zero."

"Bearing dead ahead," Data confirmed.

"The field disturbance will last fifty-five hours," Mantell continued. "If you don't return by then . . ."

"We're aware of the contingency plans," Picard said.
"The crew will attempt to reach Terok Nor, and we will
launch the *Enterprise* into a star. No technology will be
recoverable."

"Good luck, Captain Picard, Captain Kirk. And good
hunting." Mantell flashed off the screen again, replaced
by an image of the three distorted starships, now in
formation at the points of an equilateral triangle.

Mantell's voice came over the speakers. "Mark!"

"One-tenth impulse," Data confirmed.

The image on the viewscreen expanded slowly as the
Enterprise moved forward, heading directly for the
center of the triangle the starships formed.

Kirk studied the screen carefully, looking for any sign
of transition. But there was nothing. Only the ion storms
and continuous plasma lightning of the Badlands.

The three starships slipped off the screen. It would
happen any moment now, Kirk knew. He put his hand
on the edge of the life-support console, just in case—

—the viewscreen flickered and the image of the storm
suddenly jumped to show a new configuration of plasma

billows as if two visual recordings had been spliced together with no concern for continuity.

But that was all.

"Mr. Data . . . ?" Picard asked.

Kirk waited for the answer. Surely it couldn't have been that simple, that inconsequential.

But it was.

"According to the quantum signature of the plasma particles surrounding the ship," Data said, "we have just crossed into the mirror universe."

Kirk felt a shudder pass through him, a release of tension. He looked at Spock.

"You have what you asked for, Captain," Spock said.

Kirk understood. Now everything was up to him.

EIGHTEEN

———————— ☆ ————————

"I am so sorry Dr. Bashir was called away," Garak said as he placed his tray on the table in the Klingon café. "But still, it gives us a chance to become better acquainted, wouldn't you say, Doctor?"

Andrea M'Benga looked up from her padd and her mug of peppermint tea as Garak sat down across from her.

"That is, if I'm not disturbing you," the Cardassian added.

"Uh, no, not at all," M'Benga said. Though in truth, he was.

"You're certain," Garak asked solicitously. "You have the look of someone who'd much rather be sleeping."

M'Benga laughed. There was something about this tailor that made it impossible for her to believe the rumors that floated around him like storm clouds. She could believe he was once a gardener at the Cardassian embassy on Romulus. He certainly had that gentle, caring quality about him. But the stories that he had also been an assassin for the Obsidian Order—that was pushing things too far.

"I would rather be sleeping," M'Benga admitted. "But since I'm not, I'd appreciate the company."

Garak smiled graciously. "Such refreshing forthrightness. I shall do my best to keep the conversation scintillating and hold your interest."

"So how's the tailoring business?"

"It has its ins and outs."

M'Benga laughed. "There's never any small talk with you, is there?"

"Words are so precious," Garak said, "that it is a shame to waste them on the mundane. Speaking of which, have you heard from Dr. Bashir?"

"He'll be back tomorrow. Apparently it was a mix-up at an agricultural station. Some antiviral agents were mislabeled. They thought they had an epidemic on their hands. But it was just allergic reactions."

"Well, I'm glad for the people on Bajor. But poor Dr. Bashir, he'll have missed all the excitement."

M'Benga waved her hand to get her server's attention. "All what excitement?"

Garak leaned in more closely, his clever eyes never resting as he checked out the rest of the customers at the café. M'Benga was certain he was always on the lookout for customers and wanted to see who was in need of new clothes.

"Surely you've heard talk about the mysterious visitors? People in Vulcan traveler's cloaks who weren't exactly Vulcan? Sightings of a Starfleet vessel hiding in the cometary halo?"

M'Benga tried to freeze her expression, but it was next to impossible to disguise her true reaction from one as observant as Garak.

He waved a friendly finger at her. "Now, now, Doctor,

let's remember that forthrightness. You have heard the stories, haven't you?"

A huge Klingon finally appeared at the table and M'Benga asked for a fresh pot of hot rg'h tea. She used the momentary distraction to craft her answer for Garak. As long as she could keep him believing that she had heard stories and had not been actually involved with his 'mysterious visitors,' she was sure she could keep Kirk's secret.

"I've heard the stories," she admitted.

Garak sat back, nodding sagely. "Ah, and you don't wish to spread rumors. Very noble of you. It doesn't make for interesting conversation, mind you, but I understand."

Then a shadow fell across the table. "Hello . . . Garak."

M'Benga looked up at the intriguing, half-formed face of Odo, the station's security chief.

"Doctor," the shape-shifting constable added brusquely.

"What an unexpected pleasure," Garak said. "Would you care to join us?"

M'Benga thought it was refreshing the way Garak treated everyone with equal respect.

"It won't take a minute," Odo said. "I'm here about a missing-property report."

Garak smiled vacantly. "Whose missing property?"

"Yours," Odo said.

Garak kept his smile. "But I haven't filed any missing-property reports."

"Well, maybe you don't know it's missing yet."

At that, Odo placed a small, glittering black sensor relay on the table, about the size of a large earring.

"I'm afraid I don't understand."

"It's a Cardassian optical spy sensor."

Garak looked alarmed. "Do you suppose there are Cardassian spies about? On a Cardassian space station?"

Odo looked down at M'Benga. "I found it in the infirmary."

Now M'Benga was alarmed. "Where? When?"

"In the equipment above the examination table. Yesterday."

M'Benga felt her heart stop.

Odo studied her carefully. "Is something the matter, Doctor?"

"No, not at all." M'Benga knew she had to get in touch with Captain Picard. The security of his mission to the mirror universe might have been breached. "It's certainly an odd place to put a spy device."

Odo looked back at the tailor. "What would you say about that, Garak?"

Garak picked up the small device and squinted at it. "Oh, I'm not a person who knows much about such things, I'm afraid. But it appears to be a simple device. Old design. Not much range. Probably left over from the occupation."

"It was working yesterday when I found it. And it wasn't there the last time I swept the Promenade for bugs."

Garak held the device out as if to drop it into Odo's hands. Odo took it from him. "Would you like me to ask if anyone's lost a spy device?" Garak offered.

"What I'd like you to do is to stay in your shop and not get yourself involved in anything that might make you appear to be working for the Cardassians. Captain

Sisko might have a war to win, but I have a station to keep safe *and* secure."

M'Benga watched in fascination as Odo's hand suddenly changed configuration, becoming a three-fingered paw with powerful claws that snapped the device into pieces, which he then sprinkled over Garak's salad.

"Enjoy your lunch," Odo growled at the tailor. Then he directed a forced smile at her. "Doctor. We should talk about this, later, when Dr. Bashir returns."

The Klingon server was just waddling back with M'Benga's tea as Odo stalked out of the café.

"I . . . don't know what to say," M'Benga told Garak to cushion the embarrassment he was undoubtedly experiencing.

But Garak had undergone a transformation of his own. His face no longer sported its disarming smile. "You know, your problem, Doctor, is that you are far too trusting. Always accepting things at face value," he said darkly.

M'Benga didn't understand his change in mood, but right now she had problems of her own. She pushed her chair back and began to rise to her feet.

But Garak leaned forward again, and now his words were fast and crisp. "Did Bashir attempt that experiment with the trianosyne?"

M'Benga sat down heavily. *I must never discuss trianosyne with anyone,* she recited to calm herself. "I don't know what you're talking about," she said.

"No, I don't suppose you do. And that shows how powerful their hold is on you."

M'Benga could feel her head begin to swim. "I think I should go."

"I think you should come to my shop," Garak said.

M'Benga's entire body resisted the suggestion. Garak was dangerous. Anyone who wanted to discuss trianosyne with her was dangerous. They must be avoided at all costs. At all costs. At all costs.

"I can't," she said. She stood up, ready to leave.

And then Garak smiled at her with all his brilliant, heartfelt good cheer. "Are you sure, Doctor? I've just received a new shipment of colorful fabric from Betazed. I'm so sure there are some that would make fine new headbands that I've put aside a special selection just for you."

The sense of growing panic left M'Benga as quickly as Garak's mood had changed. "Well . . . well . . . that does sound nice."

"Then it's settled," Garak said as he got to his feet. "I'm just around the Promenade beside the assayer's office. We'll go there now and you'll have first pick."

"Why, thank you, Garak."

"Not at all, Doctor. I always enjoy doing a good turn for those I believe are deserving. And I find you most deserving indeed."

M'Benga basked in the warm glow of flattery. It felt good.

How nice to have made a friend like Garak, she thought as his mention of trianosyne, like so many other experiences she had had over the years, faded from her memory.

Feeling ever so much better, she followed Garak to his shop, to see just what he had for her.

NINETEEN

―――――――――――☆―――――――――――

Without bothering to hide his revulsion, Picard walked around the vessel that would carry Kirk deeper into the mirror universe—a so-called Imperial Raptor. It was a squat black shape with forward-swept wings, spiked with red talons. A gaping maw filled with bloodstained fangs was painted on both sides, as if it were a hellish beast come to devour the innocent. And the forward viewport had been outlined in lurid circles of scarlet and saffron and violet, as if a monstrous eye were perpetually leering. In a word, it was hideous.

"What kind of a world, what kind of a history," Picard said, "brings forth something like this?"

Kirk ran his hand along one of the vessel's black panels. "Terror must be maintained or the empire is doomed. It is the logic of history."

To Picard, it sounded as if Kirk were quoting someone. "Who said that?"

Kirk pointed off to the side of the hangar deck, where La Forge was holding a final briefing for the vessel's pilots, T'Val and Kate Janeway. The two Spocks were present as well. "Intendant Spock. More than a century ago. I had dared question Starfleet's decision to exterminate the Halkan race."

Picard saw the tortured expression that came into Kirk's eyes, and he knew that it didn't belong there. "Jim, if you need proof to be sure the barbarism of the mirror universe did not come about because of you, all you need tell yourself is that the Terran Empire was well established before you ever crossed over. It's not your fault."

"But the Terran Empire was destined to collapse," Kirk said. "The Halkans gave it 240 years at most. I told the intendant, 'Conquest is easy. Control is not.' The faster the empire grew, the more diffuse its power would become and the faster it would disintegrate. That's the true logic of history. But by inspiring the intendant to do something about it, I set off a chain reaction. One that led to an even more brutal regime."

"Which might have happened anyway, or another way, sooner or later." Picard knew Kirk had enough pressures weighing him down without adding an unnecessary one to his burden. "If I have learned anything from my study of archeology, it is that history has an ebb and flow all its own. And that sometimes, it is not the individual who makes a difference, it is a . . . a wave of circumstance that sweeps individuals along. That's why there are patterns in the historical record, the same stories playing out again and again."

"What does that say about free will?" Kirk rapped his knuckles on one of the panels that displayed the symbol of the Terran Empire—a fearsome sword plunging through the Earth. The panel sounded flimsy, revealing its deception. "Good thing there's no sound in space.

What's going to happen if someone scans this thing and realizes it's a duraplast camouflage shell around an advanced Starfleet shuttlecraft?"

Picard had already asked that question of La Forge, who had led the team that had constructed the Raptor to resemble other craft in this universe. The actual specifications had been provided by Radisson.

"You should be able to outrun anything local in this," Picard said. "The warp engine's been modified for high speed. It won't be efficient at low speed, and the ride could be rough. But nothing will catch it."

"Nothing that we know of," Kirk said, distracted by something behind him.

Picard turned to see T'Val, Janeway, and both Spocks coming toward the Raptor. Their briefing had ended. It was time for the mission to truly begin.

Picard shook hands with them all. "We'll take you to the edge of the Badlands farthest from the Cardassian border. And from there we'll be monitoring for any transmissions. Captain Radisson has given us clearance to take the *Enterprise* out of the Badlands, but only if I feel certain she won't be detected. So if you do get into difficulty, make sure it's in a secluded system."

Picard had hoped this last admonition would lighten the moment, but only Kirk offered him a vague smile. Janeway's face seemed locked in its permanent scowl, and T'Val remained as unreadable as any Vulcan Picard had ever encountered.

"Just fire the triggering signal fifteen minutes after we're clear," Janeway said. "We'll handle it from there."

The sensor dish has already been reconfigured," Picard said. Then he added in reassurance, "Whatever signal Tiberius transmitted from the asteroid in the Goldin Discontinuity, we'll be sending out the same one, almost as powerful."

To Picard, that was one of the riskiest parts of Radisson's plan. Days after Tiberius had disappeared at the side of the asteroid, when enough subspace monitoring records had been compared, it had become clear that Tiberius had beamed down to the labor camp to activate an intense subspace beacon.

The power couplings and the transmission nodes later discovered within the asteroid—melted by a power surge and beyond reconstruction—had produced a three-second pulse that subspace specialists said was strong enough be picked up across the galaxy. Furthermore, upon expansion, recordings of the pulse revealed it to be a highly compressed, complex code, containing the equivalent of thousands of screen displays. Unfortunately, the code, thus far, had yet to fall before the Federation's top cryptographers.

The current theory, Picard had learned, was that of the thousands of screens of information within the pulse, all except one or two were extraneous. Which meant it could be virtually impossible to pick out the vital information from the padding. In a way, Picard thought, that was similar to the problem Professor Galen had faced during his years of trying to extract the hidden holographic message buried in the genetic codes of myriad diverse species.

But whatever the message's ultimate purpose, Radisson's plan was to have Picard re-create that same message in the mirror universe. The *Enterprise* would not be able to transmit a pulse that could span the galaxy—

there were *some* limits to her powers. But it would be strong enough to be received throughout most of the Alpha and Beta Quadrants.

Radisson had half jokingly called the pulse a mating call, and Picard had seen her point. Given the extent of the operation that had created the labor camp, the duplicate *Voyager,* and the mysterious crossover device, Tiberius had to have an incredibly complex infrastructure in place in the mirror universe, with ships, supply lines, and a network of loyal workers and/or soldiers. That meant he also had to have a sophisticated communications system that could operate without Alliance interference.

Radisson's hope, and Picard and Kirk had agreed with this, was that Tiberius's communications network would pick up the signal and attempt to respond. That response would give Kirk his first point of contact to track down Tiberius. From there on, he would be on his own.

Picard saw Janeway step forward to fold down the side panel on the Raptor shell, exposing a small walkway leading to the hull of the shuttlecraft contained inside. The shell was supported by a fine network of composite struts and tension wires that La Forge had custom-configured to carry a structural integrity field.

As Janeway and T'Val now moved into the shell, Picard looked past them to see that for safety's sake, La Forge's team had removed all Starfleet and Federation markings from the shuttle's hull, just in case it lost its disguise. He knew that among the other security steps La Forge had taken to prevent the spread of advanced Federation technology in this universe was a self-destruct mechanism powerful enough to vaporize the entire shuttle, without leaving any physical remains of the vehicle—or of its passengers.

Kirk was now in the shell opening. Like Janeway and T'Val, he was dressed in rough civilian clothes, the design of which had been based on the sensor records provided by Sisko of Deep Space 9 and authenticated by Intendant Spock. The garments had even been replicated from matter obtained from the labor camp, so the fabrics' quantum signature would not betray their true origin.

Whether any of these precautions would be necessary, or, if necessary, successful, was something Picard fervently hoped Kirk never discovered. But at least the man was going into the field as properly outfitted as Starfleet could manage.

As Kirk paused in the opening, Picard walked up the short ramp to bid him farewell. "As Captain Mantell said, good hunting."

"As Captain Radisson might say, good listening for that mating call."

"I hope we're both wrong about her," Picard told Kirk. "I would hate to think so imposing a character did not exemplify Starfleet at its best."

Kirk gave him an odd look. "She's an interesting character all right. But not what I would call imposing." He held out his hand. "I'll see you in fifty hours."

Picard shook it with a smile. "Since Radisson's well over two meters tall, and as wide as the two of us put together, I'm not altogether sure I'd want to meet anyone you *would* consider imposing."

But Kirk was not smiling. "The Captain Radisson I talked with was maybe a meter and a half tall."

Picard didn't doubt Kirk's recollection, which meant only one thing. "There're *two* Radissons?"

"Or none," Kirk said grimly. "Or if there is just one, I'm betting neither of us have seen her." He stepped into the Raptor's shell. "Talk to Spock. My Spock. He's got some interesting ideas about that. Those science vessels, for instance—it's possible nothing we saw on them was real."

"Merde," Picard whispered.

"When I get back, we'll both go hunting together," Kirk promised. Then he pulled the shell closed behind him, and the ghastly Raptor was ready to take flight.

Picard stood watching as it hovered up from the hangar deck, slowly pivoted to face the forcefield pressure screen, then took off into the Badlands.

It was inevitable that his thoughts returned to Captain Radisson and Project Sign, as, for the first time, Picard began to wonder where the hunt would find more secrets hidden—in the mirror universe . . . or his own.

TWENTY

—————— ☆ ——————

M'Benga stepped into the cool darkness of Garak's tailor shop and felt instantly comfortable. She could smell fresh flowers and the clean scent of crisp new cloth. When Garak closed the door behind them, the noise and the bustle of the Promenade faded away completely, as if she had entered another world altogether.

"Your shop is quite different from how I remember it," M'Benga said.

Garak was inputting codes into the security panel by the front door. "With the windows turned to maximum opacity and the sound baffles set to high, it is a small refuge in a busy day." He turned to smile at her. "I like it."

M'Benga looked around the tiny shop but didn't see any bolts of Betazed fabric. "Are they in the back?" she asked.

"Exactly," Garak said. "In the back." He gave her a little bow and extended his hand to indicate the way past the purchasing counter to the small door leading to his storeroom. "Please."

She moved to the door. It was a quaint, old-fashioned one, with a handle she had to twist and push on her own.

Garak reached over her to open the door even wider, then put a friendly hand in the small of her back to propel her in.

She was about to say something to object to his actions when she was startled by what she saw ahead of her.

A man. Human. Civilian. In a chair. *Tied* to a chair. *Bound and gagged* in a chair.

"Garak!" M'Benga said, alarmed. The human's face was bruised. One eye swollen shut. And his right sleeve was torn back to show where something that resembled a neurocortical stimulator had been affixed to his forearm. The man stared up at her with raw fear, then pulled and bucked and tried to twist out of his bonds without success.

She started for him at once. Those injuries had to be treated.

Garak's hand was on her arm, pulling her back.

"Let me go! He's hurt! I have to treat him!"

But Garak's hand didn't relax its hold. "First, I must insist you answer a few questions."

M'Benga struggled against his grip. "That is unacceptable." She attempted to reach for her communicator. But Garak caught her other hand, effectively immobilizing her.

"Doctor, stop! Listen to me! Answer my questions, and then I'll release you and you can call ops or Odo or do whatever you want and I won't stop you. A minute of your time, that's all I ask."

M'Benga realized Garak's strength was too much for

her to overcome, unless she wanted to gamble on her Academy martial arts, and she hadn't practiced those as rigorously as Starfleet regs recommended.

She decided to risk taking Garak at his word. A few questions, and then she'd get station security in here.

"All right," she said. "One minute."

"Look at the man," Garak said. He stepped to the side, still holding her arms, so she could see the prisoner. That's what he was, she knew. Garak's prisoner.

"What's your question?" M'Benga asked warily.

"Do you recognize him?"

"No."

"Look closely, Doctor. Have you ever—*ever*—seen that man in your life?"

She stared at the man. Tried to imagine him without a bruise, without a swollen eye . . . nothing. Feeling increasingly unsettled, she glared at Garak. "I have never seen him. Now let me go."

"What if I told you you were mistaken? What if I told you you *had* seen this man before? In fact, you treated him. In the infirmary. Three days ago."

"Impossible." M'Benga began to feel herself tremble.

"Computer," Garak said. "Display infirmary surveillance recording. Three days ago. Time code: twenty-six hundred hours eighteen minutes. Look at the display screen, Doctor."

There was a small Cardassian computer terminal on the wall, flanked by racks of men's suits. An extreme wide-angle image of the infirmary was displayed upon it. The point of view was from the equipment palette over her examination table. "Odo was right," she exclaimed. "That was your spy sensor he found."

"He didn't find it," Garak told her. "Your Starfleet friends did. Keep watching."

M'Benga became even more upset as she realized that the Cardassian tailor must know about her contact with Kirk and Picard and the two Spocks. Critical Starfleet security had been breached. She had to get word to . . . to . . .

On the surveillance display, she watched herself walk across the infirmary floor. She was with the man who was now tied up in the chair. He was holding his arm as if he had injured it.

"That never happened," M'Benga said, bewildered. "This is a holographic forgery."

"Keep watching."

The man sat down on her examination table. M'Benga watched herself approach him with a medical tricorder and a tray with a selection of bone and flesh accelerators, then adjust the tricorder to read his arm. She watched herself make additional adjustments, stepping up its sensitivity, as if she hadn't been able to detect any injury.

She saw herself tap the side of the tricorder as if she thought it wasn't working properly. Then, when her onscreen self turned to see if there was another tricorder next to the table—

—the man she'd been examining tapped a small spray hypo to the side of her neck.

Reflexively, M'Benga touched her neck but, of course, felt nothing. If it had actually happened, it was too long ago.

"And that is why you don't remember," Garak said.

M'benga watched, horrified, as onscreen she saw the

man catch her as she collapsed, then spin her around and lift her onto the table. She turned away. She didn't want to see what happened next.

"It's all right," Garak said softly. "After that, you were quite safe."

M'Benga turned back to the screen. Now the man was at her main computer station, working quickly. But she couldn't see which subsystems he was accessing or what he was doing with them.

"I don't understand," M'Benga said. She was beginning to feel dizzy. "I need to sit down."

"No," Garak told her. He forced her two hands together, then held both her wrists in one powerful hand. M'Benga was vaguely aware of his other hand reaching for something on a shelf behind her. Vaguely, she thought she might be able to get one of her own hands free, but she didn't seem to have the strength. The crowded storeroom was beginning to feel close and hot and she could feel she was losing her balance.

"Hang on, Doctor," Garak shouted at her. "Don't let them win."

M'Benga began to close her eyes. It would be easier, she knew, if she just went to sleep. But then she heard the hiss of a hypospray, felt a cold spot on her neck.

Now she was wide awake. Anxious, nervous, and—

She ripped her hands away from Garak's grip.

"What the hell was that?!" she said as she slapped her communicator and . . .

She wasn't wearing her communicator.

Garak was holding it. He had taken it when her eyes were closing, when she had been about to fall asleep.

She rubbed at her neck, fully aware of the fact that

Garak was blocking the only exit from the room. "What did you give me?"

"Among other things, a very powerful stimulant."

"What for?"

"Why, to help you resist the deep psychological patterning you've been exposed to. Your tendency to faint or fall asleep at the drop of a Klingon's *arthk'R,* whenever you're exposed to certain stimuli that might make you remember . . . things they would rather not have you remember."

M'Benga's heartbeat accelerated. She knew she had some kind of synthetic adrenaline in her bloodstream. *Among other things,* Garak had said.

"Who doesn't want me to remember what?" The whole idea was ludicrous, but the surveillance tape— that was too convincing to be a forgery. The way she'd handled the malfunctioning tricorder. M'Benga knew that was exactly how she would have behaved.

"The instigator of this little conspiracy is an organization called Project Sign."

M'Benga didn't recognize the name. "Never heard of it."

"I expected not. I'll say this for them. They have the expertise to erase portions of your memory permanently, if messily. And they chose not to do that. Instead, your memories have been placed on . . . let's call it layaway. What can you tell me about Station 51?"

"It's a top-secret research lab for the . . . good Lord." M'Benga pressed her hands to her temples as her brain literally exploded with information about Station 51, Starbase 25-Alpha, the underground labs on Zeta Reticuli IV. She had trouble breathing. Her heart was pounding. She knew somehow that Garak was holding her, lightly rubbing her back, saying comforting things, but it was as if he were on the other side of the Promenade while she was wholly enveloped in entire days and weeks erased from her life and now brought back all at once.

And through it all, one face, one voice, Commodore Twining. Nate Twining.

"I chose this," she gasped.

It *all* came back.

"They came to me at graduation. Told me of . . . my Lord, they told me so much . . ."

"About what?" Garak asked intently.

"Research. Alien life. . . . There's so much more alien life than we think we know about. . . . They're among us. . . ." M'Benga couldn't help it. She began to laugh, almost helpless to stop herself.

"Is the conspiracy really that humorous," Garak asked with real concern, "or are you having a bad reaction to my homemade bi-trianosyne compound?"

"I'm sorry," M'Benga gasped. "I'm fine, I think." She wiped tears from her eyes. "It's just . . . finally knowing all that they've told me over the years. Putting it all together . . . they *lied* to me . . . all the way through it. Kept telling me contradictory things so that . . . so that . . ."

"If partial memories ever did surface spontaneously, you'd never be able to piece the whole story together," Garak said.

M'Benga leaned back against a rack of clothes, so liberated she felt as if she must be floating. How many times had she thought about a shore leave she couldn't quite remember . . . a medical conference that had bored her to tears . . . and never pursued the fact that there were whole sections of her life missing?

"Garak, how ever did you know?"

"I've heard about this trianosyne. How it is sometimes a by-product of certain memory manipulation techniques, usually for rather nefarious purposes."

"How have you heard about it? I never have, and I'm a doctor."

"Ah, but I'm a tailor."

M'Benga narrowed her eyes at him. "Garak, that makes no sense."

"It makes as much sense as anything else around here. The important thing is, you have your memories back." He pointed to the panic-stricken man tied in the chair. "And people like that won't be able to use you anymore. For whatever purpose."

M'Benga gazed at the man with her newfound knowledge. Now she remembered him from the infirmary, not just three days ago, but a week before that, and a month before that. "He's a regular," she said. She suddenly understood. "Now I know why you told Julian to try to test himself for a trianosyne spike in his blood. None of the equipment in the infirmary would have detected it. This man, or his partners, has reprogrammed everything to ignore the substance."

"Whatever this Project Sign is, it is a very thorough organization. How are you feeling now?"

M'Benga held up her hands. They were shaking. "Calming down."

"Let's test that, shall we? What can you tell me about the *children* in Station 51?"

M'Benga's mouth dropped open as something terrible suddenly tumbled to the forefront of her mind. "They

killed them! They phasered an entire shipload of innocent children." She clutched at her chest in the almost
visceral shock of the memory.

"And what of the child Captain *Kirk* described?"

M'Benga rubbed her temples as all the pieces began to
fit together to form . . . to form . . . a pattern that had
no pattern. "The child . . . I remember Kirk saying
there was a child with venom on his fingers. A Klingon
venom. No, it was Vulcan . . . ? It was . . ." It suddenly
hit her. "That's why they stole my genetic atlas." Now
the words spilled out of her, faster and faster. "The last
time I was at Station 51, I was examining the children,
their genetic structure. It was mostly human, but one
child . . . child 7 . . . he had genes from some kind of
animal on Vulcan. And . . . then the children were escaping and, oh it was terrible. Nate Twining ordered
them killed. And the EMH gave me something. That's
when I woke up on Vulcan and I thought I had—"

"Rudellian brain fever," Garak supplied, a reassuring
hand on her shoulder.

"Right . . . and just last week, I was going through my
atlas for a paper I was working on, and there it was, the
same genetic structure from Vulcan. And I had the
sudden memory of what had happened and the condi-
tioning kicked in and . . . I passed out."

Garak nodded encouragingly. "And what was that
genetic structure?"

"A Vulcan sandshark." M'Benga shuddered. "A type
of small snake in the southern deserts. Incredibly
poisonous . . . Why would a child have genes from a
poisonous . . ." The pattern suddenly began to make
sense.

Hideous, sickening sense.

M'Benga looked again at the man in the chair. "Garak, do you know who he is?"

"I know *what* he is. The rest isn't necessary. Though I think you'll find it interesting." The tailor took his hand from her shoulder and went to the man.

The man cowered as the Cardassian tore off his gag. M'Benga cringed as the man screamed hoarsely, as if he had already spent hours screaming.

Garak turned to smile comfortingly at M'Benga. "Not to worry. The shop is fully soundproofed. I find it helps me in my work."

The man's screaming gradually stopped as he hyperventilated and was forced to gulp in great breaths of air. "Don't let him near me . . . don't let him near me . . ." he panted over and over.

Part of M'Benga was appalled to see someone so badly mistreated. But another part remembered the children being incinerated by phaser fire. If this man was somehow involved with Commodore Twining's inhuman act, then perhaps he deserved whatever Garak had done to him. Perhaps . . .

That raised a whole new set of disturbing questions for M'Benga.

"Garak, *why* are you doing this?"

For once, Garak didn't have a quick or glib answer. "If I said professional courtesy, would that make sense?"

"Not really."

"Forthrightness, then. I like you, Doctor. Not in any way that should serve to cause you concern or make you think you might have a Cardassian suitor at your doorstep. But an appreciation, if you will, of your work here on the station, your unfailing civility to me, and the sweet, almost childlike way you have persisted in believing I am nothing more than plain, simple Garak, a lone tailor with a little shop on the Promenade."

M'Benga watched Garak closely and realized that for the first time in all the months she had known him, in all the conversations she had had with him, this might be the first time he was actually speaking from his heart.

"You see, Doctor, there are far too few innocents left in this universe, and when I see one such as yourself, abused by . . . by people like me, who should know better . . . well, as insane as this may sound, in my line of work, I am perhaps one of the few who still clings to the idea that there are rules by which we must abide.

"This Project Sign, they're not following those rules. And so I took it upon myself to . . . to be your . . ."

"Knight in shining armor?"

Garak blinked, then stared at M'Benga, and for the very first time ever, she saw his real smile, no artifice or calculation behind it at all.

"I think I like that," Garak said. "Sir Garak, knight of the . . . what was it?"

"The Round Table."

"The Round Table." The tailor remained silent for a few moments, as if replaying that phrase in his mind. Then he looked up again, and whatever door into his soul had just been opened an instant before, M'Benga could sense that it had closed again. He smiled at her. Warm, charming, full of friendship. But it was not the same. "Thank you, Doctor M'Benga."

"Please, call me Andrea."

But Garak shook his head, then looked at his prisoner. "We still have work to do. Listen carefully to what this man will tell you."

Garak leaned closer to the prisoner, making him pale as he tried to push away with nowhere to go. "And you will tell her everything, won't you? Because you wouldn't want me to have to start again from the beginning."

The man shook his head rapidly.

"Now tell the doctor what you told me about the children," Garak said pleasantly.

"We didn't kill them," the man sputtered. "At Station 51, we beamed them out into transporter cells. Completely enclosed chambers. Only way in or out is through transporters. That's what we did."

"I saw the phasers fire," M'Benga said.

"They were beamed out first, and then the ship was destroyed and the docking chamber sterilized. That's what the phasers were for. It's a Wildfire scenario. Full implementation. Really. You have to believe me. The children were too valuable to destroy."

"Valuable?" M'Benga asked. "What's that supposed to mean?"

"It's how these people think," Garak explained. "Go ahead, tell her the rest. About Captain Kirk and his bride."

The man sagged in his chair, and as much as M'Benga was beginning to feel real apprehension about what Garak might have done to him, she knew she also had to know what Garak had found out.

"Do you know what happened to Teilani?" M'Benga asked.

"We sent the child to her. One of the children from the ship."

"What do you mean, you sent the child to her?"

The man hung his head, defeated. "The children are

genetically engineered. Some of them have poison sacs under their fingernails. Some produce toxins in their saliva. Neurochemicals in their sweat."

M'Benga felt sick, afraid where this questioning would lead. *"Who* sent the child to Teilani?"

"We did. Project Sign."

"To kill her?!"

"No! She wasn't supposed to die. She was just supposed to get sick, go into stasis for a few months."

"Why?"

"So Kirk would do what we wanted him to do."

"What? What did you want him to do?"

The man moaned, half sobbing. "They didn't tell me. . . . It wasn't my job. . . . Please . . ."

"And that," Garak said with finality, "is as much as I could get out of him."

M'Benga's mind churned with all the things she knew she had to do, all the new memories she still had to sort through. "I should get him to the infirmary."

"He'll be fine," Garak said. "I'll take care of him."

M'Benga didn't want to think about what Garak might already have done, what he might be capable of still doing. But she couldn't allow this man to come to harm. "Take care of him how?"

Garak took another hypospray off a shelf. "The same way they took care of you, Doctor. Poetic justice, I call it. He won't . . . remember . . . a thing."

Then he offered her her communicator.

M'Benga took it, pinned it back to her jacket, but didn't switch it on.

The tailor gave her a small nod of acknowledgment. "Might I ask what you plan to do next?"

"Kirk said Starfleet's taking Teilani to *Qo'noS*. I should pass on what I know."

"But not . . ." Garak prompted.

M'Benga nodded. "Not *how* I know it."

"Thank you, Doctor."

M'Benga studied the prisoner, cataloguing all the things she could see that were wrong with him, that she should treat. Wondering what other injuries were hidden from her.

"Garak, after you've exacted your poetic justice, could you see that he ends up on my examination table? Think of that as a professional courtesy."

M'Benga could see it was a hard decision for Garak to make.

But he made it.

"For you, Doctor, anything."

"Thank you, Garak."

"No, thank you. I can't remember when I've had so fascinating a diversion. And in such a good cause, as well. Have a good trip to *Qo'noS*."

M'Benga stared at Garak. "What makes you think I'm going to go there?"

"Trust me, Doctor. A tailor knows these things."

TWENTY-ONE

☆

The call had been answered.

Twenty-seven minutes after the *Enterprise*-E transmitted a reproduction of the signal Tiberius sent out in Kirk's universe, a response was received.

It was compressed, complex, and highly directional. With the wide separation between the disguised shuttlecraft and the *Enterprise,* which remained hidden in the Badlands, the exact location of the responding transmitter was easily calculated.

Kirk was not surprised. He was going back to where it had all begun. Where *everything* had begun.

Earth.

The destination had surprised Kirk's pilots, though. Janeway and T'Val feared an Alliance trap.

"But here, Earth's a dying planet," Kirk said. He still had vivid nightmares of his first glimpse, only eight months ago, of the distorted version of his own planet of birth.

He had been running across the surface of the moon with Janeway, T'Val, and Intendant Spock. The moon of the mirror universe was uninhabited. Completely different from the moon Kirk knew. No domes, no lakes, no singing birds or children playing.

And in the lunar skies had hung a desecrated world he scarcely recognized.

On the sunlit half, it was as if a virulent mold had spread across a poisoned sample dish, mutating into warring colonies of dull putrescence. Once-blue seas, no longer dusted with swirls and arcs of soft white clouds, were now vast reservoirs of turbid brown and black and purple.

And the land—once swathed in green and streaked by dusty bands of desert brown, dramatically striated by mountain rock and glacial plains of pristine ice—was now a single smear of gray, blemished by obscuring blots and whorls of jet-black clouds.

On the night side, Kirk shivered at the recollection. It was as if civilization had been wiped from the planet. Where cities and transportation networks should have traced the continents with jewels of light was instead a scattered spray of glowing red dots—whether volcanoes or fires burning out of control . . . he hadn't been sure. Besides sporadic flashes of lightning from storms that raged across the surface, there were no other sources of light on the entire ravaged planet.

"I saw no signs of Alliance bases," he now told Janeway and T'Val as they hurtled toward mirror Earth in the masked Starfleet shuttlecraft. "What would they want with a world like that?"

"It's not that they want it," Janeway said. "It's that they don't want anyone else to have it."

"Why would *anyone* want it?"

"For a place to hide," T'Val said. "Except, of course, logic suggests that the more inhospitable a place is, the less likely the Alliance will be present there. Thus, the more likely a rebel base will be established. Thus, the more likely the Alliance will be there."

Kirk leaned forward from his passenger seat behind the pilot and copilot chairs of the shuttle. "If logic suggests that the most inhospitable places are where the Alliance will build its bases, then why would the Alliance send a false answer to our signal, drawing us to a place where we would expect to find a trap?"

He heard Janeway smother a laugh. She wasn't one for constantly working and reworking a problem. Like him, she preferred to face a challenge head on, then make adjustments as necessary. "Here's the plan," she said. "When we get to Earth, we'll be very careful."

Kirk had no argument with that, especially since they were in a Federation vessel that could outrun anything that might chase them.

For the next twelve hours of high-warp travel, Kirk's two escorts spoke very little. If Kate Janeway and T'Val had learned new things during their past eight months in Kirk's universe, they didn't seem inclined to share their knowledge or any of their experiences with him.

At first, Kirk was puzzled. Kate Janeway had a scientist's passion for discovery. This silence was atypical for her. It wasn't until the disguised Raptor was making its final approach to the mirror Earth's system, coming in from the solar south, rather than risk crossing the orbits of the planets and perhaps encountering automatic navigational alert stations, that Kirk finally realized why T'Val and the mirror Janeway were so hostile toward him.

"This was supposed to be your mission, wasn't it?" he asked. "That's why Captain Radisson was able to put everything together so quickly. She'd been planning it for months, except it was supposed to be just you two going."

T'Val gave no indication that Kirk had said anything at all, let alone that he had said something that might be of interest, right or wrong. But Kate Janeway's reaction let Kirk know his guess was close to the truth.

"So what if it was?" Janeway said. "That doesn't change anything."

"It changes everything if you two were planning on a different mission goal," Kirk said. "Why were you coming back to your universe?"

"To recontact the Vulcan Resistance," T'Val said coolly. "Set up relations between your Federation and our freedom fighters."

But Kirk wasn't that easily convinced. "You could have done that anytime. And you don't need this Imperial Raptor to do it. No. This mission was set up for a different objective. And then I came along and forced everyone to change what they were after."

Kirk knew he was right. But he didn't know why T'Val and Janeway wouldn't directly acknowledge his conclusion. What was it that they had wanted to accomplish over here? Something they wanted to keep from him.

Kirk decided to try a long shot. "Were you planning on killing Tiberius?"

"Isn't that what *you're* planning on doing?" Janeway countered.

"Only if he gets in our way," Kirk said. "I'm just here to find out what kind of poison he used on Teilani. When we have that, I'm going home. Tiberius can wait for another day."

T'Val's and Janeway's only reaction was to glance at

each other, but that was all, until Janeway announced, "Dropping to impulse."

Ahead, through the wraparound shuttlecraft viewport and the much more constricted opening in the Imperial Raptor shell that masked the shuttle, Kirk saw the Earth rush at him, expanding rapidly, as it could only for faster-than-light velocities, and then stop.

"Entering polar orbit," Janeway said.

T'Val concentrated on the sensor controls. "I am picking up one Alliance vessel in a standard orbit around the Moon. It's a . . . *Strell*-class troop transport."

"They're probably still mapping all the ice caves and tunnels we used to use," Janeway said. "As long as we don't use our transporter or phasers in orbit, they won't be able to detect us."

Kirk hoped that was true. It wasn't as if the distance from the Earth to the Moon was very far. But then, sensor technology might not be as developed here.

"All right, Captain," Janeway said. "We got you here. What's next?"

"We look for a beacon," Kirk said. "It will be low powered, hard to detect. Based on the assumption that whoever's coming to look for the base that sent the response to the signal already knows where it is."

"Then why have a beacon at all?" T'Val asked.

"For the last few hundred kilometers," Kirk said. "Once you get close enough, most Class-M planets start to look alike."

Janeway turned in her pilot's chair to catch Kirk's eye. "We could take days to search the whole planet to find something that might be transmitting only a few hundred kilometers. So if you were Tiberius, where would you hide your base?"

Janeway's approach was a good one. Kirk considered the problem. "First of all, it will be underground. Anything on the surface would be too easy to detect."

"How about underwater?" Janeway asked.

"That's too hard on spacegoing ships," Kirk said. "Organic material gets sucked into cooling vents and stationkeeping thrusters when you land. When you take off, any moisture freezes and there's the danger you'll crack open exterior access panels. And if there's a power failure, you can't stay hidden longer than your air supply can last. If it's a long-term base, it's underground."

Kirk felt Janeway's careful study of him. "All right, that was Captain Kirk being an efficient mission planner. And all you managed to do was narrow our search down to the land areas of the planet. Now think like Tiberius," she advised him. "Is he going to build his base on the tallest mountain? The most spectacular gorge? The biggest meteor crater? If he had the whole Earth to choose from, where would a man with the ego of the emperor of known space go to first?"

Kirk realized he didn't know enough about Tiberius to answer that question. But he knew where he himself would go, if he were coming home to his Earth.

"Iowa," he said. And he gave her the coordinates of the farm that had been his first home. He knew them as well as he knew his own name.

But on Tiberius's Earth, there no longer was an Iowa.

Eighty years earlier, after the mirror universe's Battle of Wolf 359, in which the Imperial Starfleet of the

Terran Empire had been destroyed by the Klingon–Cardassian Armada, the armada had advanced to Earth.

In four days of constant bombardment, the entire planet had become a wasteland. Particle beams had carved its surface. Klingon disruptors had dried the Great Lakes of North America. The rain forests had been reduced to sterile, charred timber.

Janeway guided the disguised shuttle over the area that had corresponded to Kirk's coordinates. But there were no landmarks, not even half-buried roads or the foundations of buildings that had stood for centuries. The golden state of Iowa was a black expanse of ash and destruction.

"Sensors are reporting indications of massive disruptor bombardment," T'Val said.

Janeway pitched the shuttle forward without changing its level flight path so they could see the passing, featureless landscape through the viewport. "Looks like someone else knew this is where Tiberius was born."

Even though he knew this world was but a reflection of his own, Kirk was stunned by the cruel demonstration of the impermanence of things. Someday, even on his Earth, he knew, there would be no sign of his birthplace left—the roads, foundations, all the traces of all the lives that had been lived there, would be swallowed by time, eternal darkness.

The realization stirred the flame of resistance within him. What better reason could there be to keep up the fight against the inevitable end of all things than knowing that the end was inevitable? After all, how could there be courage without knowledge of fear? Or victory, without knowledge of defeat? The very knowledge of death was what gave life meaning. The devastation of this world, this shattered picture of the shape of things to come, only made his own world and his own quest all the more precious to Kirk.

Someday all things would succumb to the dark victory of time, but not today.

He pulled himself from the depths in which he had immersed himself. He tried to think where else someone like Tiberius would go on this despoiled world.

And then T'Val said, "I am picking up a transmission pulse. Low powered. Difficult to detect."

"Welcome home, James T. Kirk," Janeway said as she set the shuttle's course to follow the beacon.

The beacon was an extremely weak, slightly irregular subspace pulse that from more than 100 kilometers away would never have been detected in the general background of subspatial static. It was coming from a tumble of old concrete slabs, half buried under drifting mounds of ash. At first glance, the pile of rubble and debris appeared to be all that remained of a small town. Yet Kirk could not remember a town or major construction so close to the Kirk family farm. At least in his universe.

After slowly circling the rubble, Janeway put the disguised shuttle down as close to the slabs as possible, then nudged the small craft forward so it would be partially concealed by an overhang.

At once, T'Val focused her sensors on the slabs and reported there was an undamaged metal construction deep within them. A long cylinder in the center of the rubble pile, extending underground at least 500 meters. She refrained from increasing the power of the sensors to look even deeper. There was a chance the spillover radiation might alert the crew of the transport ship orbiting the moon. But there was little doubt in her mind or Janeway's—or Kirk's—as to what that cylinder was or where it eventually ended.

The three of them decided the shuttle was sufficiently hidden by the overhang and its own dark appearance. They would leave it together and search together.

Kirk was amused, rather than disturbed, by the joint decision. Part of it, he was sure, had to do with the fact that neither T'Val nor Janeway really trusted him. He understood that he was, in their eyes, Tiberius, and he accepted that he always would be.

The three of them moved carefully into the pile of rubble. As the beams from their hand torches cut through the thick, polluted air, neither Kirk nor his two companions were surprised to discover that what looked perfectly random on the outside was cleverly constructed on the inside. The concrete slabs had been arranged against each other to create a protected walkway leading from the exterior to the central shaft.

Kirk's team halted by that shaft, probing it with their beams of light. It was simply a metal tube, about three meters across, and four to five meters tall, before it disappeared into the slabs overhead. T'Val reported that there was an energy source connected to something within the shaft. She said that logic suggested there was a turbolift car inside. Kirk hoped she was right. Though the walkway they had crossed was only 50 meters long, he and Janeway were breathing hard. The oxygen concentration was much lower than on Kirk's Earth. According to T'Val's tricorder, it was as if they were halfway up Mount Everest, even though the atmospheric pressure was normal.

"It's from the destruction of the rain forests," T'Val explained. As a Vulcan, she was not affected by the diminished oxygen. "The ecosystem of this world is no longer self-sustaining."

Kirk wished this image of a dying Earth, devoid of its natural vegetation, could be something transmitted to every sentient being in his own universe. A lesson about the balance of things never to be forgotten.

As they walked around the metal cylinder, Kirk was the first to find a way in on the far side—inset doors that would open onto either an elevator car or a circular staircase. Given the oxygen count, Kirk was still hoping for the elevator.

There was a scanning panel beside the doors, and no other obvious means of opening them. So Kirk did the only thing that seemed reasonable.

He put his hand to the screen.

The screen flashed blue.

The doors opened onto what appeared to be an elevator car.

Whatever waited below, it was programmed to welcome Tiberius.

Kirk stepped into the elevator, moved to the side to make room for T'Val and Janeway. They both began to follow him.

And then they cried out in pain as they were thrown back from a crackling force field.

Kirk put his hand forward cautiously. He felt no resistance.

On the other side of the elevator doors, T'Val did the same with her biomechanical hand. Rings of blue energy suddenly flared from the tips of her metallic fingers. Kirk saw her grimace slightly—an expression of unbearable pain in a Vulcan—as she leaned into the force field, trying to push her way through. Until finally her hand was snapped back, spinning her around to collide with Janeway.

"Is this kind of force field common in your universe?" Kirk looked all around the elevator car but saw nothing that might be force-field controls.

"I've never heard of anything like it," Janeway said as she struggled to keep T'Val on her feet. "It has to be selective on a genetic level."

"I do not know how such a thing can be possible," T'Val gasped. The Vulcan was still straining to draw breath.

"Let's see if we can fool it." Kirk reached out past the plane of the force field, then took Janeway's hand in his, in an attempt to pull her hand through. Perhaps whatever the force field–control sensors were picking up in his body would cover Janeway's presence.

But the instant her hand hit the force field, Janeway's fingers slipped from his as if they were covered in tetralubisol.

"It's not going to work," Janeway said as she shook her hand back and forth as if trying to restore circulation. "But look on the positive side. It must mean that whatever's down there is for Tiberius's eyes only. You could be close to what you need."

Kirk knew that what he was about to do was inherently risky. Especially to attempt on his own. But if he were to have any hope of saving Teilani, he had little time and no choice. He nodded. "I'll go down, take a quick look, and come back up to report," he said. "And I'll see if I can find the controls for this force field."

Janeway and T'Val didn't seem too sorry to see him go, though they did say they would wait for him to return.

Kirk doubted they would wait long, though. The crossover instability in the Badlands allowing the *Enterprise* to return home would last only another 42 hours. Unless Janeway and T'Val wanted to risk their lives trying to use an Alliance transporter array at Terek Nor, Kirk knew they'd want to leave within 20 hours, to give themselves a suitable safety margin.

Kirk couldn't blame them if they wanted to rejoin Intendant Spock the easy way. He'd just make it his own priority to return before those 20 hours were up, too.

"I'll be back as soon as I can," Kirk said.

Janeway and T'Val watched him without reaction.

There was only one control surface in the elevator car—a small, rectangular red panel. Kirk pushed it.

And realized he wasn't in an elevator car. Suddenly, Janeway and T'Val, the interior of the metal cylinder, and all the rubble outside its door melted into the golden shimmer of a transporter effect.

With no time to even try to stop the process, James T. Kirk was gone.

TWENTY-TWO

───────── ☆ ─────────

A timeless moment later, the universe re-formed around Kirk.

Instinctively, he braced himself for a change in local gravity, but before he had a chance to feel a solid surface beneath his feet, another tunnel of shimmering light formed around him. Again and again, the transporter effect glittered then faded, and Kirk realized he was passing through multiple transporter stations.

Finally, one room solidified around him and didn't change. He sniffed the air. The smoky scent of pollution was gone. Everything smelled cleaner. He could tell there was more oxygen in the air as well.

He looked around, blinking, letting his eyes adjust to significantly brighter lighting.

He was in a cylindrical room, almost identical to the room of just a few seconds ago that he'd mistakenly thought was an elevator car. Except where that transporter room had had a single red rectangular control surface, this one had two. A green rectangle, just above another red one. There were several possible interpretations. The most likely one, Kirk concluded, was that pressing the red control would beam him back to where Janeway and T'Val still waited for him. Where he *hoped* they still waited for him.

Before he experimented with the transporter system, though, Kirk decided to check out his current location.

As he moved toward the closed doors of the cylindrically walled room, they slid open soundlessly.

Beyond was an even more brightly lit alcove, 20 meters across, with a gleaming white marble floor and curved walls. Kirk stepped out through the transporter room doorway to see two corridors leading off to either side of the alcove. One of the corridors had a large, two-dimensional, optical photograph hanging on its wall. The subject looked familiar to Kirk, and he went to it.

And was appalled.

The familiar part of the photograph was the buildings he recognized—Starfleet Command Headquarters in San Francisco. Since the Daystrom Annex was not included, Kirk knew the photograph was an older one, dating back at least—if not more than—60 years ago, to when the annex had self-constructed itself.

But closer inspection of the image revealed that the symbol depicted on the wall of the main building, and on its banners, did not belong to Starfleet but rather to the Terran Empire. The icon was the sword of conquest savagely thrust through the Earth.

Then with a start, Kirk saw that the spindly constructions in the foreground landscape were gallows. In fact, the optical photograph showed 20 people being *hung* in front of Starfleet Headquarters, surrounded by onlookers, most in the old-style uniform consisting of brightly colored department shirts, black trousers, and boots.

The photograph was barbaric. What it depicted, unthinkable.

Then he saw the names.

There were placards on the gallows, with small though legible letters.

Kirk read the first one, felt a wave of nausea, but was compelled to read them all.

That first one said RAND. The body dangling beneath it was that of a woman, blond. Then SCOTT. DECKER. MOREAU. Several more names that meant nothing to Kirk. But then GARROVICK. MARCUS. M'BENGA. There were more.

He was looking at evidence of a purge. One that must have been conducted by Tiberius. Though he had known that the mirror universe emperor was a monster, that his namesake had laid waste to worlds, slaughtered colonists, and achieved command of the *I.S.S. Enterprise* by the assassination of Captain Christopher Pike . . . to see the evidence of his counterpart's insatiable drive for vengeance, to see it culminate in this grotesque and personally devastating spectacle—for Kirk, somehow it made Tiberius more evil *and* more human at the same time.

Kirk turned his back on the optical photograph and its atrocities. He looked the length of the rest of the corridor. Other optical photographs were hung on its walls. He had no desire to view them, unwilling to learn what other disturbing events Tiberius might have chosen to commemorate.

He stepped back into the alcove just outside the transporter room, checking the second corridor running from the opposite side. There were no photographs on those walls. He would investigate in that direction first.

The floor of the second corridor was also slick white marble. Every few meters, pairs of slender rose-marble pillars, exquisitely streaked and shaded, supported inset wall panels that hid indirect lighting strips. It was a subdued style of design that could be a century old, two centuries, or which might have been built no more than a few days ago.

And not one aspect of it betrayed a single clue as to what this installation's purpose was. Living quarters? Museum? Hidden military base?

Kirk walked on to the end of the corridor. Angled off to the side was a large door, painted white to match the walls and the floor. And, shockingly, on the floor in front of the door lay the body of a small, dead animal. As out of place in its sterile white surroundings as the photographs had been. Another reminder of decay and death.

Kirk gently nudged the small sand-colored body with the toe of his boot.

The creature—some kind of primitive, fur-covered biped, about 20 centimeters tall and profoundly overweight for its size—flopped lifelessly to the side. But it had a deceptively light mass.

Kirk crouched down to examine it more closely.

Abandoning caution, he picked it up.

It was a toy. A stuffed bear with button eyes and a stitched mouth.

And just as Kirk was struggling to make sense of it, the large white door slid open and he looked up to see—

—a young boy. Memlon's age, six or seven at most.

The boy was in white sleepwear decorated with yellow suns and blue moons. He rubbed his eyes, peered at Kirk, then held out one hand, his intention obvious.

Kirk, feeling as if he were trapped in a dream over which he had no control, offered the bear to the boy.

The boy took it by its soft cloth ear, then hugged it close.

He smiled then at Kirk. "Thank you, Daddy," he murmured.

Kirk rocked back on his heels, nearly losing his balance. Instead of rising to his feet, he sat down on the floor, staring at the child, knowing without question who the boy's father really was.

Then another tiny figure stepped up behind the boy. A little girl with curly light brown hair. "Daddy!" she said, and launched herself at Kirk, throwing both arms around his neck.

Kirk tried to push the child away. He looked past her and there was another child, and another. Beyond them, in the room past the large white door, he saw a row of dormitory beds, and more children in brightly colored sleepwear coming for him.

Kirk scrambled to his feet. For some reason he could not yet articulate, he was filled with terror.

These were the children of a monster. How could they not be monsters, too?

And yet, as they gathered around him, all reaching up, clamoring for love and attention, calling him Dad or Daddy or, even from the older ones, Father, he realized they weren't just Tiberius's children. They were *his* as well. His genetic code and Tiberius's were identical.

And then he realized the reason for his fear, something he had seen without consciously recognizing.

One child in the midst of the others. At least twelve of them, Kirk counted, though there were more beds than that. The child who stood apart was the child who had hugged Teilani, who had scratched her skin with his nail and condemned her to death.

Kirk looked down at all the little hands reaching up for him. What else were these creatures capable of?

The hands. Kirk's eyes fixed on their nails. He backed away, bumped into the wall.

They called for him, reached for him. Their hands . . .

Kirk slid down the wall, back to the floor. Saw them draw closer. Tiberius's children. *His* children. All monsters and murderers.

And then they stopped.

Their eyes opened wide. Their mouths forming O's of astonishment.

As they looked from Kirk to what was beside Kirk.

And Kirk didn't even have to turn his head to know what that was. Who that was.

His search was over.

James Tiberius Kirk stood with his hands on his hips, looking down the corridor at his beloved children, having no need for the man on the floor beside him to look up so he could be identified.

"James, I'm so impressed with you. Have you said hello to . . . *our* children?"

Kirk slowly stood up, holding onto the wall for support.

Like a warrior, Tiberius assessed his opponent's condition. Better than it was the last time they had met. But not good enough.

"Back to your crèche," Tiberius ordered. He clapped his hands commandingly. *"Now."*

Instantly, as if stung by a lash, the children retreated through the white door, to safety.

And then Tiberius and Kirk were alone, face-to-face. They stared at each other.

Tiberius was the first to see fear.

"I have been reading about you," Tiberius said with a smile. "About your so-called exploits. I never would have thought vengeance was something you had the stomach for."

"Try me."

Tiberius shook his head. Such an empty threat. "Be careful, James. We're not in spacesuits. There's no schedule we have to keep. And I *am* your better. In all things."

Interesting, Tiberius thought as he studied Kirk's reactions. The way he had responded to the word *schedule.* Could it be that Kirk was on a schedule? And if so, what kind?

"You murdered Teilani," Kirk said fiercely.

Tiberius permitted himself a gloating smile, secure in the knowledge that before this day, or at least, this encounter, was over, James T. Kirk would be dead, and all the universes would know of Tiberius the Triumphant. "If that's the way it makes you feel, if it inspires you to take this kind of foolish chance, then I almost wish I had tried to kill her."

"Don't lie to me, you bastard!" Kirk shouted as he lunged at Tiberius.

Tiberius shot out his right hand so quickly that his weak counterpart's attempt to deflect it was much too late. The blow caught Kirk on the side of his head. Before the weakling could fall to the floor, Tiberius's knee connected with Kirk's jaw. Only then did Kirk strike the hard marble floor.

"I don't need to lie to you," Tiberius said scornfully.

"I don't need to do anything to you, or for you, or because of you. Except to hold you in the contempt you deserve."

Kirk stared up at Tiberius. "Liar," he spat through the blood streaming from his cut mouth.

"Are you that eager to die?"

Kirk got to his feet with surprising speed. "If that's what it takes."

Sighing at the drawn-out nature of the hunt, Tiberius decided he might as well try to deduce what had brought Kirk here. He wouldn't mind knowing just how Kirk had managed to locate his most secret base. Perhaps he wouldn't kill this pale ghost version of himself. Yet.

"Come with me," Tiberius said peremptorily. "I have something you might enjoy."

Then, to cement his disdain for the man, and his utter disregard of Kirk's abilities, Tiberius turned his back on his counterpart and started down the corridor, to the section of his base that held his private living quarters. Kirk was too much the coward to attack him from behind.

Tiberius felt a foreign emotion invade him. The thought of finally disposing of this wretched, imperfect copy—when he was through toying with him—was turning this into the sweetest day of his exile.

Why, he almost felt happy.

TWENTY-THREE

☆

Kirk limped along in Tiberius's wake.

His head ached, the inside of his lip was split, and at any other time in his life, he would have jumped Tiberius the instant his back was turned and strangled the pompous, self-righteous, murderous monster without a second thought.

But he needed Tiberius alive. At least until he had the antitoxin Teilani needed. Tiberius might survive another few seconds past that moment. But only seconds.

They reached the alcove outside the transporter room. Kirk watched Tiberius walk past the terrible photograph of the hangings at Starfleet Headquarters without paying it a moment's notice.

As he came to it, Kirk couldn't help himself. He paused to check the photo for another name. MCCOY. And found it. *How is that possible?* he asked himself. That identical people can have such different lives?

"Old friends?" Tiberius asked. He had turned back to see Kirk looking at the photograph and walked back to join him, as if they were on a tour of an art gallery.

"Do you *have* any friends?" Kirk asked grimly.

"How can I?" Tiberius replied. And to Kirk it sounded, incredibly, as if his counterpart was actually being sincere. "I once was, and will be again, absolute master of life and death throughout known space. *Everyone* wants to be my friend, James, to curry favor, to bask in some slight reflection of my glory. But if I were to allow that, choosing one or two favorites or familiars here or there, how could I be fair with my subjects? How could I be honest? Come along, James. So much to do, so little time."

Tiberius started down the corridor again.

"In my analysis of your woefully inadequate career," he continued, "I believe I have identified many of your flaws. Chief among them, your foolish persistence in believing that you are like ordinary men." Tiberius glanced back over his shoulder. "You are *not* like ordinary men, James. You never have been. *We* never have been. But only I have been able to rise above your shallow concerns about being a man of the people."

"Do you ever shut up?" Kirk asked.

They had come to another large white door. Tiberius placed a hand against the scanner plate on the wall beside it, and the door silently slipped open.

"I hope you realize," Tiberius said, "at some dim level of your perception, that the only reason I have allowed you to live this long while insulting me, is because I do respect you."

"Why didn't you respect Teilani?"

Tiberius paused in the open door. "Incredible as it may seem to you, I don't care about your Klingon-Romulan hybrid concubine. Intendant Picard, on the other hand, seemed to find her remarkably attractive, but if he did anything to Teilani, it wouldn't be fatal."

Kirk suppressed his rage. It would not do to assault his counterpart again. Tiberius was better trained, more practiced in hand-to-hand combat. He would have to choose his time precisely. He might not be able to outfight his opponent, but Kirk was certain he could outthink him. Once the antitoxin was his.

But until then, he still couldn't let this smug bastard continue to lie, unchallenged.

"If you don't care about Teilani, why did you send one of your children to poison her?"

For the first time, Kirk felt he had said something that Tiberius was interested in.

"I did no such thing."

"I was there. I saw it. I recognized the child in your . . . crèche."

Tiberius took on a serious expression. "Which one?"

"I can't be sure. A boy. Eight years old. He was in pajamas."

"Where did this take place?"

"Don't play games with me! You *know* where it took place."

Kirk saw Tiberius's face flush red, as if his temper had gained control of him. "Assume I *don't* know. Assume one of my eager commandants decided he'd make my day by sending an assassin after Teilani without telling me. Do you have sufficient imagination to do that?"

"Chal," Kirk said. But he'd be damned before he'd let Tiberius escape responsibility for what he had done.

"A backwater world. Of no importance in your universe. A lifeless cinder in mine. What did this child do to Teilani?"

"Poisoned her," Kirk said. "With a Klingon nerve toxin."

Again, Tiberius took on an expression of legitimate interest. "Follow me. I have something to show you on my computer."

Kirk wasn't certain what was going on, but finding out where Tiberius's computer was could definitely provide him with an edge. He followed Tiberius past the exhibition of atrocities depicted in the photographs on the wall. He couldn't help but notice one.

"Ahh," Tiberius said as he saw what Kirk was looking at. "One of my personal favorites."

The small name plaque on the image said PAVEL A. CHEKOV. But what it showed was a desiccated body in a transparent tube. Then Kirk remembered what that tube was. An agony booth.

Tiberius preened as if proud of the photo. "I believe you share in some of the glory of that day. That week, actually. My good friend at the time, Mr. Spock, informed me that Chekov moved against me while you were conducting your laughable masquerade on my ship. When I finally returned to the real universe, I found poor Chekov in the agony booth, as punishment, but my torturers were at a loss because of the leniency you had shown him.

"So I made leniency my showcase. I had the agony booth set to medium intensity. Think of a dull toothache throughout your body, in every part. Bearable, but most uncomfortable. And then I kept Pavel in it. It took thirteen days for him to die. It had a bracing effect on my crew. Set a new standard throughout the fleet."

"In my universe, he became head of Starfleet."

"Which could explain a great deal about your Starfleet, don't you think?"

Kirk didn't want to engage this beast in any topic of

conversation other than the one that had brought him here. "Where's the computer?"

Tiberius pointed through the door. Kirk entered.

The computer was on a console before him. It looked like a standard Starfleet system, the kind he'd expect to see on a starship. Past it, on either side of the long narrow room they had entered, Kirk saw transparent display cases. At the end the hall, Kirk saw a pair of bright red sliding doors that made him think of the original *Enterprise.*

Tiberius went to the computer console and input a series of commands, angling his body so Kirk couldn't see what his authorization codes were. When he stepped away again, there was a visual sensor recording of the boy who had attacked Teilani. The same one who was in the crèche on the other side of the alcove.

"That's the boy," Kirk said.

"You're certain?" Tiberius asked. "Perhaps it was this boy?" He pressed a control on the console and a new image appeared.

"That's the same one," Kirk said.

"Or perhaps this one?" Tiberius asked.

Another new image. But again, the same boy.

Then Kirk looked at his hands, said the word that answered his questions. "Clones."

"Exactly. Three of that young one. And what might be of interest to you is that one of him is missing in your universe. I sent a signal to activate a number of secret bases and assets over there. The group of children *he* was with never reported back."

Kirk tried to process that information. "What are you saying? That someone just decided to use that boy to kill Teilani as a coincidence?!"

"Someone who knew *how* to use him, yes. That seems a reasonable assumption."

Kirk didn't understand the choice of words Tiberius had made. "What do you mean by *use?*"

"You don't know?"

Kirk shook his head and stepped to the side as if avoiding confrontation, but he did so to give himself a better look at the keyboard. "Right now, it seems I don't know anything."

"That's a start," Tiberius agreed. "As I said, I can't have friends. No peers. You can't imagine the disappointment you were to me. But still, I have to make preparations for the future. We both seemed to have achieved a second chance at life. Perhaps we'll get a third. Who knows? But in the meantime, I created clones."

Tiberius grinned. "Oh, not exact duplicates. Replication drift can be dangerous, and I was looking to the long term. So they're all half me—half us—and half various other people whom my research showed had satisfactory genes. And when I began adjusting their genetic heritage, it seemed a simple matter to enhance it here and there. Multiplied strength, vastly increased endurance. Hyperintelligence. And . . . a built-in method of self-defense."

Kirk waited for the rest of the explanation he knew would come. And it did.

"I borrowed here and there from other successful species."

"Species?!" But then Kirk knew the answer before Tiberius could continue. "Poisonous ones. The toxin wasn't *painted* on the boy's fingernail; he *produced* it."

"Mystery solved. Let's go down there."

297

"No!" Kirk insisted. "It's not solved. Who set that child on Teilani?"

"What does it matter? You said she's dead."

"She's in stasis. You must know what toxin the boy produced. You must have an antitoxin!"

Kirk didn't like the way Tiberius remained in place, folded his arms, and began to smile, horribly.

"You think *I* have the capacity to save Teilani?"

Knowing the terrible door he was opening, Kirk gave the only answer he could. "Yes."

Tiberius laughed, the sound hollow, mocking, to Kirk. "Just one small detail overlooked, James. Why would I *want* to?"

There was only one thing Kirk had to offer. "You want to kill me."

"I do. And here you are. Not much of a bargaining chip, I'm afraid." Tiberius walked closer to Kirk, watching him closely. "But you are serious? You want to save Teilani. You *have* to save Teilani. No matter what the cost?"

Kirk hesitated. He feared what Tiberius might be suggesting.

But more than that, he feared what might happen if he did not hear more.

"What do you want me to do?" Kirk said, and with those words he knew his soul was forfeit to Tiberius.

From his counterpart's triumphant smile, Kirk was certain Tiberius knew the same.

"Come with me," Tiberius said.

He turned his back on Kirk again and walked halfway down the line of display cases, stopping in front of one that had a small figure in it.

Kirk joined his counterpart to look inside that case.

And was almost sick.

"Balok?!" he said.

"The one and only. Brilliant scientist. Lonely starship captain. And an extremely disappointing ambassador from the First Federation. He does, however, make an excellent trophy."

Kirk was overwhelmed by the butchery before him. The figure in the case *was* Balok, the diminutive alien who had tested him and his crew back during his first five-year mission. The encounter had marked the beginning of a still ongoing, if unconventional, relationship with the First Federation. But here, in this universe, Balok was a *stuffed* specimen in Tiberius's chambers of horrors, his mouth permanently twisted into a smile as he perpetually contemplated the glass of *tranya* that had been wired to his lifeless hand.

"Before I was finished with him," Tiberius said affectionately, "Balok gave me many secrets. I think you saw the Tantalus field at work. That was one of his. Captain Pike seemed far too eager to keep all the spoils of the *Fesarius* for himself, so I used the Tantalus field to rid the *Enterprise* of him, earning his rank for myself."

Tiberius frowned, as if recalling a terrible defeat. Kirk enjoyed the sight.

"But after a time, torture seemed to have little effect on him. From what my men and I could translate from his ship's computers, there was a vast base of Fesarius-class ships just outside Imperial space. I used all my skills to make him reveal what I wanted to know, and in the end, before he died, so pathetically and alone, he told me where the base was located."

Kirk could guess what had happened. "He lied to you."

"Imagine my disappointment."

Kirk looked at the mummified body of the little alien. He *could* imagine Tiberius's rage. This was the result of it. Absolute insanity.

"So my question for you, James T. Kirk, is do *you* know where the First Federation base is?"

Kirk nodded. Of all the questions Tiberius might have asked of him, that was one he could answer.

"Do you have the antitoxin that can save Teilani's life?"

Tiberius matched Kirk's acknowledgment.

Then he held out his hand.

"I believe this could be the beginning of a most profitable relationship," Tiberius said. "Something to give each of us what we want most."

Kirk looked at that hand for long moments.

It couldn't just be a yes-or-no situation, to accept that hand or not. There had to be a third option. There always was a third option.

But not this time.

Because there was no more time.

Kirk took Tiberius's hand in his and shook hands with the demon who dwelled within him.

Because of what he did at this moment, Teilani might live.

But James T. Kirk was utterly and hopelessly defeated.

FIRST FEDERATION

☆

There was an ebb and flow to history. Certain stories played out again and again. Similar patterns arose from the chaos.

One of those patterns was the principle of non-interference.

In some places, at some times, known as the Prime Directive.

The First Federation was immensely old, immensely advanced, and had long ago learned the dangers that could result when a race was given technology it did not discover by itself.

In the universe of Captain Kirk, Balok had been delighted by his discovery of the Federation. He had eagerly taken on an exchange officer, Lieutenant David Bailey, late of the Starship Enterprise.

Bailey had proven most informative.

Humans and their associated races in the United Federation of Planets were not ready for some of the more startling technologies of the First Federation.

So Bailey was treated as an honored guest and returned

home a better being for his experiences. Diplomatic relations were established, but at the highest levels, the representatives of the First Federation told those of the new Federation that, in most cases of scientific exchange, their own principle of non-interference would apply. The worlds of the Federation could not expect to share the wonders of the Fesarius until they had achieved similar breakthroughs of their own.

The Federation was committed to the Prime Directive, and so it could not question the First Federation's position.

Relationships were cordial. Cultural exchanges were frequent. But Fesarius-class ships were rarely seen.

There was a base, however. One the First Federation had abandoned until the day the Federation became more of a technological equal.

The base existed in a hollow asteroid, a forward supply station, waiting for the day the relationship between the two starfaring cultures could truly be established on a more balanced footing.

In the mirror universe, the base no longer existed. After Balok's tragic encounter with the Enterprise, the First Federation withdrew from all contact with the Terran Empire and, later, the Alliance. Balok's people would return to that region of space, but only after the age of barbarism had ended and a more progressive, hopeful system had taken its place.

But in the universe of Captain Kirk, the base had been left intact. Lieutenant Bailey had seen it. He had forwarded reports to Captain Kirk. Captain Kirk had passed those reports to Command. Eventually, all the reports were classified and filed away, and the location of the

First Federation base became covered by the security oaths of the people who had learned the truth.

But on a galactic scale, on a universal scale, truth had many levels.

To save Teilani, Captain Kirk now made preparations to bring Emperor Tiberius to that base.

But the location of that base was not known merely to humans.

In the ebb and flow of history, it was known that, in time, Kirk would arrive at the base. And it was now known that Tiberius would arrive with him.

So preparations had been made.

And in addition to all that Balok's people had left behind, one more artifact had been included.

An obelisk, with raised pictograms that described a tonal language.

In this region of space, the race who had left it had many names. Sometimes, they were known as the Preservers.

Some of their artifacts were believed to be billions of years old.

But this obelisk, flashing with flares of silver light for anyone who might be present to see it, had been put in place only six years earlier, at the time of an unexpected event on Veridian III.

And it would remain in place, until Captain Kirk arrived to read its message.

Those who were sometimes called the Preservers had not gone away.

They waited for the pattern to unfold from the chaos.

They waited for their encounter with Captain James T. Kirk.

And the waiting would be over soon.

James T. Kirk

will return in

Star Trek® : Preserver

For further information about William Shatner,
science fiction, new technologies,
and upcoming William Shatner books, log on to:

www.williamshatner.com